# Big & Bossy

*A Fake Engagement Second Chance Romance*

Boulder Billionaires

Mia Mara

Copyright © 2024 by Mia Mara

All rights reserved.

No part of this book may be reproduced in any form or by any electronic or mechanical means, including information storage and retrieval systems, without written permission from the author, except for the use of brief quotations in a book review.

# BIG & BOSSY

Boulder Billionaires Book One
*Billionaire Boss / Fake Fiancé / Second Chance / Enemies to Lovers / Forced Proximity*

**What could be worse than my ex walking in on me half naked? How about being fake engaged to him and taking his orders 24/7.**

Jackson Big shows up in my life after 10 years.
And offers, no, *orders* me to work for him.
It's going to be fun making his life hell.

So here I am in his office, waiting to see him again, my stomach in knots.
And instead of keeping my cool, I spill coffee all down my blouse.
I do my best to quickly clean up, standing there just wearing my thin bralette.

And that's when the door opens...

And the man who crushed my heart walks in.
My bare torso in full view.

In his eyes, there's a hunger and longing that sets my heart pounding.
And I can't help but notice how sexy he looks in a suit.

So he gives me his shirt.
And now we're both half naked.

He's definitely got something BIG planned for me.

Because, somehow, he's now my boss and I'm wearing his ring on my finger.

# Chapter 1

## *Jackson*

I hoped that relocating my headquarters to Boulder, Colorado was going to be worth all the goddamn effort.

I needed sleep, and I needed a glass of whiskey.

"Jack," someone called from behind me.

*Put your fucking game face on. Pretend you want to be here. Pretend you aren't two seconds away from throwing yourself off this goddamn building.* Slapping a grin on my face, I turned. Before me stood Will, Head of Development, with a clipboard clutched to his chest. "Yes?"

"You asked for an update on the campus."

"Shit, sorry, yes," I sighed, leaning forward on the back of one of the shittiest office chairs imaginable. I hated the environment we were working in. The space came furnished but the lights were horrible, the atmosphere dingy. "Update me."

"Construction should be finished in the next day or two. Electricity was finished yesterday, water the day before that. Internet and elevators will be finished by Friday. All that's left is the interior."

"Are we up to code?"

"Yep, the Boulder City council has given us the go-ahead to open up." Will clicked his pen, jotting something down on his clipboard before using the tip of it to shove his glasses farther up his face.

"Perfect. Thanks," I said, standing up straight.

"You know, sir, we could look into hiring another company for basic furniture and decorators. It could be less costly. We could get in touch with IKEA—"

"Absolutely not," I seethed, directing my glare to the bridge between Will's glasses. "I don't know how many times I need to tell you. I don't care about the cost. I want L&V Interiors, and we will get L&V Interiors."

"Yes, sir."

The meeting I was in, if it could even be called that, was about Infinius—our latest development in the tech industry. Infinius was an AI-powered software that was becoming drastically more useful every day. People wanted to buy it, wanted to know what it's capable of, and potentially invest in it.

But mostly, people wanted the chance to speak to me.

I'd made the jump from my family's business within the private military sector nearly six years ago. "It'll collapse," they told me. "The tech industry is flooded."

Sure, Mom. That's why I had been on Forbes' thirty-under-thirty for the last two years.

After my graduation from NYU, I spent a few more years in New York working as my parent's New York connection before moving back to Chicago and starting my own company. I'd visited Boulder a few times—once with Mandy before things went haywire, and the rest on business trips. Colorado had always been somewhat of a haven for me—I spent most of my winters in Vail, skiing or lounging around with Wade, my best friend.

Boulder had two things I needed more than anything.

The first and more sensible thing was that Boulder was tech-central. I'd never been one for the beach, so Silicon Valley was low on my list, but the mountains, the national parks in Colorado... those were what drew me the most along with the amount of tech companies.

The second and less sensible thing was easy in theory but difficult in practice.

Mandy.

She had moved back here after graduation.

And I hadn't seen her since *that* night.

I pulled my phone from my pocket. The lone notification on my screen was one I got at least once a week like clockwork—a text from my mom, asking the exact same thing she always did.

*Are you free this weekend, honey? I've found an excellent woman that I'd love to set you up with on Saturday.*

I swiped the notification away, needing desperately to not think about what 'excellent woman' meant to my mom. In the back of my mind, I knew she was only trying to help, but I didn't want any help and I definitely didn't want whatever woman she had in mind.

I had moved to Boulder for a reason.

A knock on my door dragged my attention away from

the distracting thoughts, and a second later, a mop of blonde hair poked into my office.

"Jack," Angela, my assistant said, shuffling her body between the frame and the slightly-open door before shutting it behind her. "I just got a call from L&V Interiors."

My back went rigid as I slid my phone back into my pocket. "Okay."

"I know you said you wanted both owners in attendance…"

My fingers clenched around the armrest of my chair, my jaw steeling. "Don't say it."

"I'm going to say it, Jack." She crossed her arms over her chest, her expression stoic. If she wasn't such an excellent secretary, I'd have fired her long ago for her attitude. "Only Mr. Voss will be there."

"You're fucking joking, right?"

"No, I'm not joking."

"Call them back. Insist Ms. Littleson be in attendance as well," I snapped.

"Jack."

"Angela."

"Do you honestly expect me to do that?" She leaned back against the door, arms still tightly crossed against her chest. "You want me to embarrass myself by calling back?"

"Yes," I replied. I leaned back in my chair, then slowly lifting one foot after another, I placed them onto my desk, crossing them at the ankles. "Tell them the meeting won't go ahead if she's not there, and as such, the deal will be off."

"Fuck's sake," she grunted, pushing off from the door and opening it once again. "You're lucky you pay me enough to deal with this shit."

*If she doesn't attend, the whole thing is pointless. All of it. Entirely, horribly pointless.*

# Chapter 2

## *Mandy*

"No."

"Mandy. Come on."

"I said no, Harry." I grabbed my sweater from the counter in our back office, shoving it into my bag as quickly as I could. I almost wished I'd left my hair down today, at least then I could use it to shield my face from Harry's too-hard gaze. "I'm not doing it. End of discussion."

"They insisted you be there," Harry said, leaning his ass on the table as if I hadn't told him off for doing that exact thing a million times.

"Yeah, you said that."

"No," he replied, crossing his arms over his broad chest as I peeked at him through the corner of my eye. "They called back. They said that if you don't show, they'll pull out."

The expression 'seeing red' was suddenly far too real for me. My hands clenched around the straps of my bag, my jaw muscles straining. *He can't do that. That's not fucking fair.* "What did he say exactly?"

"Well, it was his secretary, I think. But she said that if

you don't show up, they'll hire someone else to do their interiors. We can't afford to lose them as a client, Mandy. They're the biggest contract we've got." Harry sighed into the silence that hung thick between us, the little puff of air sending one of his face-framing curls flying upwards. "You have to go."

"He's just doing this to be a fucking asshole," I snapped. I was so ready for the day to be over—it was ten past five, and normally, I'd be sitting in traffic right now, blasting my radio, soaking up the last rays of sunlight before it hid behind the rocky peaks. But no. I was in our business' break room, knee deep in bullshit. "I guarantee if you call them back and tell them that I have some previous engagement, he'll suck it up and back off."

"I think you're the only one who has to suck it up, Mands. We have to keep this contract, and I'm not going to risk losing it. It's our only way to be noticed outside of Boulder," he urged, throwing his hands up, emphasizing he had no other ideas.

He was right, though. This contract was the best one we'd ever received, and we'd barely had to fight for it. If we wanted to get bigger, to have a shot in Denver, Aspen, or hell, even outside Colorado, we'd have to keep J.B. Tech as a client.

I'd only agreed to it in the first place on two conditions —Harry would be the sole representative between our businesses, meaning I wouldn't have to see *him*; and J.B. Tech had to give us enough business to fund us for at least the next year.

And one of those conditions was already falling apart.

I fought the burning in the backs of my eyes as I turned to Harry, my hands starting to cramp from their vice-like grip on my bag. "I can't do it, Harry. I don't want to see him. I don't."

"I know. I know you have a history with him, but just this once, you have to look past it."

I threw my bag over my shoulder. "I need to think about it," I mumbled. "Please. Just give me a day."

Harry sighed as he collapsed into the chair beside the table, shoving his hands through his hair in frustration. "Fine. You need to tell me by tomorrow, okay? I want to call them back sooner rather than later."

———

The clinking of glasses, low music, and scraping of silverware on plates wasn't enough to keep my mind off the upcoming meeting with J.B. Tech and every single thing that came with it. Even Amanda's buzzing praise of our new product lineup as she babbled at me over dinner wasn't enough. My mind kept traveling back to him, to why he was insisting on my attendance. I hadn't seen him in ten years. Why now? Why me?

"Mandy."

I looked up from my empty serving plate, locking eyes with Amanda as she sipped her fruity cocktail. "What?"

"Were you even listening?"

*No. Of course not. I have bigger problems than your boss sleeping with his secretary.* "Of course I was."

She rolled her eyes at me as she shoved the little tiki umbrella into her straw, stirring around the colors in her glass. "I've known you since we were, like, five. I know when you're lying. Your nostrils flare."

Instinctively, I covered my nose as I let a glare seep through the facade I was desperately trying to keep up. I hated when she was right.

"What's going on?" She pressed, resting her chin on her intertwined knuckles as she leaned forward on the table. "You're normally attentive. Something's gotta be bothering you."

I chewed the flesh of my cheek as I thought about the best way to bring it up to her. She'd been there every step of the way, through the rise and fall and rise again. "You remember Jackson?"

Her body stiffened as she narrowed her eyes. "I haven't heard that name in a long time. Have you been, uh, thinking about him recently?"

"Not intentionally," I mumbled, slumping back in my seat. "You remember how we got that massive client? The one that's moving their tech business to town?"

Slowly, Amanda's eyes widened, the realization I'd painfully had to make a few weeks ago sinking into her now. "Don't tell me it's J.B. Tech."

"It's J.B. Tech."

"Fuck," she spat, sitting upright. "Can you at least avoid him?"

"He's insisting I attend the first meeting or he'll pull the contract," I explained. Just saying the words made the pit in my stomach grow larger, stealing my appetite. I wanted to be home, in my bed, with my face shoved into the pillow and a scream ripping from my throat. "We need the contract."

"Oh my God, what a fucking psycho," she said, her body recoiling. "He shatters your heart into a million pieces

*Big & Bossy*

and then expects you to just agree to see him ten years later? At a business meeting of all things? I mean, fuck, if L&V needs the cash I can have my mom wire it to you. Don't go near him if you can help it."

I sighed the best chuckle I could muster. "That's a lovely offer but if my business is going to stay afloat, I'd rather it be because of me and my hard work."

"I get that. I do. But if it's between seeing Jackson fucking Big and your business going under, I'd rather you didn't have to—"

"Don't worry about it, okay? If it comes down to it and I have to work with him, I'll just make sure his life is a living hell," I laughed. *If he thinks abandoning me in the middle of the night after taking my virginity is an okay thing to do, then he can withstand my bitchiness.*

"Okay, okay. But I'm serious. If you need the money—"

My phone buzzed loudly from the table, preventing her from finishing the sentence. We stared at the screen in tandem, the number unknown to either of us.

I didn't normally answer unknown numbers.

And I don't know what compelled me to this time.

"Hello?" I asked warily, holding one finger against my open ear to dampen the sound of the restaurant.

"Hello. Mandy."

The breath in my lungs suddenly felt more like ice than warm air. I knew that voice. Knew it all too well, even though it had changed, matured, deepened. "Hi," I breathed.

"I heard you were having a bit of a hard time deciding whether or not to come to our meeting," he drawled, the sound of a pen tapping against wood just barely seeping through the phone. "I'd like to make it a little easier for you."

"I—"

"I don't think you can afford not to come, Ms. Littleson." The click of the pen, the typing sounds of a keyboard. "L&V Interiors. Owned by Miranda Littleson and Harry Voss. Currently valued at approximately five hundred thousand dollars. Three shareholders—your mother, Gianna Palton; Amanda Holston, nice to know she's still around; and Tracey Holston, who I can only imagine is Amanda's mother. I don't think your shareholders would be happy to know the actual valuation."

The idea of the plate of spaghetti I'd ordered was suddenly nauseating. "Excuse me?"

"Those numbers aren't exactly correct, are they, Mandy? Your reported income in the last two years has been significantly lower than that. Business slowed down, and with no new, big contracts..." he continued, the creaking of leather faint in the background. "You'll be at the meeting."

"Jackson—"

Silence, then the sound of a beep. I pulled my phone away from my ear, the call gone, nothing but my lock screen filling the space that his number had taken.

"The fucker hung up on me."

*And to think I used to call him panda bear.*

# Chapter 3

## *Jackson*

Showtime.

I'd planned everything, right down to the last detail. I wasn't going to let a single part of this slip through my fingers, she wasn't going to get away that easily. I needed to see her, and I needed her alone.

The streets were quiet as I pulled my car into the parking lot. Twenty minutes late, exactly as planned. Mandy and Harry should already be inside. Sliding my phone from my suit jacket, I dialed Angela, the sound of her voice seeping through my car speakers after almost going to voicemail.

"What."

"Are they all set up in the meeting room?" I asked as I double-checked the contents of my briefcase. *All in order.*

"Yes, obviously."

"Can you grab Mandy and bring her to my office, please?"

"Jesus, Jackson," Angela huffed. "This is insane. You know that right?"

"I'll give you a bonus this month," I offered, disconnecting the Bluetooth from my car and shoving my phone between my shoulder and my ear. "Tell her I need to speak to her alone first. I'll be upstairs in a few."

"Fine."

I hung up the phone as I stepped through the cheap sliding doors of the building. Boulder didn't allow for high-rises, so our hired office was on the fourth floor. The bottom floor, though, had a cafe.

And I was going to make use of it.

---

"Good morning, Angela," I grinned as I plopped a hazelnut latte onto the front of her desk. "You will, of course, still receive a bonus. Consider this an extra thank you."

Angela wrapped her fingers around its warmth, her lips curled back in a sneer. "This smells like hazelnut. I don't like hazelnut."

"You did last month."

"I changed my mind. I like vanilla bean, now."

I narrowed my eyes at her before rolling them as dramatically as I could. "You just love being difficult, don't you?"

"Not as much as you do."

*So lucky you still have a job.* "Is Mandy in my office as I requested?" I asked, bracing myself with my hand on her desk. "Or did you conveniently forget?"

"No, she's in there." Her nonchalant tone made the semi-relief I felt from Mandy being nearby shrink. "Have fun."

"Thank you." I clutched my black Americano in my hand as I stepped away from her desk, heading back toward what passed as a private office in this drab, horrible building. My heart quickened its pace with every step I took, nearly doubling when I saw a shadow move behind the closed blinds of my office window.

I quieted my footsteps, taking my time, not wanting to set off immediate alarm bells for her. The handle of my briefcase felt heavy in my hand, as if the weight of the world was resting in my palm. In a way, it was.

The woman I'd loved, the woman I'd hurt in the worst possible way stood on the other side of that door, waiting for me. Sure, it was only because I'd threatened her, but something in my gut knew she would have come either way. I knew a part of her was excited to see me too. I hoped.

Fingers shaking and breaths coming too fast, I turned the handle.

Five foot five, slender in the way an athlete would be, chestnut brown, curly hair hanging low around her shoulders. All things I absolutely should have noticed first, things a normal, sane man would have noticed first. No, my eyes went directly to her bare torso, her flawless, exposed skin from the waist up covered only by a thin bralette. *Where the fuck is her blouse?* She hadn't heard me come in.

Unsure of what to do or say, I cleared my throat to get her attention, her surprised shriek nearly making me jump. In one swift motion she turned, and right away I noticed her white blouse clutched between her fingers, covered in what looked like coffee. Her eyes were wide as saucers, locked on mine in a state of fight or flight. Even through the obvious mortification oozing from her that she so desperately tried to hide, she looked as beautiful as she did ten years ago. More so, even, and considering the state of her appearance, I had to keep myself from thinking with my cock for once.

I turned my gaze from her as soon as our eyes met. I didn't want her thinking I was a creep and an asshole all wrapped in one although I was certain she already did.

Closing the door behind me, I dropped my briefcase onto the floor. Without letting myself think too hard or too quickly about it, I shrugged my suit jacket from my shoulders, popped off my cuff links, and loosened my tie.

"What the fuck do you think—"

"Oh, calm down, Mandy." I unbuttoned my shirt, keeping my back turned in a desperate endeavor to keep her from seeing my chest. She didn't need to know about the tattoo yet.

I slid the sleeves down my arms before chucking the loose piece of fabric at her blindly.

"That stain won't come out. You might as well just take my shirt," I said, feeling the heat of her eyes on my back. I was bigger now, stronger, more of a man than I was at twenty-one. I was in the top ten of America's Top Bachelors, actually.

"Thank you," she mumbled, the only other sound that of rustling fabric as she slipped it on. Our eyes locked as I stepped around my desk, one arm covering the top of my chest, and within a split second she cast her gaze down to her lap. "I can't have a meeting with you if you're going to be shirtless the entire time."

"I'm not expecting you to." I leaned forward, keeping my eyes locked on hers to keep her from paying attention as I opened the bottom drawer of the saddest-looking desk in existence. My backup shirt was neatly tucked in at the bottom, underneath a handful of papers and folders. I plucked it out and slipped it over my head.

"Why...?"

"What?" I asked, plopping my ass in my chair as I stared her down.

"Why didn't you just give me that one?"

I blinked at her as I adjusted the sleeves, my mind entirely blank. Something about seeing her in my dress shirt was too much, making it far too hard to think. A heavy silence fell around us, the only sound that of our combined, awkward breathing. This was already not going to plan.

"Fine, if you're not going to answer me, then we might as well get on with it," she sighed, fingering the little holes in the sleeves where the cuff links had held it together. "Why did you have your secretary bring me in here alone? Why can't I have Harry with me?"

I narrowed my gaze as I tried not to stare at the way her fingers worked, tried not to wonder what else they did in the confines of a dark bedroom. "Would you have preferred Harry be in here as you scrubbed your shirt of its stain in nothing more than your bra?"

"You're not a psychic, Jackson."

The sound of my name coming from her lips made my skin crawl in the best possible way, made my heart skip a beat in my chest. "No, I'm not," I admitted. I chose my words carefully, my tone carefully, to come across as strongly as I could. "Truthfully, I wanted to speak to you alone first because I want to ensure that you're going to be professional about us working together." *And I just wanted to see you alone after ten years of hiding from you.*

"Oh. Absolutely not." She leaned back in her seat, crossing her arms against her chest. "If you're going to force me to be around you then I will be actively trying to make your life a living hell."

"I would appreciate it if you wouldn't do that," I snarled, keeping my voice as even as I could.

"God, you sound like an old man. What happened to you? Did abandoning me in the middle of the night age you by thirty years?"

I steeled my jaw as I forced myself to look away from her. *I deserved that.* "I'm doing my best to be level-headed here, Miranda. Level-headed and professional."

"Was it professional to call me up and tell me that you know I'm broke and making me come to some ridiculous, unnecessary meeting?"

"Was it professional to undress in your future boss's office?" I snapped back.

Mandy's face went red, whether from embarrassment or irritation, I had no idea. "If we're going to work together, *Mr. Big*, you will not be my boss. You'll be my equal."

"Mr. Big?" I scoffed, my jaw nearly twitching from restraining the urge to clench it. "Don't fucking call me that. Call me by my name. You said it two minutes ago. And as for me being your boss, that is absolutely the case."

"If you're going to try to boss me around then this entire thing is doomed from the start," she quipped. "I'm not going to listen to you. All pink interiors are what you wanted, right? Top to bottom, pink carpets, pink tile, pink paint, pink desks—"

"Enough." This wasn't going how I wanted, not at all, but I suppose that was on me. "You will be professional. You will listen to me when I give orders. Do I make myself clear?"

"*Crystal*, Mr. Big," she hissed through her teeth, her hands fidgeting in her lap. "Doesn't mean I'll actually do what you say. But I will listen."

Irritation boiled in my blood as I shoved myself up on

my feet, my hands planted on the desk in front of me. I leaned toward her, my muscles flexed, my temperature rising. "Miranda Littleson, I will be your fucking boss. You will accept that. You will deal with whatever that means for you if you want to keep this contract and your goddamn business afloat. What I say goes. What I tell you to do, you do. I say 'jump', you say 'how high'. Do you understand me?"

Wide eyes met mine as she watched me loom over her. "Yes."

"Fucking perfect. Now get back to the meeting room before I change my mind."

I watched her practically scurry from my office. I needed a moment alone, I needed time to collect myself. This wasn't going to plan, and I was being far too harsh on her. I was cornered. There was nothing else I could have done, but I didn't want to do it this way. I wanted her to want this. But I was doing what needed to be done, right?

*No. You're being an ass, Jackson.*

I sighed as I collapsed in my chair. I *was* being an ass. I needed to tone it down before she walked away for fucking good, her own business be damned.

I needed to win her back.

# Chapter 4

## *Mandy*

My head felt too heavy, too bogged down with whatever the hell had just happened. All I could do was stare at the clock and watch the second hand move, listening to the seconds tick away. That was somehow louder in my mind than the words coming from Harry's mouth, though the incessant clicking of Jackson's pen one chair over managed to seep through the fog plaguing my ears.

I could still feel the warmth in my cheeks from what had happened in his office—the embarrassment of being caught without my shirt, the anger from his threats, the disappointment that ran far too deep within myself for agreeing to all of this. It didn't help that I could feel the little bit of warmth from his skin still on the fabric of the shirt he'd lent me, that I could smell his cologne, the same cologne that he wore during university.

"So, if we're in agreement," Harry said, the words slowly filtering in through the fog. "Then we'll be in charge of the communal spaces, the offices, and the executive rooms. You'd like them all to be uniform in design, correct? So it's all cohesive?"

"Yes," Jackson responded. The word almost sounded biting, as if he'd prefer it were me up there with the clicker and pointer.

"Do you have a color and design scheme?"

"Colors should match the company's logo and branding, which I've included in the paperwork I have here for you. Design scheme: think minimal but sleek, futuristic but not tacky. We're a tech company, so it should *feel* like a tech company." Jackson lifted the briefcase he'd walked in with onto the table and opened it. He pulled two stacks of alligator-clipped papers and slid them across the desk. "You'll find all of the details in there from color to design to building plans and layouts. You two will also be given express permission to be on site from security so you can see it for yourselves."

Harry took the stack of papers and flipped through them quickly, scanning each sheet with his eyes. "This is more than enough information," he chuckled. "Normally our clients don't give us this much."

"I like to be thorough."

*I shouldn't have taken this contract.* Even though he was thorough, even though it would be fairly easy for us with the amount of specification he had, this was a horrible idea from the start. I doubted his threats held any actual venom behind them, though based on our last interaction before today, hurting me seemed fairly high on his list of things he enjoyed doing. But I'd never known him to be vindictive. It was a new low for him if that was his plan.

Being this close to him again, his scent on the shirt I was wearing, brought up too many memories of the past. All those nights at the arcade, all our time spent studying side-by-side in the library, him reading over his engineering textbooks as I poured over my interior design ones. Late-night coffees, the occasional party, our last night together...

I hated thinking about that night.

I'd given fucking all of myself to him. I'd let him in. I'd slept with him. I had agreed to be exclusive, whatever that meant in college. I'd done it even though I knew better. I'd seen firsthand, time and time again, my mom getting fucked over by men she slept with, dated or married. All but my dad. But men like my dad were few and far between, and I didn't stand a chance of finding one as good as he was.

I definitely wouldn't find it in Jackson.

"Is that everything?" I asked, directing my gaze at Harry rather than to Jackson.

"I believe so, yes. For now anyway." Jackson sighed, leaning back in the creaky leather chair he was sitting in. "I would appreciate it if you two could keep me updated during the beginning stages."

"Of course, Mr. Big," Harry said. He gathered the paperwork in front of him and stuffed it into his bag. "We'll be in touch."

I stood before he dismissed us, feeling like a disobedient child getting out of their desk chair before the bell rang. I didn't want to stay a moment longer—I did not want to be around him, his cockiness or his moodiness. He stopped me before I'd even reached the door.

"Miranda," he said. I hated when he used my full name; actually, I hated when anyone used my full name. "I'd like my shirt back at the earliest convenience."

I dug my fingers into the sleeve of the shirt, gripping it to keep myself from swearing at him. "No problem, Mr. Big."

*Big & Bossy*

———

As I drove along route seven, my windows down and the stereo on, I had two options: Take the next left and head back to the office, force myself to be a person for the rest of the day, and have to talk to Harry about everything that happened while wearing Jackson's shirt. Or I could take a right instead, head home, and go for a run, allowing every single annoying thought in my mind to be stomped out with each step.

Option two sounded much better.

At the red light, I pulled up Harry's number from my contacts on my Audi's screen.

"What's up?" He asked through the speakers. "Couldn't wait til we got back to the office to chat?"

"I'm going home," I stated blandly, switching across lanes to the far right. "Can you handle the rest of today's work on your own?"

"Oh. Is this because of the meeting?"

"I don't want to talk about the meeting, Harry."

"Okay, then. Sure. I'll handle it. But don't dwell on him, okay? He's an asshole," he said. I could hear the clicking of his turn signal through the phone and it was grating on my ears. "I'll handle as many interactions for you as you need."

"Thanks, Harry," I sighed. "I'll see you tomorrow."

———

Jackson's shirt was on the floor before the door had even shut behind me. I wanted it as far away as fucking possible. The temptation to burn it itched at the back of my mind.

*You can do this.*

No, I can't. This was a horrible idea, a horrific, terrible, awful idea. My eyes burned as if I'd spent the last two hours crying, which I probably would have if no one else had been around. I was thirty-one years old, for God's sake. Why did I still become so easily upset about a guy who broke my heart ten years ago? I should be stronger than this. Harder.

And why is he even in Boulder to begin with? He's not from here. If I remembered correctly, and I absolutely did, he's from Chicago. Mr. Big-shot could've moved his business anywhere. Silicon Valley was the perfect place for tech millionaires and billionaires so why not there? Why here? Why me? Ugh.

I slipped on the first pair of leggings I could find and changed my bralette to a sports bra, heading out of the house before I could think about anything else. I needed to run, I needed to clear my head.

I ran to the park first, my empty stomach already screaming at me to go back home and eat. I never ran when I was hungry, I knew better. But I hadn't been able to bring myself to eat anything earlier, not with that dreaded meeting hanging over my head. Every attempt nearly made me vomit.

Each step on the pavement made me feel a little bit better, even if I knew it wouldn't last. Every slap of my sneakers on the concrete chased away the bad, helping me to wade my way out of the fog, turning night to day in my mind. I knew I could do it, I would figure out a way through. I just had to keep running.

What Jackson and I had was good, great, even, before he

fucked it all up. We could be friends again I suppose, if we both wanted to. *No, we couldn't.* I swatted the idea away before it fully fledged. *What I want is revenge.*

Revenge. Now there was an idea.

Things began to become even more clear. If I was going to do this, if I was going to work with him for the foreseeable future and have to listen to him and heed his orders, I was going to make it as hard as possible for him in ways he couldn't imagine.

He'd told me too many times what his weakness was when it came to women—short skirts and long hair. He went absolutely fucking mental when I'd show up to our dates with barely anything covering my ass, and my usual, unruly tresses sleek and silky. I could use that to my advantage. He hated to be teased. My thoughts were becoming diabolical.

My ankles and my knees began to hurt, and as the sweat began to pour down my back from the intense afternoon sun, I knew how I could fuck him over. He didn't get to hurt me then show back up ten years later as if it was totally normal and try to destroy me all over again. I would make every second a living hell for him. I would show him who the real boss was.

# Chapter 5

## *Jackson*

What passed as a coding lab in the building was abhorrently sad. I knew for a fact that it had an effect on our employees—barely any natural light, low ceilings, drab fluorescent lighting—but I still expected better than the shit I was being given.

"Making this many mistakes is unacceptable," I stated, pointing toward the screen behind me. "There was never this much of an issue back in Chicago. I know you all are better than this."

Mumbles of "sorry, sir" echoed throughout the room. I knew I was being harsh, knew I was nit-picking. But our investors expected better, *I* expected better, and goddammit, why was Mandy still in the back of my mind?

"I need perfection," I snapped, turning off the monitor. "Don't make me tell you again."

Everything in me was telling me to shut up and go back to my office. I was irritable, angry, and frustrated all because of Mandy. Part of me wanted to cancel the entire thing, move everyone back to Chicago, rip up my contract with

L&V. and never think about her again. But I'd put so much effort into this, I'd risked everything.

Everything for someone who would rather I didn't even exist.

Slowly, methodically, I made my way back toward my office. I needed to get away from all of it, even for an hour, but I knew I couldn't. I had a reporter waiting for me, I had people to please, a business to run. I just didn't want to do any of it.

"Jackson?"

I turned, expecting Angela to be staring at me with hatred but instead I was met with my spitting image. Black hair, much longer than mine; tanned skin; a scowl that could curdle dairy.

My sister.

"Jesus, did Mom send you?" I snarled, turning away from her as an instruction to follow me.

"Obviously." Her heels clacked on the tile as she walked. "You're expected at brunch this weekend. Mom said you haven't responded to her text."

"I didn't respond because I'm not going," I snapped, turning on the ball of my foot to face her. "I'm busy. She knows that. I can't believe she sent you all the way out to goddamn Colorado just to convince me, and it's even worse that you agreed to do it, Tiana."

"You know mom has her ways." Her eyes glanced around the dimly lit hallway, her young face scrunched up. "This place is shit. I hope you're not staying here."

"I'm obviously not staying here. We're building a new office, which, by the way, you'd already know if you paid any attention during our weekly 'family' calls." The door to my office felt like a barrier between me and the journalist, and although I'd much rather stay out in the hall and chat with my annoying little sister, I was already late for the interview. "Tell Mom I'll consider it. I have to get back to work."

"Fine," she groaned, tipping her head back in frustration. "You're the worst. And your attitude is shit, Jack."

---

"So, Jackson. I think I'll start with the question every woman in America wants to know..."

*No. Please, no.*

"Why are you still single?"

I sighed as I leaned back in my chair, my irritation already flaring. Every single time I got interviewed it was always the same shit—why are you single, do you have any women in your life right now, what's your idea of a perfect date.

You'd think with the number of times I was asked about my love life that I was Taylor Swift and not the head of one of the biggest tech corporations in America.

"To be honest, Clara, I've been far too busy with our latest AI model, Infinius."

"It's Claire."

"Okay, well, to be honest, *Claire*, I've been too busy with Infinius," I repeated, preventing myself from rolling my eyes as I said the words.

"We'll get to Infinius later. What I and the readers are desperate to hear more about, though, is if you're seeing anyone," she explained, her lips tilting upward as she dragged the clicker of her pen along her bottom lip.

"No, I'm not," I clipped, sitting forward in my chair and resting my elbows on the desk. I knew I'd have to tell her eventually. It always went down like this until I answered their incessant questioning, leaving little to no time to actually talk about the things I was proud of and about the company. "Can we move on now?"

"Of course we can. Just a few more questions on this topic though." She slowly shifted her position, uncrossing her legs then crossing them the opposite way and slightly leaning forward, emphasizing her chest. I fucking hated it. "What do you look for in a woman? What's your type?"

"How is this relevant?"

"It's what our readers want to know."

"Jesus," I sighed. I rubbed at my eyes, pushing just a little too hard on the socket and making a headache bloom beneath the surface. *Not you,* I wanted to say. "Brunettes," I replied, and she perked up as she pulled her brown, straight hair over her shoulder. "Curly hair. Dimples. Tanned, but in a subtle, natural way. Athletic body, not too tall."

Her grin faded as she started to realize I was not, in fact, talking about her. "Sounds like you have someone in mind."

*Shit.* "No. I just know my type," I explained. My back and shoulders began to ache, the irritation of my current predicament forcing pain upon myself from flexing too much. I could feel every inch of fabric on my skin, could feel the lining of my sock against the tip of my toes. I hated it. I wanted out of there.

"Now that you've moved to Boulder..." she started, and oh thank God, I think we're on the right track, "...do you plan to involve yourself in the dating scene here?"

I clenched my hands into fists to keep from making an outburst. I knew how to handle the media, how to deal with them, to answer politely and be civil. I learned at a young age since my family was always in the public eye. But with the stress of moving my company and Mandy being so goddamn stubborn, it was harder than usual. "Probably not. At least not until I've got all the quirks worked out with the new campus."

She nodded as she jotted something down on her pad of paper, slowly inching her body back into a relaxed position and not one that was meant to tempt me. "Speaking of the new campus you're building, will you be hosting a grand opening? Maybe some sort of soiree to announce yourselves to the area?"

My brows lifted in surprise as I realized this wasn't another question digging into my love life. "I... hadn't thought about that. We've got some time until we open, so maybe once we get there I'll consider it. We're still in the process of sorting out the interiors—"

"Will it be open-invite? Will you be in attendance?"

*For fucks sake, it* was *just a ploy to get a date out of me.* "I don't know yet as I haven't planned it."

"Right." More notes, more pen scratches, and all I wanted to do was escape back to my apartment. "You said you were sorting the interiors. Are you hiring outside help or a Boulder-based company?"

"Boulder-based, actually. We've hired L&V Interiors. They'll be working closely alongside us to perfect the inside of the building." Her pen scratched again in tandem with the sound of my foot tapping the floor. "Would you like to know more about Infinius?" I asked.

"Yes, in a moment." She leaned forward, pulling a second notepad out of her bag. "I have a few questions specifically from the readers if that's okay with you."

"The same readers who are so intensely obsessed with

*Big & Bossy*

my love life?" I snapped. Her answering glare nearly made me recoil, but I pulled my irritation back. "Sorry."

"You're one of the most eligible, and wealthiest bachelors in the country. Of course you're going to have women wanting you, Jackson Big," she explained, her tone tense, almost as if her patience with me was waning.

"I understand that."

"Perfect. So, first question. Have you dated any women outside of the public eye?"

Sighing, I resigned to myself that this was always going to be where the questions led. "Yes. I'm not public with my relationships."

"But you are single, correct?" She asked, that pen dragging again along her lips. If she was trying to entice me, it wasn't working.

"Yes."

"Are you looking?"

"In a sense," I answered, not entirely sure how to form a response to that kind of question based on my current circumstance.

"Would you ever date someone that wasn't in the same tax bracket as yourself?"

I snorted. *What an absurd question.* "Obviously. Do people really ask that?"

"They do," she confirmed, that air of professionalism making a return.

The questions only got worse—What's your favorite sex position? What color do you like best on a woman? Butts or breasts? Perfect first date? It was a miracle I didn't lose my absolute shit with her.

I spent the majority of the last five minutes of the meeting talking her ear off about Infinius, but she barely wrote down a word I said. It was pointless, and I was beginning to believe it would always be that way.

As she walked out of my office, her ass far too large for the skirt she was wearing and clinging on for dear life, I had a thought. One I'd never considered before, one that maybe my mother with all of her scheming had thought of long before me. If I had someone, anyone, by my side, surely the media would stop asking questions. They'd have to.

As much as I wanted that person to be Mandy and to have a second chance with her, that seemed way too far off to consider. I had to think of something else. Something fake. I didn't need to be getting involved with anyone on any real terms, didn't need an actual relationship. I could make one up, one that would satisfy my mother and the media, hopefully stop their incessant questioning over who I was sleeping with. Hopefully it would also fulfill my own desire to get them off my back.

The question left, then, was the most important one.
*Who?*

# Chapter 6
## *Mandy*

The repeated sound of my heels clicking against the drought-ridden sidewalk was the only thing keeping me sane as I walked to The Buff. Jackson had sent me an email, cc'ing Harry, requesting our presence at one of the nicest cafes in Boulder. He'd said he wanted to "talk business," but it felt a lot more like he just wanted to get under my skin.

I hated that it was working.

I'd enacted my plan, though, and I'd be damned if I let it fail. Harry would be exceptionally confused why I'd shown up in a short skirt with my long hair down considering my usual business attire was slacks and a blouse with my hair in my everyday bun. I would explain it away later.

I plucked my phone from the front pocket of my purse as I stood outside the doors of the cafe. I didn't want to go in alone. I texted Harry.

*I'm here. Where are you?*

I stared at the screen for what felt like minutes as I waited for Harry's three little dots to dance across the bottom of the screen.

## Mia Mara

*Shit, I didn't tell you, did I? I was... how do I put this nicely? Uninvited.*

I couldn't believe it. Jackson. He wouldn't.

But then again, he did force me to meet with him alone first. What was stopping him from doing that exact same thing again?

I slipped my phone back into my bag as I stepped through the sliding glass doors of The Buff. I'd never been there before, not by choice, but because it was notoriously difficult to book a table. It appeared its reputation held true as I made eye contact with the hostess at the podium, her eyes narrowing as she looked me up and down.

"We don't take walk-ins," she sneered, leaning forward on her soapbox. "You're welcome to call and try to book a table though I know reservations are full for several months."

The temptation to roll my eyes was stronger than when I had to speak with Jackson, and that was saying something. "I'm meeting someone who I'm positive is already here."

Her brows furrowed as she looked me up and down once again. "We don't have anyone expecting company."

"The reservation should be under Jackson Big," I said, keeping my voice as level as I possibly could.

A flash of surprise cut through her glare and I followed her gaze as she turned her head to the side. Not too far off in the distance, a lonely Jackson sat at a private table, the rest of the seating around him empty. *If it's this hard to get a reservation, what the fuck did he do to empty half of the restaurant?*

Jackson looked up from his menu, likely feeling the weight of eyes on him. Within seconds he was on his feet walking toward us, his composure and professional demeanor waning as I caught him glancing down at my exposed thighs not once, not twice, but three times.

"Mr. Big, is this who you were expecting?" The hostess asked, the pen between her fingers twirling aimlessly. "She doesn't match the description—"

"Yes, it is," he answered, cutting her off with an edge to his tone. He stopped before me, clad in an all-black business suit with a matching black button-up shirt. His dark hair was pushed away from his forehead, highlighting every obnoxiously gorgeous, angular line of his face. Time had only been kind to him. "Hello, Miranda."

My lip twitched upward in a sneer at my full name. "Hello, Mr. Big."

"I said... fuck it. It's fine. Come on." He turned on one foot, not even waiting for me as he started walking back toward his table. I followed, cursing myself for every step, every click of my heels.

He didn't even pull my chair out for me.

He sat before I did, every movement precise, keeping his eyes forward as much as he could. *That will only get harder with me sitting across from you.*

"Why did you uninvite Harry?" I asked, unable to stop it from coming out of my mouth. It was all I could think about since I saw Harry's text. Well, that, and Jackson's jawline. Fucking annoyingly unreal.

He sighed as he leaned forward on the table, his chin resting perfectly against his joined hands. "I figured it would be best for us to discuss some aspects of our working arrangement alone. Do you have a problem with that?"

I watched as his eyes lingered on my lips, my curls, my neck. Then lower, to my collarbone and chest. "I have a problem with you inviting him and then rescinding your invite."

"I didn't think you'd come if he wasn't invited." The words came so easily, so simply for him. I hated it. What did I ever see in this asshole? "I would argue that my assumption was correct. Wouldn't you?"

"I would argue that that's entirely manipulative and rude," I snapped back.

"Not incorrect, though."

"Did you bring me here solely to prove your theory correct or do we actually have things to discuss, Jackson?" I asked, shifting slightly in my chair and pressing my breasts together with the inside of my biceps. His tongue moved slightly across his lips, his gaze wandering, and *yes, that's perfect, this will work.*

He cleared his throat as he forced his eyes back to mine. "We do have business to discuss, yes," he said, sliding a menu across the table toward me. "But I suggest we also eat."

"I'm not hungry," I lied, placing two fingers on the opposite side of the menu and sliding it back to him. "I thought you wanted to meet here since it's better than your shitty rental office, not because you actually wanted food."

"That is half of the reason." He smirked at me as he pushed it back. "The other half is because I'd like to have a meal with you. So pick something out and order it. It's on me."

"Aren't I supposed to be buying your meal? I mean, I'm supposed to be convincing you to use our services. Normally that comes with the territory."

"Does an employee normally buy dinner for their boss?" He shot back, the edge of his mouth curling up in a smirk.

"I'm not your employee," I said, mostly under my breath as I flipped the menu open in front of me.

Our small talk as we ate consisted entirely of nothing. Empty chats, business stats, and weak attempts to pretend that we didn't hate each other. Jackson ordered something with scallops, and I ordered the cheapest thing on the menu—the kid's portion of chicken tenders and fries.

I was not about to let him own me because of one expensive meal.

Jackson wiped his mouth with the cloth napkin he'd placed in his lap as he leaned forward once again. "So, the designs."

*Fucking finally.* "Yes. I've drawn up a few ideas and some mood boards for you to have a look at. Hold on," I said, leaning over in my chair just enough that my ass lifted from the seat, giving him a good view of my hips and a bit of thigh as I rummaged through my bag.

"No need," he interrupted, his voice hoarse. "I prefer to see things in person."

I sat upright, my breasts bouncing as I did. "What does that mean?"

"I think the best way to gain insight into what I'm after would be to travel to a few different tech headquarters so that you can get a grasp of how I want the office to look and feel," he explained. His hand moved under the table and I chose to believe that he was brushing away crumbs and not adjusting himself.

"You know Google has an image function, right?"

His answering chuckle felt insidious. "I think seeing the places in person would be best for your creative endeavors."

"So you're willing to spend God-knows-how-much in

order to send me and Harry to a load of places just to get inspiration?"

The smile that spread across his cheeks was hollow, foul, evil. Or maybe I just wanted to see it that way. "No, princess. You and I will go. Money isn't an object for me."

I couldn't stop myself from physically recoiling from his words. "What?" I breathed, slouching back in my seat, my posture and presentation failing. "No. Absolutely not. Why can't Harry come? You just said money wasn't an object."

"Harry isn't needed," he said simply, his smile lowering as he realized I was not happy about this. "Besides, I think we need time to work out our kinks. You're obviously still angry with me, and that's fair, but—"

"Fuck you," I seethed, my nails nearly breaking from the force I gripped the table with. "I'm not traveling with you. Especially not alone. I don't want to spend a single second that I don't have to with you."

"Mandy—"

"Oh, *now* you call me Mandy? Absolutely not. What is all of this, anyway? You tortured me ten years ago and now you want to come back and finish the fucking job?"

"Mandy, calm down. You're getting worked up over something that doesn't have to happen," he hissed, his voice an angry whisper. The wait staff had started to stare and suddenly it made sense why he'd booked out an entire section.

"*I'm* getting worked up? How the hell did you expect me to act when you decided to waltz back into my life as if nothing happened?"

"Our history doesn't need to play a part in our working relationship now," he said sternly, the hand supporting his chin balling tightly into a fist. "I don't see why you can't move past it."

He didn't understand. He didn't care.

"Calm down so we can figure out how to move forward with this."

"You think I want to move forward? Do you think for one second I'd be doing any of this if I had any reasonable say? I wouldn't. I'd have run for the hills from you by now, Jackson."

"Oh come on. It can't be that bad to work for me," he snorted, his attempt at bringing the conversation back to a calm chat failing miserably.

"Do you know what your employees say about you?" I pressed, the anger in my bones beginning to splinter. "They say you're a goddamn asshole. They say you care more about your profits than them as people. If you didn't pay them as well as you do, they'd be running too."

His answering blink told me he didn't bother to read half the shit that came out about him and his company in the news.

"They say you're cold-hearted, Jackson. And you know what? I believe them. I have every reason to believe them, and you know that damn well," I said, the venom seeping from my lips without a second thought. I'd wanted to put him in his place for so long, had thought about what I'd say to him for the last ten years if I ever ran into him, but this was not what I had pictured or practiced.

"I'm not coldhearted," he snapped, the irritation showing on his face once again.

I couldn't stop the laugh that escaped from my throat. It was raw and angry, full of ten years' worth of heartbreak. "You fucking abandoned me," I said quietly, low enough so that only he could hear. "You are a glacier, Jackson Big, and you don't even care."

His jaw clenched as he watched me, his eyes hard as

steel as they stared into mine. If I looked long enough, I might be able to see what he'd been to me before. My rock. My person. My everything. "You didn't think that ten years ago," he said.

The backs of my eyes began to burn as I forced myself to my feet. I shook my head, trying to shake away the memories that were bombarding me from every angle. It was just too much. All of it. I grabbed my bag from the floor, ready to go, but I stood firmly in place.

I knew why. There was something left unsaid, still something hanging in the back of my mind. It itched. It burned. It had to come out, and I knew there was absolutely no way of stopping it. I could say it and be free. I allowed every ounce of anger I had left, every pent-up emotion that had built over the last ten years to surface. Too loud. Too angry.

"I don't know how I ever let myself love a man like you."

# Chapter 7

## *Jackson*

The air wasn't as fresh and the birds weren't as active, there was a "polluted" feeling in the atmosphere that started to give me a headache as I sat in my rented Ferrari outside my parent's house. I'd adapted to the elevation, nature, and fresh air of Boulder already.

What I hadn't adapted to was my parents' incessant need to have me attend family gatherings.

I hadn't even packed a bag. I had no intention of staying —I didn't want to be around my parents for any longer than I needed to. It wasn't that I didn't love them, they were great in their own ways, solid in their parenting, and loving toward me and Tiana. But they were overbearing, too involved, and being around them for too long posed its own risks. The same risks I'd abandoned so I could live my life the way I wanted to.

I sighed as I pushed open the driver's side door. The house stood tall in front of me, its pillars, large windows, and stone facade boasting the money they had. Not that I had any room to judge, but even I didn't go as far as they did with showing off my wealth. As a kid, I'd get lost in the house, wandering from room to room on Christmas morning, until I found the tree that actually had presents under it and wasn't just there for decoration.

"Jackson! You came!"

My mom stood in the center of the double door entryway, leaning on the frame in her apron and dotted slacks. *As if you're actually cooking and haven't hired chefs.*

"Shut the door, Kate, you'll let the cool air out," Dad grumbled, coming around one side of her to take a peek at me. "Oh, good, Jack's here."

"You act like I had a choice," I mumbled. I walked up the front steps toward my parents, the lines and creases in my suit from my flight far too apparent. I noticed the grimace flash across my mom's eyes as she caught them.

"I can have Henry grab your bag from the car," Mom grinned, one arm coming out as she moved toward me, inviting me for a hug. I gave it to her.

"I didn't bring one." Her thin frame always felt so much thinner when I hugged her. "Who's Henry?"

Dad rolled his eyes, his posture tight. "The new help. Your mother is in love with him."

"I am not," Mom hissed, pulling back from the hug to hit my father in the gut with the back of her hand. "What do you mean you didn't bring a bag? I've got a whole weekend of fun planned out for the five of us. You're not staying?"

"Five of us?" I asked.

"Fred's here, too." Finally, a small crack of a smile emerged on my dad's face. It wasn't often I got to see that, and the idea of Tiana's boyfriend being there was what brought it on. "The three of us are going golfing tomorrow. You can borrow my clubs."

"I'm not staying. Just here until tomorrow morning." I stepped between the two of them, the aloofness of the house already making me feel uneasy. The grand double staircase stood in front of me, marble flooring everywhere. It felt like a show house, pristine and perfect all the time. Not one speck of dust or a hint that anyone lived there or ever set foot in it.

"Tomorrow morning?" Mom echoed as Dad shut the door behind her, the sound echoing throughout the obnoxiously large hall. "For God's sake, Jackson, if I didn't know any better, I'd think you hated your own family."

"I'm just busy."

"Too busy for your family?" Mom pressed.

"Too busy for most things," I grumbled, as I followed the sound of hushed, giggling voices coming from the second of three living rooms. Mom said something behind me as I walked, her words blurring and vanishing before they even registered. I was thinking about Mandy again. Thinking about that painfully short skirt she'd worn, the little ringlets of her hair as she unknowingly twirled it around her finger, the sheer audacity she had to show up like that.

Not to mention the sheer audacity she'd had to say all of those awful things about me. She'd think twice about that if she knew what I'd done for her. The hell I'd put myself through.

It made my chest ache just to think about, right beneath the little spot that marked me forever as hers.

"Jack! Nice to see you, man," Fred called from the sofa, one arm around my little sister's shoulders and his chin pressed against the top of her head. "It's been too long."

"It has," I deadpanned, too tired to pretend to be

enthralled by any of them. "You should come out to Boulder."

"Nah, too many rocks," he joked. I tried not to take offense as my dad burst out laughing at his arguably horrible one-liner. "I do think Colorado is in our future though. Tiana loves it out there."

Mom's lips twitched upward as she watched the two of them giggle and squirm on the couch. Tiana was always friendlier around Fred, always sociable, happy. A stark difference from her usual angry facade that she definitely didn't learn from me.

"Honey," Mom cooed at my father as she untied her spotless apron from behind. "You remember that thing we bought for tonight? Why don't you go get it?"

"The Dom Perignon? Now?"

"Yes, Paul."

Fred's brows rose as he looked between the three of us. *Already?* he mouthed at my mother, and she nodded in return.

"What the hell is going on?" I mumbled.

"Shh."

Dad came around the corner, a bottle in each hand, and behind him, one of the many helpers around the house carried a tray of champagne flutes. "We haven't even had dinner yet," Dad grumbled, his shoulders slumping forward as he started working on opening one of the bottles.

I sat down on the corner seat next to him, reaching out one hand, requesting the other bottle. He handed it to me without a word. Every twist made my fingers wish they were doing something else, something far more mischievous, something that involved a lot of Mandy and very little clothing. *I don't know how I ever let myself love a man like you.*

She loved me at one point. That was enough. It had to be enough to fix things.

"Fred..." Mom urged, stepping around my father to take a seat next to me. She smoothed out the lines on her slacks, shooting a glare over to me suggesting I do the same. *No.*

Fred shifted in his seat across from us, slipping out of my sister's embrace and standing up straight as he cleared his throat. "Tiana," he began, and as I watched his hand reach into the pocket of his jeans, I noticed he was trembling. "The last two years with you have been the absolute highlight of my life—"

The cork popped in my hand so loud that the room stopped. I thanked my nonexistent gods that it didn't fizz and spray everywhere.

"You've become so ingrained in my life that I can't see a future without you in it. I know we've had our ups and downs..." *Is he really doing this now? Is that why they waited for me?* "...and I know that things aren't always easy. But between us, I think we can handle the world together."

My chest warmed as I watched Tiana's eyes light up when Fred dropped down to one knee. Mom sniffled beside me, as if she hadn't known this was coming, but obviously she had. Dad was too entranced by the champagne to actually pay attention.

"Tiana Big, will you make me the happiest man alive and agree to be my wife?"

That got Dad's attention.

"You didn't ask—"

"Shh," Mom hissed at my father.

Fred's hands shook even harder as he pulled the box from his pocket, opening it in front of an anxious Tiana. Even from where I sat several feet away, I could see how much the ring shone.

"Oh my God, yes, yes, yes, a million times yes!" Tiana squealed as she lunged for him, her arms wrapping tightly around his neck. The smile on her face was larger than I'd ever seen—even bigger than it was the Christmas she got the life-size Barbie dream house she'd been begging for.

A new record for the books.

Mom clapped beside me as Dad side-eyed her, his excitement hidden behind his irritation that no one had told him. *Join the club, Dad.*

"We can have that Colorado wedding you've always wanted," Fred said, his face buried in the crook of Tiana's neck. "I'm sure your brother knows all the good spots."

"I'm sure Tiana knows more places than I do," I chuckled. She'd been planning her wedding since she was a kid and knew what she wanted before she even knew what marriage truly was. She'd made sure the entire family was clued in on her plan.

"Now it's your turn," Mom joked, nudging me with her knee as she wiped the tears from her eyes.

"Mom," Tiana groaned, pulling back from Fred as she slipped the ring over her finger. "Can't you just let me have my moment without dragging Jack's love life into it?"

"No, no, I'm serious. You know, my friend's niece just got back from France. If I message her now I could probably talk her into coming over this evening or maybe tomorrow morning before you have to leave."

"Mom, please," I sighed. "Can we not do this again? You know how much I hate—"

Tiana's phone dinged from beside her on the sofa.

A second later, Dad's.

Mom's and Fred's went off at the same time.

Mine buzzed in my pocket. And then buzzed again. And again.

All around us phones were going off, over and over, alert after alert.

"What the fuck?" I pulled my phone from my pocket, my family going absolutely silent as they collectively stared at their screens.

It was Samantha in Public Relations. I opened the message, and within a second a photo and a link filled my screen. *Lover's Quarrel: America's Most Eligible Bachelor in the Doghouse.*

Clear as fucking crystal, the photo they'd used was of me, eyes wide at the table, a furious Mandy standing on the other side. *No. Fuck no, they were watching?* Beneath the headline was a video. I hesitated with my thumb over the play button, the terror already sinking into my bones, but before I could press it, the sound filtered out of Tiana's phone.

"I don't know how I ever let myself love a man like you."

My mom's.

"I don't know how I ever let myself love a man like you."

Fred's.

Dad's.

Mine.

*I don't know how I ever let myself love a man like you.*

# Chapter 8

## *Mandy*

Every angry stab of pain that shot through my feet, my ankles, my calves, and my thighs reminded me that I was okay. I was alive, I was in control of myself, and I was not a puppet. I was not Jackson's little plaything that he could manipulate and force to do his bidding or spend time with him. I could handle this. I *had* to handle this.

"Daydreaming again?" Harry huffed from beside me, sweat building on his forehead as he tried to keep my pace. He'd done alright on the flat path, but now, as we ascended higher on the Shadow Canyon Trail, he was struggling with the uphill. I figured he also wasn't used to running on trails; he generally pounded cement or a treadmill.

"Maybe," I chuckled, slowing my speed to give him time to catch his breath. "All this shit with Jackson has just been eating away at my brain. I think I'm down to my final ten brain cells."

"Better make sure those ten brain cells are your interior decorating ones."

Harry's hand wrapping around my arm made my fight

or flight response kick in for a fraction of a second before I realized he was asking me to stop running altogether. Every time he touched me I couldn't help but think that it was something more than just an innocent gesture. He'd always been there for me ever since my final year of university, always by my side, almost as close to me as Amanda. But that hadn't stopped him from trying to lay it on me at our graduation. Hadn't stopped me from reciprocating, either.

I'd told him time and time again during those early years that I was broken, that I wasn't relationship material, that I had my own troubles and heartbreak to deal with. I made it abundantly clear. He also knew what Jack had done to me. But there was still a part of me that thought there might be a chance he hadn't moved on from our one night spent together all those years ago, and he still had feelings for me even though our relationship was purely platonic now and had been for eight years.

"What's wrong?" I asked, turning on my heel as he leaned over himself, hands braced on his knees as he desperately sucked in breaths. "Are you okay?"

"Fine," he wheezed. "Can we turn back?"

"We're closer to the parking lot if we keep going from here." I pulled my hydration pack off my back and forced the spout into his mouth. He sucked greedily, taking in every drop of water he could and breathing heavily through his nose between swallows. "You sure you're okay? I can call for assistance—"

"I'm fine, Mandy. Let's just take it slow the rest of the way back to the car." Slowly, he lifted himself back upright, his face red and dripping.

"If you're sure."

"I'm sure," he grinned, taking one big deep breath as he

shook himself out then adding, "You should really start running more, seemed like you were struggling to keep up."

My eyes had never rolled so hard.

---

The whizz of the blender was like white noise in my head, clearing it for a few seconds as I watched the bits of fruit, yogurt, and spinach get smaller and smaller. Around and around it went, smearing against the edges, turning dusty pink in the jug.

"I think it's good, Mandy," Harry chuckled as he wiped the back of his neck with a sweat rag. He'd followed me back to my house after I'd offered him what he so dutifully called 'running aftercare.'

Releasing the button on the blender, I watched as all the little particles slowed and stopped. I missed the noise already. "This is my secret recipe, you know," I joked, sending him a half smile as I poured out enough for both of us. "You can't ever tell a soul what you saw me put in here."

"Strawberries, spinach, yogurt, and apple juice. Really creative. Genius, if you ask me."

"Shut up," I chuckled. I leaned onto the white kitchen island, my exposed lower back drying from the cool air in the house and watched as Harry hopped up onto the bar stool. Realization hit me like a ton of bricks. "Oh my God, I'm so sorry. I completely forgot about your date last week. How'd it go?"

He laughed as he sucked up the smoothie through a straw, wincing as he got a big chunk of spinach. "I was wondering when you'd remember. It's fine, you've had your own stress going on. It was good. We had a great time, she seemed super into me, but she, uh... she didn't return my calls after. Don't know what I did."

"Oh, Harry, I'm sorry." I reached across the island, grabbing his hand with mine and giving it a little squeeze.

"It's alright. I'm just a little sick and tired of every date I go on ending badly, you know? I'm starting to wonder if I'm some self-fulfilling prophecy now, ruining it before it even gets a chance to start." He squeezed my hand back, a little harder than I had, as he looked down at our overlapped fingers.

"Don't be silly. There's absolutely someone out there for you." My phone buzzed in the pocket of my leggings but I ignored it. "You're an incredible guy. You will find someone that matches your vibes and I promise, you'll be happy."

Harry mumbled something under his breath, too quiet for me to hear. I didn't press him on it. What he felt was his business and if he didn't want to share it, he didn't have to—I just wished I could make him feel better. I wished he didn't doubt that there was someone out there for him. I wanted him to be happy, and just because I was happy without a significant other didn't mean everyone else was.

He downed the rest of his smoothie before hopping off the bar stool.

"Bathroom still where it used to be?"

I chuckled. "Obviously."

I watched as he walked off down the hall, his legs still shaky from the run. My phone buzzed again in my pocket, and then again. *It's not important. If it was, they'd call.* Emptying our glasses into the sink and giving them a quick wash, I tried desperately once again to keep my mind off of

Jackson and our argument, off of whatever the fuck his end goal was with all of this.

*Buzz.*

*Buzz.*

*Buzz.*

"Seriously?" I grumbled, sliding my phone from my pocket and wiping the sweaty screen on a paper towel. My screen was lit up with Instagram notifications, from both my personal *and* professional accounts. Tags. Comments. Likes. Messages. "What the fuck...?"

I flipped open the notifications, navigating over to the tags. Picture after picture popped up, then video after video, all of the same scene—Jackson, sitting back in his chair with a smug but surprised look on his face. Me, standing up, leaning over him, angry. A direct shot from somewhere off to the side, both of us clearly in view. My hand shook as I read the captions.

*Jackson Big's girlfriend rages at him.*

*Jackson Big's off the market?*

*In a shocking new video, Jackson Big's new girlfriend Miranda Littleson is already angry with him.*

*Jackson Big, America's once most eligible bachelor, might have deserved the lashing he received.*

*Jackson Big gets his ass handed to him by his new girlfriend.*

The shaking moved from my hand throughout my body, tremors racking every inch of me as I clicked the little play button. "I don't know how I ever let myself love a man like you," I heard my voice shouting through the speaker of my phone, the clip playing twice before moving on to the next one, the exact same scene. Over and over.

It was past tense. They had to know it was past tense. Right?

I scrolled the comments, my eyes burning as I read them one by one—some supportive, some mean, some attacking my body, others attacking my hair, and some of them actually praising me for putting him in his place. This was bad, this was really bad.

My phone lit up again, my mom's face and her name, Gianna, filling the screen. A video call. It had to be about the news, there was no way she'd call me out of the blue like this. I declined the call.

Messages started pouring in, requests from reporters and shocked emojis from people I hadn't spoken to since high school. My phone was buzzing out of control, unable to keep up with all of it. My mind couldn't keep up with it either. *How did he let this happen? Was this on purpose? What the fuck does he want with me?*

"Mandy," Harry said, his voice filtering in from somewhere on my left. I could barely move, couldn't even open my mouth. Fight or flight had fully hit me now, and I'd done the one thing I always hoped I wouldn't, the secret third option—freeze up. "Mandy, what's going on?"

Shaking, furious, I turned my phone screen to him.

"What the...?" He snatched my phone from my hand, scrolling to a video and pressing play.

"I don't know how I ever let myself love a man like you," I heard myself say again. And again.

"Holy shit," he mumbled, scrolling.

My phone buzzed again in his hand, the screen lighting up with the same unknown number that had called me last week. I knew exactly who it was. I grabbed my phone back, swiped to answer it, and brought it shakily to my ear.

"Explain," I hissed. "Now."

A sigh from the other end.

"Jackson fucking Big, tell me what the hell is going on or so help me God—"

"Calm down. It'll be fine. We'll fix this. I don't know how this happened or how this got out but we will figure it out, okay? I'm in Chicago right now but I'll be back tomorrow morning. Meet me at seven. I'll send you the location," he was rambling, his own voice shaken and surprised. I hated that it made me feel even an inch better about the situation.

"I don't want to see you," I lied.

"I get that. But we need to meet with my PR team, okay? First thing in the morning."

"I want it fixed now," I choked, my voice cracking. I could feel the tears building in the corners of my eyes. I didn't want to cry, not about this, not about him.

"I know. I know, princess, but it's getting late and there's nothing we can do about it tonight," he sighed. In the background, I could hear giggling and the clinking of glasses.

"Are you... are you *celebrating* this?" I snapped, sucking in a breath and holding it.

"No," he said quickly. "My sister just got engaged. I'm sorry. This is horrible timing."

It was too much. Far too much for me to deal with, too much for my already fragile heart when it came to him. "Okay," I whimpered. A warm hand met my shoulder, rubbing me softly, trying to calm me. "Tell Tiana congratulations. But you better fucking fix this."

## Chapter 9

## *Jackson*

The bags under my eyes were clear proof that I didn't get a lick of sleep. Dodging questions all evening from my prodding family was hard enough, but trying to sleep knowing what Mandy was going through was worse. I'd taken the first private jet I could book—four a.m. I hadn't even said goodbye to my family, quietly leaving the house and heading to the airport.

I clutched my cup of coffee in my hands as people started filing into the room. My entire PR team had flown in at short notice, and I'd waited until the absolute last minute to tell them where to meet. We didn't need the press following them or Mandy, not when I was already being watched like a hawk. Another article about me had already hit by five a.m., a picture of me boarding the private jet, heading back to my girlfriend as they'd titled it.

Mandy stepped through the doors last, her wild hair up in a bun. Her eyes were as dark as mine, a cup of coffee in her hands. She wore her oversized NYU hoodie, the one she wore almost constantly back in the day, and a pair of joggers. Too early for anything else.

I'd booked an office space under a false name just outside of Boulder to give us enough privacy to deal with this.

"Hey," I sighed, turning the office chair next to me to offer it to her. She didn't even fight me as she collapsed into it, and even though I knew it was mostly because of her exhaustion, I wanted to believe that she was growing fond of me.

"Hi," she mumbled. "Didn't get any sleep either?"

I shook my head. "Not a second."

"Is it bad that it makes me feel slightly better?" She breathed a slight chuckle, her eyes staring down at her cup, her name written in swirly writing along the top.

"No, it's not bad, Mandy."

Samantha, my head of Public Relations, took her place in front of the group. "Right. Let's get this over with," she said, turning on the projector and lighting up the wall with article after article about us. "This is bad, guys. Really bad. Media shitstorm-level bad."

"We know that" I sighed, leaning back in my chair and practically hugging my cup against my chest.

"I don't think you do, Jackson. This is worse than every single time before," she clarified, clicking something on her laptop and pulling up the video. Mandy winced as it played three times for emphasis. "Every other time the media has suspected you of dating someone, we've been able to either bury it under the rug or scrub it per your requests. This is different. This is a video, Jackson, and worse yet, she's saying she loves you."

I watched as Mandy breathed in a shaky breath, her eyes still glued to the lid of her coffee. "I meant it in the past tense," she mumbled, and dammit, that hit me right in the heart. I knew that's what she meant but it hadn't stopped me from wondering if maybe it was still present tense. "They have to know that."

"Sorry, Miranda, but they don't know that. Maybe next time you're shouting at Jack, be more precise with your words," Samantha clipped, her irritation at the entire scandal seeping through. This was making her job harder, I knew that. But it wasn't an excuse to talk to Mandy that way.

"Don't talk to her like that," I snapped, locking eyes with Samantha's bloodshot ones. "I pay you to deal with stuff like this. Not to be rude to someone who was just speaking her mind and trying to clarify things."

I tried to pretend not to notice the weight of Mandy's eyes on me. "Thank you," she mumbled.

Samantha looked between me and Mandy, her glare wavering on me. "Even if you meant it in the past tense, it doesn't matter now. Trying to clarify the situation will only make people more intrigued and more likely to spin things in ways you might not want."

"So what do we do?" I asked.

Jason from the media team spoke up next. "Well, as requested, we had a meeting last night over Zoom and have been in contact all morning trying to figure out the best way forward," he said, standing from his chair and taking his place next to Sam. "The only possible thing we could come up with to get through this is something that I don't think either of you will like, but it's often used to sway the media and the public on their opinions in situations like these. It may buy you some time to figure out whatever is, uh, between you two."

"There is nothing between us," Mandy muttered.

I had a feeling I knew what was going to come out of their mouths. I had friends that had tried certain tactics to get the media off their backs when it came to questions about their love life. Hell, I had a few of my own. But involving Mandy in such an idea felt like way too much, it felt wrong. She'd fight it every step of the way, kicking and screaming before she agreed, even if deep down she knew it was the best way to get the press to give us a drop of privacy.

"Are you suggesting a fake relationship?" I asked, setting my coffee on the table before my grip made the cup explode. From the corner of my eye, I watched as Mandy stiffened, her tired eyes going wide.

"Yes," Jason said, clicking into the next slide that Sam had arranged. It included headlines of celebrities, different instances of announcing a fake relationship to build up excitement and then letting it calm down. "Better yet, engaged. You'll probably get a few interviews, a bit more press, and then it'll die down until you announce whatever comes after that, be it a wedding or breaking up. From then on, things should die down."

"No."

I turned to Mandy, watching as she desperately tried to take a breath. "Mandy," I sighed, the temptation to reach out and comfort her nearly overwhelming my senses.

"No," she repeated, her hand shaking as she set her coffee next to mine. "Absolutely not. I'm not doing that."

I'd be lying if I said it didn't disappoint me to hear her say that. I knew it was a bad idea, knew that I was a shit person for wanting it, but a fake relationship with her would mean more time with her, more opportunities to make things right. I wanted that more than I wanted anything.

Well, maybe not more than I wanted her.

"I'm not a pawn," she said, her voice growing a little

louder. "I'm not going to pretend to be your fiancée, I'm not going to pretend to be your anything."

"Miranda," Sam hissed, her irritation growing. "This is the only thing I can offer you. If you want some semblance of peace, this is your only option."

"It's Mandy," I grumbled.

"Whatever, I don't care." She stood ramrod straight, her stark gray eyes flashing, her breaths quick and shallow. "I don't fucking care. I'm not doing it."

"Mandy," I pressed, shifting up onto my feet. My chair rolled back unintentionally too quickly, crashing into the wall behind me. "You're overreacting."

"Can you at least listen to the benefits?" Sam asked, her tone far too similar to one of an annoyed mother chastising their child. "People will believe it—"

"I don't want them to believe it," Mandy barked, her head snapping in Sam's direction so quickly it made the bun on her head begin to shake loose. "I don't want to be associated with him. I don't want this. I don't want to do this." Her bottom lip quivered, her shaking hands trembling harder. "I'm not doing it. I'm not."

I hated seeing her like this. It had been ten years since I'd seen her this worked up, this stressed out, and that had been right in the middle of midterms. But this wasn't midterms. This was far more serious. "Mandy," I breathed, wrapping my fingers around her biceps and turning her to face me. She didn't even flinch. "Look at me. Deep breaths."

"There will also be benefits for you, Miranda. You'll get Jackson's personal protection team and plenty of good press for your business," Sam continued.

"She gets my team no matter what she decides," I hissed at Sam, not taking my eyes off of Mandy.

Mandy's eyes went glassy as she stared up at me. I

hated this. I didn't want her to have to deal with any of it, even if it meant something positive for me. "I can't do this, Jack."

"Okay. What do you suggest instead?" I asked softly, resisting the urge to drag my fingers up her arms and take her face in my hands. I knew there wasn't another option, and I knew she'd come to that realization sooner or later. But she had to do it on her own. She had to make the choice for herself.

"I... I..." Mandy stammered, her heart hammering so hard in her chest that I could feel each pulse in her arms. "I don't know. I'd prefer this hadn't happened in the first place."

"I know," I sighed, holding eye contact with her, watching as the tears welled up. She didn't blink, didn't want them to fall. "Unfortunately, J.B. Tech hasn't invented a time machine yet, so that's not in the cards. But this option, this unfortunately shitty option, is the best we have right now. It's the best thing for both of us. I don't like it either."

"I hate it," she snapped, the anger seeping back into her, the softness she'd shown me for a millisecond disappearing. "I hate you."

The words hit me like a bullet to the chest. I recoiled, releasing her arms. "You hate me?"

"Of course I hate you," she choked, rubbing at her eyes and forcing the tears to retreat. "I don't want to spend another goddamn minute in your presence, let alone be your fiancée. I'd rather jump off Bear Peak."

I didn't want to get angry with her. I wanted to help her, to make her feel better, but if she was going to attack me I was going to argue right back. "You'd rather kill yourself than spend time with me?" I laughed, the anger in my blood beginning to boil. "Fine. Let's take a drive, princess. Bear Peak isn't far."

Her eyes widened with rage, and I could see the little blood vessels getting larger in the whites. "Fuck you," she spat, taking a step toward me. "You'd love that, wouldn't you? Out of your hair, out of the press, dead in the middle of Rocky Mountain National Park—"

"You think I want that?" I was livid. I leaned in closer, our faces just inches apart, our breaths mingling. "I am trying to *help* you. Neither of us can change what's already happened, but this is the only way forward."

"I'm not doing it." She grabbed her coffee from the table, stepping with one foot toward the door. I grabbed her, stopping her and pulling her closer. Again, she didn't fight me.

"Listen to me," I snarled, each word dripping with a venom I didn't want to have to use on her. She'd given me no choice. "It's better to lay with the devil you know than the fucking sharks that will come for you if you don't. They will consume you alive, do you hear me? You might hate me now, but you'll hate yourself even more if you invite the hell they will force on you."

"Let go of me—"

"Listen and I'll let go," I said sternly, loosening my grip just a hair. She could've wriggled free at any time if she wanted to. "You've never experienced what they can do. If I were you, princess, I'd be careful how I talked to the one person who can get you through this nightmare—me."

Her bottom lip trembled again either with rage or frustration. It melted my heart, but I held my gaze, my sternness. She needed to understand. These were not schoolyard bullies we were talking about. This shit could get really nasty, really quickly.

She opened her mouth, and from the look in her eyes I could tell that whatever she wanted to say was far harsher than anything she'd already said, but lucky for both of us she shut it again. "I'll think about it," she mumbled, tearing herself away from me and stepping out the door.

## Chapter 10

### *Mandy*

My house had never been so loud.

Camera shutters, knocks, my doorbell going off every five minutes. The sound of people mingling or shouting, faces appearing outside my windows. I'd closed every blind, blocked them off with every curtain, turned on music louder than I could stand, and still they swarmed, yelling my name, shouting questions that I had no intention of answering.

I was furious. I hadn't stopped shaking since the meeting this morning. Jackson had called me multiple times, and each time, I'd sent him to voicemail. I refused to save his number in my phone; I had unintentionally started to remember more of his number with every call he made. But I'd never tell him that.

I didn't care about his promises, he was the reason I was in this position to begin with and I'd be damned if I bowed to him now, even if he did show me a smidgen of kindness when the panic set in. I hated myself for bending to it so easily at the time—I will not allow myself to be so vulnerable again.

My phone rang beside me, this time lighting up with a familiar face and name instead of Jackson.

*Mom.*

"Hi," I answered, my voice betraying me already and cracking on the only word I could manage.

"I'm outside," Mom said. I could hear the camera shutters and talking through the speaker. "Can you let me in? I've brought you some groceries and other things I thought you might need seeing as you're stuck inside."

I chuckled as I wiped my nose. "Yeah," I said, "Of course I'll let you in. Don't talk to them."

"I would never."

I hung up the phone and made my way to the front, the din from outside getting louder with each step away from my bedroom. As soon as I swung open the door, men and women from everywhere began to lunge toward it. Some with cameras, some with microphones, venomous words spilling from their mouths. In the middle of it all, Mom stood strong, groceries in hand and a smile on her face.

I grabbed her and quickly pulled her inside, slamming the door in their faces and locking it.

"Thank God you're here," I sighed, wrapping my arms around her and pulling her to me. "I didn't want to subject some poor delivery guy to the frenzy out there."

"Oh, honey, of course I'm here," she cooed, dropping the bags at my feet and hugging me tightly. "Why didn't you answer my calls yesterday?"

"I was too freaked out," I sighed. I pulled away, getting a good look at her. I was her spitting image, just younger, right down to the bags under her eyes that told me she hadn't slept well, either. "I'm sorry."

"It's okay. You've got bigger problems than making sure your ma is kept up to date," she chuckled.

*Big & Bossy*

She followed me as I picked up the bags and carried them to the kitchen. They were heavy, filled to the brim. *How long was she expecting me to be trapped for?* One by one, I started pulling the items from the bags, filling up my fridge as Mom sat at the breakfast bar.

"So, pardon my curiosity," she started, resting her chin in her palms. "But is it true? What they're saying, I mean."

"No," I sighed. "It's not true, Mom. That's the problem."

"Can't you just tell them that?"

"I've tried. The ones outside don't believe me and I doubt that any others will." *Blueberries, freezer. Bread, counter. Yogurt, fridge.*

"That guy you were with... his name sounds familiar," she said, flipping open her phone. "Jackson Big?"

"He's famous," I explained, hoping to put a stop to that line of questioning before it went any further. I put what was left of the bags on the counter to sort later as I watched her study whatever photo she had up on her phone.

"No, I know that. But didn't you date a Jackson in college?"

"No," I lied.

She narrowed her eyes at me as she turned her phone around, a photo of me from ten years ago filling her screen, one arm around Jack's waist and a smile as wide as the Pacific Ocean plastered on my face as I stared up at him.

"He was a friend."

"Friends don't look at friends like that," she said simply, pushing her glasses up her nose as she locked her phone. "I used to look at your father that same way. I remember who he was to you. So be honest with me. Is it true?"

I sighed. I hated this, all of it. Even my own mother didn't believe me. "No, Mom, it isn't true. Yes, I dated him.

No, we're not together now. What I said in that video was meant as past tense."

She pursed her lips together, her hands reaching out to grab mine like I'd done to Harry yesterday. "But you did love him at one point."

"I don't want to talk about that—"

"You know," she said, her hands squeezing mine as she locked eyes with me, "Sometimes I worry that the things I went through after losing your father affected you. I don't want you to end up like me."

"I've completed steps to make sure I won't," I deadpanned, letting go of her hands and standing up straight. "I can't get hurt by love if I don't let myself feel it."

"I don't want that for you, either," Mom insisted. "A love like I had with your father is once-in-a-lifetime. If for a second you think you have that, you need to hold on tight to it."

I couldn't keep the scoff from crawling up my throat as I crossed my arms over my chest. "You think I love him? I detest everything about him. You know what he did to me. You know what I went through."

"I do know that" she nodded, her eyes growing softer as she took in my defensive posture. "I think a lot of your anger and fear comes directly from the feelings you had for him back in college and how much he hurt you."

"No," I snapped. "What I felt for him then is completely gone now. He won't ruin me. Not again."

---

Mom agreed to stay the night with me. She watched out the front window as I gathered spare blankets and pillows for her to sleep on the couch, her eyes wide as she stared at the news crews and paparazzi still stationed outside.

"You can't live like this," she mumbled. "What are you going to do, Mandy?"

I sighed as I lifted the comforter high, spreading it across the plush sofa. "I don't know. Jackson offered me a solution but I don't know if I'm going to take it."

She turned, brows furrowed. "What did he offer?"

"He wants us to pretend to be engaged. He said it would get the media off our backs for a little bit."

Even in the dim light of the room, I could see the concern on Mom's face as she walked toward me. "Honey. I say this because I love you and not because I'm trying to push you to do anything, but if Jackson genuinely thinks it would help, why don't you want to do it?"

"Because I don't."

"Miranda. Doing nothing has to be worse than trying something," she said. Slowly, she lowered herself onto the sofa, her bones creaking as her age showed a little. "I know you have a right to be angry with him—"

"My anger is entirely justified," I interjected.

"I know."

"Do you?" I snapped, clutching the pillow between my fingers as the image of his face popped up in my mind, his soft expression as he looked down at me this morning when I panicked. *Why did he have to be kind to me then?* "He spent months building my trust. He knew I was wary of relationships, he knew that I was terrified of being in love because of you and Dad. I trusted him. I gave myself to him. And then he ran before I even woke up."

"Honey—"

"He hasn't even had the decency to explain himself!" I laid the pillow down on top of the other to keep myself from trying to tear it in half. "He knows exactly what he did to me and he hasn't even apologized."

Mom took a deep breath as she laid back on the couch, shuffling herself under the comforter and pulling it up to her chin. It suddenly felt like the tables were reversed, like I was tucking her in and she was just a child who didn't understand. "I know that. But he's trying to help you now. Maybe that's his way of apologizing."

"If that's his way of apologizing, he can shove it up his ass."

"Mandy."

"Mom."

"Just think about it. I can't always bring you care packages and spend the night. I have my own life," she chuckled, cracking a smile at me.

"I don't know. I think maybe the best thing is to just get out of the contract and put as much distance between him and me as possible. I hear Bermuda is nice year-round," I joked, forcing the smallest smile to my face just to make her feel better.

"If you move to Bermuda I will never forgive you," Mom laughed. "I'd never see you!"

"Only because you're scared of flying." I leaned into the motherly role, placing a little kiss on her forehead. "Go to sleep. You can put on rain sounds or something on your phone if the press is too loud."

"What a strange sentence to come out of my daughter's mouth."

I chuckled as I got up. Even though I didn't like my situation, having her here and talking things through with her made me feel at least a little better about it all. I would get through it, I was sure of that. I'd been through worse.

As I got myself ready for bed, showering, brushing my teeth, and doing my skincare, I couldn't keep my mind from wandering back to this morning. Jackson had been far too kind to me. I almost wished he hadn't—at least then I could still be entirely justified in my anger. But he knew before I did that my anxiety was peaking, and he remembered from all those years ago that reassurance was my ticket to calming down. It hadn't worked, but he'd tried.

And I hated that.

My phone dinged on the countertop as I finished applying my night oil. I'd managed to set up my notifications to only show the things that mattered instead of the litany of pointless ones.

*I'll cut you a deal, Mandy. If you're willing to go through with this, I'll ensure you get whatever you want, no strings attached. Name your price.*

*You know it would help both of us.*

I sighed as I picked it up, double checking the number. Definitely Jackson.

I'd finally saved his name in my phone.

# Chapter 11

## *Jackson*

Mandy was good at many things: interior design; studying;, dancing; running; and, most annoyingly, stressing me the fuck out.

Six days. For six goddamn days she's ignored my calls, stayed in her house, and worked from home. If she was attempting to get around the problem with the press by hiding, it was only making them chomp at the bit that much more. Headline after headline stated, 'Jackson Big's new girlfriend hides from reporters'. They wanted answers. They wanted a *story*. And even though she was keeping in contact with the planning committee of J.B. Tech who were under express orders not to speak about her to the media, her silence with me in particular was beginning to drive me insane.

And that is why I'm sitting in the back of my driver's car outside of her office building. I heard she'd finally gone in to work today.

"I think it'd be beneficial if we went through the parking garage and you entered from the rear," my driver, Steve said, starting up the engine once again as we stared at the swarm of reporters standing outside the front of her building.

"No need. This shouldn't take long."

Agreeing to the engagement was almost certain at this point—she'd be insane to deny it, so what harm could it do if I just waltzed right in?

I unbuckled my seatbelt, got out, and brazenly walked to the building's front door, cutting through the sea of people as cameras snapped and microphones were shoved in my face. Ignoring all of it, I casually stepped through the front doors into reception.

"Oh my God." The woman behind the desk stared at me with wide eyes, her face pale. "You're Jackson Big."

"Which floor is L&V Interiors on?" I asked, ignoring her shock as I stepped up to the elevators.

She blinked at me, not quite comprehending my question. "Uh. F-floor two," she stammered, her fingers wrapping tight around the necklace she wore. "No, sorry, floor three."

"Thanks."

The doors closed and the elevator began to rise, dinging once, twice, three times before opening again. I knew exactly what to expect on the other side.

Mandy stood there, her wildly angry face almost distracting me enough to not notice how incredible she looked. Her hair was down again, hanging about her shoulders in perfect curls. Her black blouse hung loosely over her shoulders, tightening a bit over her breasts, and was tucked into a short, loose plaid skirt. No tights. Simple heels.

*Was she expecting me?*

I stepped through the elevator doors, steeling my jaw to keep myself from thinking about how much I desperately wanted to bend her over a desk and fuck her senseless. My cock, however, did not seem to get the memo, and I had to focus to get the blood to retreat.

"What the actual fuck, Jackson?"

Just seeing her like this was threatening to distract me entirely, but I forced myself to focus on her face and only that. "Well, if you hadn't ignored my calls and messages, I wouldn't have been forced to make an unannounced visit."

She pushed her hands into her hair and took a deep breath to try to calm herself which only placed more emphasis on her chest. Screw just fucking her—I needed more than that. I needed to *claim* her and fuck the stubbornness right out of her.

"I need an answer, Mandy. You can't just leave me in limbo like this." I said. "What'll it be?"

She groaned in frustration as she turned away from me, the noise only exciting me more. I needed to get a handle on myself, and I needed to do it quickly. "Follow me."

We walked in silence down the quiet hallway, each door leading to a different set of small offices. I let myself watch the way her curls bounced with every step, the way her skirt swayed around her upper thighs, until she opened the last door on the left and ushered me through.

The space was small and not what you'd expect from an interior design office, but it was beautifully decorated. Two individual offices on either side, a break room at the back, his and hers restrooms. It was cohesive and professional throughout, modern with its color blocking and scattered foliage. "Harry went home at lunch. We can talk about this alone, just you and me. I don't want to deal with your PR team right now."

I nodded. The space between their offices was set up with a small waiting area, two plush modern sofas and a table between them.

"Do you want a drink?" She asked, moving back toward the break room and leaving me in the waiting area. "It's Lagavulin you like, right?" she called out. "Harry's got some back here. It's not the twenty-six so you'll have to settle for the eight, okay?"

*She remembered that?* "That sounds amazing. Yes please," I said as I took a seat on one of the sofas, leaving plenty of space if she decided to sit next to me.

I sat in silence until she returned, two glasses of Lagavulin Eight in her hands. She set them on opposite sides of the coffee table, taking a seat across from me and crossing her legs as she leaned forward. "Okay. Let's talk."

"I assume you have questions," I said, picking up my glass.

She didn't reply. Instead, her fingers wrapped slowly around the half-full glass of whiskey in front of her, lifting it to her lips before downing it in one gulp. She closed her eyes and took a deep breath, clearly calmer than when I first arrived.

"*If* I say yes... how will this work?"

My mouth watered as she leaned back, uncrossing and re-crossing her legs. I swear she gave me a peak of what was under her skirt, but it was too quick to be sure. "Well for starters, we'd have to pretend to be head over heels over each other," I began, my gaze locked on her legs. "We'll need to do a public proposal announcement, maybe a few interviews. And you'll be my plus one at my sister's wedding in two months."

In truth, I had no idea if it would take that long for the media swarm to die down. It could be less, could be more, but my mother and Tiana had insisted I bring her when they'd seen the news. Said it would be dramatic.

Mandy twirled her hair around her finger as she

watched me like a hawk, her lower lip clutched between her teeth. "*If* you say yes, do you know what you'd like in exchange?" I asked.

She leaned forward, crossing and uncrossing and crossing again. *Fuck, she has to stop doing that.* "*If* I say yes, I'd like you to introduce me to potential clientele. Take me to a few networking events. Sell me. Make my business boom, Jackson Big, and we *might* have a deal."

"That's all you want?" I asked. I lifted my glass to my lips, taking a hearty sip and feeling my control dwindle just a hair. "You can have anything, and you want clients?"

"Yes," she replied as if it were obvious.

"Deal."

"Wait. Not a deal yet," she drawled, her lips twitching up at the corner. "I'm assuming that pretending to be in a relationship with you is going to include some... intimate things in public. I want to know how far you expect us to go."

*Jesus. I can't talk about this with you, not now, not when my cock is doing half of my thinking and my control is slipping.* "Don't tell me you're already excited to kiss me," I teased, the words falling from my tongue like molasses, soft and smooth. Too much, but I didn't care.

She scoffed, her cheeks reddening. "You wish I was. Don't let your ego get the best of you, Jackson."

I chuckled as I stood, my mind swimming with far too many thoughts of having her in my arms, my lips against hers, my cock... *Stop. Calm down.* "It won't be any more than what you typically see in photos of other couples in the public eye. Kissing, holding hands. Looking at me like you want me, but based on that blush on your cheeks, that one shouldn't be hard."

Her blush deepened, this time with what I was sure was irritation. "I'm practicing," she lied. "Don't fool yourself."

"Is that right?" I asked, stepping around the table that separated us. I leaned forward, holding my weight with one hand on the armrest and the other on the back of the sofa, caging her in. I could smell her perfume, see her chest rising and falling, the goosebumps breaking out along her neck. "Just practicing, princess?"

"Yes," she breathed.

I leaned in a little closer, our breaths mingling, and lifted one hand to her cheek. My heart raced in my chest just from touching her, from being so close to her. "Then I hope you don't mind if I practice a little myself."

Her pulse thrummed beneath my fingertips as I brushed them along her jaw, her throat, the back of her neck. So soft, so warm.

"No one's in here to take our photo, Mandy. You can tell me to stop," I whispered, brushing my nose against her cheek as I greedily took in more of her scent. I could smell the hint of Lagavulin on her breath, could practically taste her perfume . "But you don't want me to stop, do you?"

She breathed in, rough and shaky. "You're an asshole, Jack."

I rolled my eyes, moving swiftly before she could object, wrapping one hand around the small of her waist. I hoisted her up off the sofa, the little shriek she made only making it that much better and exciting me even more. I carried her over to the large window that separated her personal office from the seating area and pressed her against it..

She looked up at me, confusion blaring in her half-lidded eyes. I didn't want to step away. I'd take what I could get, even if it was only a drop.

"Jack—?"

I couldn't stop myself.

I needed her.

I needed this.

I pressed my lips to hers before I could talk myself out of it.

# Chapter 12

## *Mandy*

*I genuinely think I'm falling for you, Mandy. Like, really falling.*
   *Please don't call me panda bear during sex.*
*I could fall in love with you so easily.*
*You're the best thing I've ever called my own.*
*That face you pull when you're so engrossed in something is the sexiest thing I've ever seen.*
*You're going to haunt me forever, aren't you?*
*I want you, and I want you for real.*

One by one, memory after memory hit me like a ton of bricks. His scent, his skin, his warmth, his lips—it was too much. Distracting enough to send my guard crashing down, allowing myself to become enveloped in him.

My body betrayed my mind.

Before I could even register what I was doing, my lips were pressed against his lips, my body pressed against his body. My arms wrapped far too naturally around his neck, pulling him closer. He sighed into me, that faint taste of whiskey on his breath mixing with the familiarity of his mouth. His body had changed in the last ten years, had grown stronger, manly. I'd barely been able to keep myself from looking at it, but with him now in such close proximity, I couldn't keep from feeling it nor did I want to.

"Fuck," he grunted, one arm snaking its way back around my waist, forcing me to arch into him.

I could feel my heartbeat pounding against my ribcage as he kissed my lips, my jaw, my neck. My breath caught in my throat when his free hand roamed, crossing the border where my short skirt met skin, wrapping his hand tightly around the muscle in my thigh and lifting my leg. Jack held it to his hip, forcing me to hook myself on him, and dear God I knew damn well if he went any farther, I wouldn't fight it.

"Mandy, your two o'clock is here." Sarah's voice cut through the speaker beside my head loud enough to shock me to my senses. "Would you like me to send them up or are you still busy?"

My arms fell from Jackson's neck, my hands shaking as the sinking realization hit me. I let him kiss me. "Oh my God," I breathed. I dropped my leg, forced myself to take a deep breath and let it out slowly.

Jack's arms reluctantly released me. He took a step back, putting much-needed space between us, and the smile that crept across his lips was so smug that I wanted to slap it off of him. "I don't think we'll have a problem with the intimate aspects of this."

"Oh shut up, Jack." I needed to respond to Sarah. But I didn't have the nerve to do it, didn't have the willpower to leave this weird little moment Jack and I had cultivated. I watched him with bated breath as he pushed his hair back, fixed the collar of his shirt, and adjusted the hard bulge pushing through the front of his pants, a cocky smirk on his face.

He leaned forward and I turned, convinced he was diving in for round two, but instead he pressed his finger against the speaker's button beside my head. "Send them up."

"Jack," I hissed.

He chuckled as he stepped away, leaving me slumped against the wall, shaken and confused. "You might want to fix your makeup before they get here. Your lipstick is a bit smudged."

A second later, he was out the door.

---

My two o'clock came and went in a blur. I shouldn't have accepted some of the ludicrous things that Angela, my client, wanted me to do for her home. I definitely should have quoted her more money. Or at least said no to her myriad of requests.

But I didn't do either.

I didn't know what to think, do, or say. My brain was too full of fog, too focused on what I'd allowed to happen between Jackson and I. *Why did he kiss me? Why did I let him?* It pinged around in my brain far longer than I wanted it to, sitting heavy like a stone in my stomach.

I was trying to rattle him, not provoke him. Wearing skirts and letting my hair loose was a step outside of my comfort zone, one that I was willing to do because I knew how much it affected him. I wanted to make *his* life a living hell, not my own. I wanted him to see what he'd left behind and what he could have had, not make him want it again.

Maybe that was naive of me.

Or maybe he was playing along. That was the only explanation that made sense and it was the only one that put my mind somewhat at ease.

Harry had tried calling me a few times. I didn't answer. I couldn't bring myself to look at my phone, not with the countless amount of emails popping up every second trying to get me to comment on my 'relationship' with Jackson. Constant DMs and tags on social media, half of them derogatory... I didn't need that in my head.

---

By six o'clock, the crowd downstairs still lingered. They knew I hadn't left yet and, apparently, they were convinced they'd get a comment from me the second I stepped out the door. *Fucking vultures.* I paced my office, trying desperately to think of a plan of how I could sneak out without being caught, but it didn't seem there was one.

*When was Jackson's protection going to start?* I groaned to myself as I sank back into my chair, resigned to sleeping here if I had to.

The door to our private offices opened. I straightened, a chill going down my spine as I realized any of the people downstairs could have easily come up, Sarah wouldn't be able to stop them. It wasn't exactly hidden which floor we were on.

I grabbed my phone from the desk, prepared to enter the three numbers we're taught from birth to know by heart, as a shadow loomed at my doorway. Before I could scream, Harry's head popped around the corner. "Still here?"

I breathed a shaky sigh of relief, my body still flooded with adrenaline. "Shit, man, you couldn't have called out?"

"I didn't know you were here," he chuckled. "What's with you? You usually aren't so easily spooked."

I leaned forward on my desk, dropping my forehead onto my arms. "I thought one of the vermin downstairs had gotten in."

He sucked in a breath as he stepped into my office. "I didn't even think about that. Sorry, Mands."

"It's okay," I sighed. "I just can't fucking leave. Not with all of them swarming down there."

"Do you want me to help you get out?" Harry offered, plopping himself into one of the two chairs that sat opposite my desk.

"No, it's okay, I've already ordered a U-Haul to bring all of my furniture here. I'm moving in and never leaving," I joked, peering up at him between the strands of curls that hung over my face.

"Probably didn't help that Jack showed up earlier," he snapped, a blip of anger crossing his features. "It's all over the tabloids. What did he want, anyway? Was it about the project?"

*Should I tell him?* The temptation to warn him of what I'd apparently agreed to gnawed at me, told me it was better for him to find out from me than to see it in the tabloids as he had with Jack's visit. "No," I started, lifting my head from the desk as if it were a bucket of cement. Harry was one of my best friends. My business partner. He deserved to know the hell that I was about to go through and how much it might affect him. "It wasn't about the project."

But Harry was also overprotective. He wouldn't be

happy about this—he'd make stopping it his number one mission. And it couldn't be stopped now. But he'd find out sooner or later...

"What was it then?"

My phone buzzed, the digits I'd typed before disappearing entirely and the words "Jackson Pig" taking their place. I snorted at myself for the adjustment I'd made to his name as I grabbed it, swiping to answer his call without even thinking twice. "What do you want, Mr. Big?"

"Always so eager to speak to me. I heard you're still at work. Are you ready to leave?"

My ears perked up at that. *Had he figured out a way to get me out?* "Yes. Absolutely I'm ready to leave."

"Good," he said. "Get your stuff and go downstairs. My driver is waiting for you out front. Be seen, but don't talk to them."

My stomach dropped. "What? I thought you were sneaking me out—"

"Nope. That's not how we're playing this, princess. You're going to walk out, head held high, and show them that their presence doesn't bother you," he drawled. "I'll see you in a bit."

"Wait, what? Where are you sending me?" Silence. "Jack?"

I pulled the phone from my ear, seeing that he'd hung up.

# Chapter 13

## *Jackson*

*Jackson Big of J.B. Tech may be hard at work on his new project dubbed Infinius, but behind the scenes, he's been working even harder to hide his single status. Has that all changed now?*

I scoffed as I skimmed the article. Line after line it talked about my love life, my preferences in women—physical characteristics, body type, personality traits—and how they just happened to match Mandy. Hardly anything was said about the campus, the project, or my move to Boulder. Just nonsense that people want to read. *Why do they insist on printing this shit?*

I exited the news app, too annoyed to finish the article. I didn't care if they ended it with something about the project or who the most "eligible bachelor in the country" was dating. I dreaded the headlines that would be coming out after tonight, how little they would focus on my accomplishments, but I needed the media's surge so we could breathe when the tide waded out.

A little itch of a thought formed in the back of my mind, nagging me, telling me this was the worst idea I could have ever come up with. If anyone from ten years ago saw it and realized who I was, they could put the pieces together. Possibly put a threat out against her. Take her—

The sound of knives and forks scraping against plates and glasses clinking together snapped me back into the moment and my attention turned to something—some*one*—else. Mandy walked through the doors of the Flagstaff House Restaurant, wearing the little black dress I'd left in the car for her. Briefly, I wondered if she'd changed in the backseat and if Steve had had the decency to pull over and step out instead of watching through the rearview mirror.

She looked otherworldly as her irritated gaze found mine. I was seated in the back, against one of the many windows that overlooked the city below from Flagstaff Mountain. I'd had to shell out thousands to ensure the seats around us were empty, save for a few that I knew would belong to reporters and journalists. I didn't want them close enough to hear us, just enough to see us.

I almost regretted letting anyone else see just how amazing she looked, though.

The satin swayed against her skin as she crossed the floor toward me, her long curls bouncing about her shoulders and breasts. I hadn't left heels for her; hadn't needed to, not when I saw the ones she was wearing earlier. They matched perfectly.

"Why are we at the fanciest restaurant in town?" She grumbled, sliding into her spot next to me as I beckoned for her to leave the chair opposite empty.

"Because I wanted to have dinner with you, sans the screaming match that happened last time."

"I have no problem screaming at you in a fancy restaurant." One of the straps on her dress fell down her shoulder. "Is someone else joining us?"

"No," I answered, slipping a finger beneath the strap and lifting it back into place.

"Then why am I sitting next to you?" Her glare could cut glass as she flinched from the brush of my fingers.

"Because I wanted you close."

"Whatever," she huffed, picking up the menu in front of her and studying it like it was written in another language. "Where are the prices?"

In the center of the table, a bucket of ice held a bottle of champagne. I plucked it from its home, popping the top off as silently as I could. "Places like this don't tend to have prices on their menus. If you're here, you can afford it. Simple as that."

She glared at me as I poured her a glass. "How much are we talking? I only have so much excess I can spend right now."

"I'm paying," I said simply, glancing across the room at those I knew were meant to be watching. "Try to look at least a little bit like you want to be here, Mandy."

"No," she chuckled, lifting her glass to her lips and taking a sip. I knew she would never admit it, but I saw the glimmer of satisfaction as she tasted it. "I don't have to pretend with you, right?"

"It's not for me," I said quietly, my hand twitching in my lap as I glanced at her bare thighs. *Touch them.* I cleared my throat to distract myself as I nonchalantly nodded in the direction of the reporters. "Press is over there. This is a publicity dinner."

She looked at me, her eyes glassing over. "This is a publicity dinner?" She asked, the glass in her hand shaking just slightly. I gave in to temptation in the hopes it would calm her, snaking my hand across my lap and grasping her knee gently.

"Yes," I whispered, trying desperately not to think about the little electric spark that shot through my hand when I touched her skin. *So soft. I remember other soft parts of you, princess.* "They shouldn't be able to hear us as long as you don't shout at me. But try to look like you're happy."

"You could have warned me," she said, her face turning upward in a soft grin but her tone dripping with venom. "Do you always have to be so cryptic?"

"You would have fought me on it if I told you it was public."

"I'll fight you on it anyway."

"I don't doubt that" I chuckled, giving her thigh a quick squeeze before moving my hand away.

One of the waiters, clad in a tailored suit and a silk tie, stepped up to our table. "Have we decided on our choices for the four courses tonight?"

Mandy glanced at me, a small nod of her head telling me to go ahead. "I'll have the venison pate, duck breast, filet mignon, and macerated raspberries, please."

The scratch of a pen on paper filled the silence between us until he turned to Mandy. She glanced down at the menu, her eye catching on something in particular. "Can I have the salad, Maine lobster, wagyu, and the cheesecake? Please."

I chuckled as I realized that she'd chosen the two items on the menu that had the extra charge star next to them, upping the price of her attendance by nearly double. It didn't bother me in the least.

As the waiter turned and walked away, Mandy seemed to sink in on herself. Whether it was because of my presence, the intimacy that occurred between us, or because of the eyes glancing at her every two seconds, I wasn't sure. But I didn't want her to feel awkward. I wanted this to still be a nice dinner, even if it was for the press.

"How are things going with the planning for the new campus?" I asked, turning my body toward her and resting my chin on my hand. "Do you have any new ideas?"

Her brows rose, a little twinkle in her eye shining. "Yes," she said, a grin lifting her lips. "I've got a few ideas."

"Tell me about them," I said. I let my wants get the best of me again, placing my hand on her thigh.

"Well, for one, I was thinking of possibly adding in a canteen," she started, and already, I could tell how much she loved to talk about her work. I didn't mind it—I loved watching the way she moved, the excited little gestures she gave, the way her face lit up. It felt like the Mandy I knew before, not the one that had turned into an angry, bitter woman. Though I suppose that was mostly on me. "I don't know if you had one before at your Chicago offices, but from my research, having a place where your employees can go to get lunch and hang out is really good for morale."

"We had one," I said, lightly tracing the tips of my fingers in slow, little circles on the inside of her thigh. "It was small. Couldn't fit more than ten or so people at a time, so something large enough for a good portion of the staff to take their break in would be great."

"I can definitely make that happen with the floor plans you gave me," she grinned, her eyes meeting mine for half a second before looking down to my fingers caressing her leg. It was like a mask slipped back into place. Her body stiffened, her eyes lost their spark, her brows furrowed. When she spoke again, her tone was harsher. "That is, if you don't want to make a million changes first."

"Why would I?" I asked, removing my hand, not wanting that to set her off.

"Well, you seem to have a problem with committing to things, Jackson."

*Ouch.* Her words hit me quick and fast, tearing open a little gash in my chest that I'd spent years trying to patch back up. My hands balled up in my lap, my knuckles cracking as I forced myself to open them back up, flexing my fingers. "Don't do that. You have problems, too." She opened her mouth to speak, but I cut her off before she could. "Don't. If you snap at me, Miranda, use your words and paste a smile on your face."

Her jaw quivered as she forced a fake smile. "Most of my problems are your fault," she seethed, the duality of her expression and the venom from her words conflicting. "So if we're going to talk about *my* issues, we should start with you."

"Me?" I scoffed, grinning right back at her. "I think we both know that the root of your distrust comes from things that happened far before I entered your life." I was not going to let her walk all over me and blame me for everything that had gone wrong in her life. We both knew that there were other reasons why she struggled with trust and besides, I'd risked so much for her. So much that she didn't even know about.

She leaned forward, her too-happy face less than a foot from mine. "You're right. I didn't and still don't trust people. But you shoved the knife further in and fucking twisted it when you came back into my life."

"At least I'm bringing profit to your failing business," I snapped, regretting the jab as soon as it left my lips.

"Fuck you, Jack."

"Not unless you beg."

"Real mature."

"Don't be a prude, Mandy," I spat, chuckling as her

happy mask broke a little. She glared at me, the mask breaking even more, and *fuck* she'd always looked so sexy when she was angry. And with her this close... "You showed me earlier there's still a part of you that wants that."

"We were practicing."

"For what? When we're alone? Grow up and admit you liked it," I hissed, leaning even closer, enough that I could smell the hint of champagne on her breath. "You liked when I kissed you. You came to life in my arms. Just admit it, Miranda."

Her lips parted as her eyes flicked back and forth between mine, her breathing just a little too rough, too heavy. Having her so close, with that stupid half-happy, half-angry expression and that satin black dress, was too much. She was too much. She'd always been too much for me.

I wanted to take her right there on the fucking table.

"Why did you leave?"

It hit me like a bucket of cold water. I recoiled, pulling away from her, dropping my mask entirely. I wasn't expecting that, didn't want to talk about it. "It doesn't matter," I breathed, knocking back the rest of my glass of champagne before filling it too full so that it spilled.

It was the wrong answer. She leaned back in her chair, every trace of emotion gone from her features. The waiter came with our first courses, and not a word was said. She was drawing in on herself, cocooning, and I needed to say something, anything. *Is this what you were like when it happened?*

"Even if I tell you," I started, unable to watch her any longer as she folded into herself, "it's not like you'll understand, Mandy. All you need to know is that I did it for you."

## Mia Mara

Mandy picked at her cheesecake as she stole little glimpses at me. She could try to pretend that she hated me as much as she wanted, could pretend like I meant nothing to her anymore, but I knew deep down there was still something there, still a spark.

Dinner went by in silence, not a peep from either of us between our argument and dessert. We ate, we sipped, and we pretended like the other didn't exist. I needed this night to go smoothly, I needed the press to have something to talk about other than our complete, awkward silence. I needed to initiate phase two. I was already planning on doing it tonight and our current state proved that it was more important now than ever.

Without saying a word, I slid my arm around Mandy's waist, pulling her and her chair closer. She flinched, her eyes locking with mine for the first time in nearly an hour as she did her best to disguise her confusion.

"What are you doing?" She asked, her body instinctively leaning away from me. I pulled her back.

"Phase two," I mumbled, placing a small kiss on her temple. She flinched again.

"Jack, please, I can pretend to like you right now but I'm just not in the mood to be close—"

"Come here," I snapped, painting a smile on my face as I looked down at her, "or I'll make you."

Her eyes went wide, her brows furrowed as she struggled to keep that mask in place. I kicked my chair out from under me, dropping down on one knee in front of her, and releasing her waist to search through my pocket instead. "Jack, what the fuck—"

"Smile, princess," I hissed. I pulled the little wooden box from my pocket, flipping it open so she could see the ring sitting atop a bed of moss. "They're watching."

# Chapter 14

## *Mandy*

I couldn't say that I hated everything about our dinner together. There were moments that felt real, moments that flowed easily as if there hadn't been ten years of separation between us. But there had also been moments where I wanted to die, where I wanted to climb inside of myself and never crawl out.

I twirled the ring on my finger absentmindedly. It was, annoyingly, exactly the kind of ring I would want. A rose gold band, molded to look as though it was made of twigs and wood, little leaves surrounding the dusty olive musgravite stone. I'd never wanted a diamond, and the rarity of this made me wonder just how much he'd forked out for it. It looked like nature, like home, and it was absolutely something I wanted to wear for a lifetime.

Not that I would be.

I wasn't expecting a proposal last night. I knew our deal included a fake engagement, but every part of me wished he'd warned me in advance. It was hard enough being in front of the press for an extended period of time, pretending that I was enjoying our dinner together, but having to fake my excitement for something I'd once dreamed about but now loathed? It was awful, gut-wrenching. I hated it. Faking liking him was hard enough on its own, but faking being in love, accepting a proposal... it was too much. Especially when half the time I just wanted to strangle him.

I needed to constantly remind myself not to latch on to those moments where it felt like it had before, all those years ago. This was one hundred percent fake. The desire I saw in him last night was bogus. I couldn't let it affect me, not again. I was only teasing him to rile him up. Nothing more.

It couldn't be anything more.

"What the fuck does that mean?" Amanda asked, her face screwing up in confusion. "Saying 'I did it for you' just feels like an excuse, Mandy."

"I know. I have no idea what he meant." I stared down at the ring, the shimmer of it under the soft glow of the restaurant's lights almost hypnotizing. "He said I wouldn't understand and he was right."

Amanda sighed as she plucked a plate off the serving cart, placing it in front of me. The restaurant she ran closed after their afternoon menu to prepare for dinner, and waiters and hostesses were shuffling around us, preparing for the evening service. I'd figured now was as good a time as any to sneak in to see her—with it being closed, the paparazzi couldn't get in to snap their obsessive little photos of me. Amanda was the head chef here, and whenever I showed up like this, she always liked to force-feed me new recipes. I never complained.

"It feels weird wearing something on my ring finger," I mumbled, unable to tear my gaze away from it even with the fancy little portion of gnocchi in front of me. "Doubly weird that it's probably obscenely expensive and I need to be careful."

"Never thought I'd see the day when you got engaged," Amanda snickered, sliding into the seat next to me and stabbing a gnocchi with my fork. She lifted it to my mouth as she made little airplane noises.

I glared at her as I opened my mouth, happily receiving the little parcel of potato and garlic. "I'm hardly engaged," I said around a mouthful of food. "I don't think this counts."

"It counts more than anything else you're likely to do." She popped a gnocchi into her mouth, humming her approval to herself. "If only it were real."

I fake gagged and watched her cheerful expression drop, slight horror taking over. "No, no, that wasn't about the food. The gnocchi is great. It was the idea of actually being engaged to Jackson that made me gag."

"Thank God. You scared me," she chuckled, plucking another plate off the cart and sliding it in front of me. This one looked like calamari, with small bits of breaded something and two dips to choose from.

"Calamari?" I asked.

"Something like that."

"Nope. Absolutely not. Do not serve me rocky mountain oysters, Amanda," I laughed, pushing the plate away . "I have never and will never have a taste for bull testicles."

"But you're engaged to one." She held back her giggles as she reached across, plucking one of the " "oysters" off my plate and popping it into her mouth. *So gross.* "Seriously, how are you feeling about everything?"

"Like I want to launch myself off of Bear Peak."

"It can't be that bad. It's not like you actually have to marry him," she said, her voice going soft as she realized that I really was struggling.

"No, but I have to spend time with him. Too much time.

I have to pretend to be in love with him. And I don't really have another option."

"What, you can't back out?"

"Well, not now. I've already said yes and it's already being printed in the papers. If I had said no, who knows what would have happened to our contract? Who knows if the media would have ever stopped hounding me?" I placed my elbows on the table, burying my face in my hands like a child. "I couldn't say no."

Amanda rubbed my back gently. "You'll get through this. It's only temporary."

"I don't want to get through it," I scoffed. "This is going to be so obscenely hard, Amanda. Especially with my mind playing tricks on me and his incessant cockiness. I know it'll be worth it in the end, I'm sure of that, but I might just entirely destroy myself in the process."

"You won't. I promise. It'll be hard but I'll be here through all of it and so will Harry."

Having them by my side wouldn't fix the anger. It wouldn't fix the sadness, the irritation, the nasty feeling in my gut that had been brewing since we'd kissed in my office. Those were things I'd have to weather on my own, and god fucking dammit, I didn't want to. I didn't want to have to face this. How could I pretend to be in love with him now when ten years ago that was my reality, a reality that ended with my heart being shattered?

My phone pinged in my purse as Amanda's manager stepped up to the table. He mumbled something to her, and she turned to me, an apologetic look on her face. "I'll be right back."

I nodded, watching her step away as I slid my phone out. A text notification from Jackson sat at the top of my screen above all the others from the media that I had ignored.

*I'm picking you up at noon tomorrow for a date. Wear pants.*

I rolled my eyes at his demand. Absolutely not, I thought, opening up the message to reply to him.

*You're coming to my house?*

*Is that a problem? They already know where you live.*

*It's fine. Anything I need to know before you arrive? A wedding, perhaps?*

*Haha. No. Just wear pants.*

Amanda reappeared in front of the table, her lips pursed. "I need to get back to the kitchen for a bit. Will you be okay?"

"That's fine," I sighed, gathering my jacket and purse beneath my arm as I stood. "I'll head home. Jackson's just texted me that we're apparently going on a date tomorrow, so at least you'll have good reading material in the following morning's newspaper."

"Oh God. What is it this time?"

"No idea. But I plan to annoy the shit out of him the entire time," I replied, flashing her a grin. "Have a good night." She gave me a quick hug before taking off toward the kitchen at rapid speed.

The way my mind kicked back into overdrive as I left the restaurant nearly made me jump. Every thought came pouring back in, a million possibilities, a thousand ways it could go wrong. I had no idea if it really was worth it, despite what I'd told her, not when my own sense of self was on the line.

The warm glow of the street lamps and the few, quick flashes of a camera lighted my way as I walked back to my car. This was going to be my new normal, at least for a while. I needed to get used to it, and it had to work.

I'd given Jackson what I swore to myself I never would; I'd given him the power to be able to destroy me once again, heart and career. And a part of me, a horribly naive part of me, didn't regret it.

# Chapter 15

## *Jackson*

My Harley-Davidson CVO hummed beneath me, its newly remodeled backseat an addition I never thought I'd end up making. But Mandy needed somewhere to sit, and if I was going to turn this into a long-haul situation, I wanted her to be able to ride it with me.

I kicked the foot out and turned it off, letting the heat from it warm my legs as I watched the pool of press people mingling about her front door. They were already beginning to turn, their cameras snapping as I pulled my helmet over my head. I smoothed my hair so I wouldn't have a helmet-head for the photos they'd inevitably take.

My black riding jeans, white shirt, and leather jacket weren't my normal attire when getting photographed. In fact, I don't think they had a single photo of me on my Harley—it was my me-time activity. No one could see my face if I had on a helmet, so I didn't draw attention. A breath of fresh air.

I almost regretted exposing myself with it as I stepped up to her door, cutting through the sea of people. *I can always buy a new one, a different model that they won't recognize.* Two knocks and the door swung open.

I was going to kill her.

"I said wear pants," I grumbled, stepping through the door and shutting it behind me before the reporters could pick up on my irritation.

"What, you don't like short skirts anymore, Jackson?" She smirked, leaning onto the back of her sofa as she played idly with her curls. "Are they too much for you to bear?"

I glared at her as I looked her up and down. Any other day, the little black, pleated skirt would be my favorite thing she could possibly wear. But unless she wanted potential burns on the inside of her calves and for the paparazzi to get an eyeful, it wouldn't do. "We're going on my bike. I suggest you put on jeans or something."

"Bike?" She asked, pushing off the sofa and sensually strolling slowly over to the window. *Fuck, she's wearing heels, too.* She shifted the blinds, peeking between them. "Oh. I've never been on a motorcycle before."

"There's a first time for everything."

"Do I need a helmet? I've probably got one in my garage, but it's for riding a bicycle, not a motorcycle." She turned to me, that little skirt swaying too much, revealing a flash of her upper thighs in the blink of an eye.

"I brought a helmet for you," I said, my voice far breathier than I expected. *Get it together, Jackson.* "Go change, I'll wait. No heels and put your hair up."

The snap of cameras pinged around us as I showed Mandy where to place her legs in order to not get burned. "These two pipes right here are the exhaust," I explained, propping her booted feet up on the pedals for her. "Don't touch them. It can burn even through your jeans."

"Okay," she said, the helmet flopping forward on her head as she nodded.

"Shit, that's too loose, isn't it?" I stepped closer to her, a whispered *sorry* under my breath as I lifted her chin with my knuckle. Her eyes went wide as she looked up at me, a perfect little photo-op, and I tightened the latch under her jaw. Just the brush of my fingers against her skin put my senses into overdrive. "There we go. Nod for me, princess, so I can see if it's tight enough."

She obeyed without hesitation. It didn't move.

"Perfect." Satisfied with the positioning, I threw one leg over the bike, sat down, and kicked the stand back up. "You'll have to hold on to me," I said over my shoulder.

"What?" She asked, her brows furrowing. "I didn't agree to that."

"Do you want to fall off while I'm going eighty miles per hour?"

"No."

"Then hold on tight." I placed my helmet on my head, clicking the visor down. One swift turn of the key and my bike roared to life, the warm hum radiating up through my legs and pelvis. The crowd of paparazzi parted, giving us an easy exit, and as I revved the engine with my hand, Mandy's arms flew around my waist. The feeling really shouldn't have been as exciting as it was but the instant her arms wrapped around me I felt a rush of adrenaline.

. . .

We drove around the outskirts of town before making our way through the peaks, down along Boulder Canyon Drive then all the way to Barker Reservoir before turning back. I made sure to check in with her occasionally, shouting over the surprisingly warm winter wind and the roar of the engine, and every time I looked over my shoulder she was smiling bigger than I'd ever seen. It was a smile I didn't deserve, but one I planned on working hard to keep.

As we made our way back into the center of town, her arms seemed to grow tired from holding on for so long. They fell downward, each hand resting on the upper part of my thigh, her chest leaning against my back. The ring I'd given her shone brightly in the afternoon light. I almost had to pull over from how fast my heart was racing just from the sight.

If things were different, if I hadn't grown up in the business that I had, maybe we could have been doing this for the last ten years and I wouldn't have had to walk away.

I placed my feet on the asphalt as I pulled up to a red light. It had just turned, and I knew damn well how long this one took to complete its cycle, so I gave myself a moment to relax. I leaned back into her, and she didn't seem to fight it. Her warmth was enough to drive me wild on its own.

"Where are we going now?" She asked, her tone gentle even as she shouted over the roar of the engine.

I lifted my visor so she could hear me better as I turned my head toward her. Without thinking my hand found her thigh, resting gently. She didn't flinch. "I figured we could go on a walk around Pearl Street. Maybe some quick shopping if you're up for it. Mostly for the press."

"Okay."

We fell into a shockingly comfortable silence as we waited for the light to change. Slowly, easily, I traced little circles on the outside of her thigh, wishing I'd let her wear the skirt instead so I was touching skin instead of jeans. She rested her head on my back, sighing into me, and fuck I wanted to hear that sigh in another context. I wanted to touch her so badly. I wanted to drive us to someplace private and fuck her on the back of my Harley.

The light changed, knocking me back into the present moment. I had to move but the mental strength it took for me to let go of her thigh was almost unnerving. As I began to drive again, I felt her chin on my shoulder and her breath against my neck.

---

Holding her hand was something I wished had happened naturally. But it was for the press, for the occasional snap of a photo that came as we walked down Pearl Street, the light turning low as the sun began to set just below the peaks.

"You can talk to me, you know," I whispered, leaning down toward her ear.

"There's not a lot to say. We're engaged. Surely you know everything about me."

I snorted a light laugh as I stood up straight. "We can talk quietly, princess. They don't have to hear."

"Why do you keep calling me that?" She asked, her head snapping in my direction. Her fake smile was plastered on but no one would be able to tell the difference in photos. "It's not like I still call you panda bear."

Just hearing her old nickname for me was enough to knock the air from my lungs.

"Jack?"

"Sorry," I rasped, clearing my throat. "Old habits die hard, I guess. Would you rather I didn't call you that?"

She looked up at me, her eyes wide with far too many unasked questions behind them. She didn't speak as she turned her head away from me. "You said we could do some shopping, right?"

My mouth was suddenly as dry as a desert and I licked my lips before answering her. "Uh, yeah, of course. What do you want?"

She tugged me toward a store before I could even catch a glimpse of what it was. Lululemon. I should have guessed.

I stood by her side as she browsed the items in silence, the little reprieve from the press a chance to act fairly natural. Before I knew it, her arms were full of workout clothes and she was headed toward the checkout counter. I followed her silently, trying harder than I thought would be necessary to not stare at her body as the woman behind the counter scanned each item of clothing. Higher and higher the number on the screen ticked, hundreds, then just over a thousand. *She's expecting me to pay, isn't she?*

"Your total is one-thousand, two-hundred, ninety-eight dollars and ninety-nine cents," the woman said cheerfully, likely excited about the store's commission sales from this purchase alone.

Mandy's hand went to her pocket. "Oh, Jack, I seem to have left—"

*Beep.*

She stared at my phone against the card reader, the sale

going through in the time it took for her to catch on. "You paid for me?"

"Don't act like you weren't going to ask," I mocked, chuckling as I kissed the side of her head for good measure. I scooped up the handles of the bag and took the receipt from the far-too-happy sales associate, dragging Mandy back out of the store by her hand. "I doubt you go on thousand-dollar shopping sprees often."

"What's that supposed to mean?" She snapped, pasting her happy face back on as we entered the sea of more press.

"It's not an insult," I said. I gave her hand a gentle squeeze. "I just knew you were going to ask me to pay. It's fine, I'm happy to."

"I could have paid," she grumbled, reaching across my chest toward the bag. "At least let me carry it, you old-fashioned goon."

I laughed as I held it away from her. "Absolutely not. And that's not just because the press will smear me for making my fiancé carry her own bags. I can see it now— *America's once Top Bachelor not so much a catch as we thought.*"

The giggle she let escape forced my heart to skip a beat. It was a real one, a happy one. Another mental image I'd keep. "You're ridiculous."

"Is that a bad thing?" I asked, squeezing her hand again as I looked down at her. *So fucking beautiful.*

"No. Yes. Maybe." She shrugged. "Can we sit? My legs are, like, weirdly exhausted from the motorcycle."

I led her across the street toward an empty bench as the street lamps began to flick on around us. The press was starting to get bored and thinning out, and I wanted a chance to actually just enjoy being a normal human with her when we could actually speak.

I propped the bag between my legs as we sat, her thigh brushing against mine, and put my arm around her. "Do you think it's working?" She asked softly, her head lolling onto my shoulder. *It's just for the cameras if any are left. Don't get excited.*

"If my PR team is right, then yeah, it'll start working soon. They'll run out of things to focus on. Right now, though, we're the hot new ticket in town. It'll die down." I drew little circles on the side of her arm, the little freckles peeking out as her skin erupted in goosebumps. "Are you cold?"

"What? No," she lied.

I rolled my eyes, leaning away from her enough to slide my leather jacket from my arms. I wrapped it around her shoulders before resuming our position. "You don't have to lie."

She hummed, sinking back into me far too easily. "You mentioned traveling. Are we still doing that?"

I nodded. "Yes. I was thinking we could head to New York, maybe Chicago. I've reached out to a few well-known architects in those areas and asked if they'd give us a tour of some of the best-designed buildings. I think it'll be good for inspiration."

Mandy fiddled with her ring, spinning it around her finger, studying it. It looked too perfect on her, and I'd be a liar if I tried to say that it didn't make my chest warm to see her wearing it. "Okay. I'll go with you."

I chuckled, placing a kiss on the top of her head. "Thanks for not fighting me on that this time."

"Oh I will absolutely still fight you on it," she smirked, lifting her gaze back up to me. The temptation to lean down and kiss her was too much. "Don't you worry."

"Then why aren't you?" I breathed, unable to resist the

urge to take her face in my hand. She sighed, turning into my palm.

"I just don't want to right now."

The walk back to the bike was short. I put her things into my saddlebags, locking them up tight before getting out our helmets. She watched me from the sidewalk, a sleepy grin spreading across her cheeks as the sunlight faded quickly. She looked far too beautiful, too tempting.

"Come on, princess," I cooed, holding out a hand for her. "Your chariot awaits."

She laughed as she stepped off the sidewalk, and as if in slow motion, I watched her foot land the wrong way. She grabbed my hand, falling forward too fast. I dropped the helmets, scooping her body up with my arm before she could hit the ground, one hand in hers and the other around her torso.

She looked up at me, her eyes twinkling in the streetlight, and dear God this woman might be the death of me. She blinked, confused, it all happening too quickly for her to comprehend.

*I could kiss her. Right now. I could say it was for the press.*

My heart thudded painfully in my chest as she wrapped one arm around my shoulders. It felt like time stopped as I watched her, the Mandy I knew all those years ago held so firmly in my grasp. Slowly, she lifted herself, closer to my lips. *Let her. It has to be her choice.*

Our breaths mingled for half a second before she stood upright, narrowly missing my lips. The blush on her cheeks made me believe that she'd felt it too, the pull, but the smug smile she gave me told a different story.

*Such a fucking tease.*

## Chapter 16

### *Mandy*

My heels against cement echoed through the large, empty space as Jackson and I walked through the new campus together. A lot was still needed. They had the basics done—water, electricity, Wi-Fi. But it was still bare bones inside. A perfect, blank canvas that I could have my absolute way with.

"You said you wanted to add a canteen," Jackson said, turning down one unfinished hallway and into a room that still had construction going on. "I've added this room specifically for that purpose. It's still being built, obviously, but I'll get the blueprints over to you so you can start designing."

I looked up at him, the smug little grin on his face far more annoying than dashing. "You added on a whole new section just because I suggested a canteen?" I asked, jotting down a reminder to myself in my notebook to wait for the blueprints.

"I seriously consider all of your ideas, Mandy," he said. He led me further down the hall, toward a large, open area where the space widened out in an impressive angle. "This, I think, will work best for the main offices. I'm thinking long tables in the center, enough space for nine or ten programmers to fit on either side. We want to give them lots of space. And no cubicles—they serve no purpose for creative minds trying to collaborate together."

Note after note, I wrote down his ideas. It was nice to see the way his eyes lit up as he spoke about the campus he envisioned, what he wanted for his employees, and how much he wanted to do right by them. He might be a tyrant at times, but he did care.

He looked absolutely ridiculous in his suit with a bright orange hard hat on his head and I couldn't suppress the chuckle that escaped.

"Why are you looking at me like that?" He asked.

I shook my head. "You just look silly in that hat."

The side of his lips tilted upward as he let out a chuckle of his own. "Yeah, so do you. You're lucky I haven't made any jokes about it yet."

"You have hard hat jokes just ready to go at any time?" I laughed.

"Of course I do. Maybe if you weren't so stubborn and *hard*-headed I'd tell them to you."

I snorted as I turned to him, his arms outstretched, his chest wide open as he spun in place. Above him, the skylights filtered in drop after drop of sunshine, illuminating him so perfectly that I inwardly gasped. *I want to climb him like a tree.*

Attraction had never and would never be a problem with him. He'd ticked off every box ten years ago, and even though he had changed and was no longer the man I'd fallen in love with, he was still a force to be reckoned with. Beneath the layers of his tailored suit was a strong and built physique, one I'd seen firsthand when he'd literally given me the shirt off his back.

I hadn't been able to stop myself from looking. I tried averting my gaze but I knew he could tell my eyes were glued. If anything, the attraction to him now was stronger than it had been when I was twenty-one, and I knew that he was aware of that as I watched him turn back toward me, his chin lowered, his jaw cut, the smallest bit of stubble poking through on his cheeks. I knew it from the way he looked at me.

"Don't like my joke?"

I narrowed my eyes at him. "Your joke was fine."

"Then what was that glare you just gave me about?" He asked. The sound echoed through the massive room as he took a step toward me, his scent swirling around me, invading my space. The same scent as the one on his shirt when he'd given it to me.

*Fuck. I can't let him know I was thinking about him.* "I was just coming up with ideas for this space. Maybe some art pieces hanging from the ceiling since it's so high up. That kind of thing."

"Oh." He turned his head upward, his eyes catching the light, his face lit from above as if a spotlight had fallen on him. I could see the gears in his mind turning, could tell he was envisioning it himself. It wasn't a bad idea—I'd seen something similar in other large offices, but it had tumbled out of my mouth before I could actually think about what that would entail and the amount of money that would need to go toward that type of decor.

"I love that."

"Seriously?"

"Yeah." He nodded as he slipped his phone from his pocket, snapping a picture of the ceiling and its skylights. "We could even hire someone local to create something custom. Make it a community thing. We could have it as the centerpiece when we launch."

I wasn't expecting anything like that to come out of his mouth. It was far too sweet, down-to-earth, and thoughtful for someone with their head so high up in the sky. "Really?"

"Yes. I think something like that would fit nicely in this space and it would help with morale as well," he explained, his jaw ticking as he looked about the room. "It's a great idea, Mandy."

---

By the time we'd finished walking the expansive campus, it was nearing five o'clock and my notebook was filled to the brim with ideas and requests—half from him, half from me. Seeing the site in person had done a lot more good than I expected, especially with him in attendance. Would I have preferred to tour it with Harry instead? Maybe, maybe not. I wasn't quite so sure anymore.

"You didn't show me your office," I mentioned, making idle chatter as we handed in our hard hats. "Is it not finished yet?"

"The space is already laid out. I just don't know exactly what to do with it yet," he admitted, one hand gently resting between my shoulder blades as he ushered me toward what would become the parking lot. "Isn't that why I'm here?" I asked with a chuckle. I stepped faster, letting his hand fall away. "Surely it'd be in your best interest to get my opinion."

"Maybe but it's my space, you know? I want it to feel

like me. I'll let you know when I'm ready for you to work on it." He smiled tightly at me, the same one he used to give when he was stressed out of his mind from class and claimed nothing was wrong. "Would you like a coffee?"

*What? Where the hell had that come from?* He nodded toward the small, white shipping container ahead of us. From the sliding window on the side, a young man in an apron leaned out, coffee in hand, offering it to the construction worker in front of him. "Uh, yeah, sure. How...?"

"I hired one of the local specialty baristas to make coffee for the guys. They don't need to pay or anything, it's just to keep them energized and warm while they're working. It's actually really good coffee," he explained. He leaned against the side of the shipping container, his arms crossed over his suit-covered chest. "Are you still a latte girl?"

*How and why did he remember that?* "No," I chuckled, stepping up to the window.

The man in the apron leaned forward onto the counter, a friendly smile plastered to his face. "What can I get ya?"

"Oat milk flat white, please."

"And one black Americano," Jackson tacked on, coming up behind me far too close. I could feel his breath on the back of my neck as he placed his order. After a moment the barista came back with our drinks. "Let's sit," Jack whispered, his breath gliding past my ear.

I followed him over to the small seating area around the back of the shipping container. It was just a few chairs and tables, but it was a nice little space for the people that worked for him to take a break and enjoy their coffee. Despite the rumors of how much of a dictator he could be when it came to running his company, he seemed to actually care about his employees and wanted them to be happy. Maybe they were just rumors after all.

We sat in slightly uncomfortable silence sipping our coffees, my hands wrapped around the warm cup in the fading sunlight. I didn't know what to say to him, didn't know how to act since people were mingling around, workers turning in their hard hats for the night and shrugging off their brightly colored safety vests. I didn't know if I was supposed to be playing the role of Jackson's adoring fiancée or if I could just be myself, be the designer. I'd worn the ring just in case.

"It's good to see how far you've come, Jack," I said, the words slipping from my mouth before I had the chance to consider them. I had to commit now, otherwise, he'd just get cocky. It still hurt like a bitch to admit it, though. "You've... done some amazing work over the years. And it's clear as day that you care a lot about your employees."

"Thank you," he chuckled, his fingers sliding back and forth along the side of his coffee cup. It was nearly impossible not to watch, not to get transfixed by it. "That might be the nicest thing you've said to me in ten years."

"Oh, shut up."

"It's true," he laughed, that same smile not quite reaching his eyes. "In all honesty, Mandy, I'm impressed by you too. Your portfolio is astounding, and the testimonials that L&V has received speak for themselves. You've grown a lot, princess. It's amazing."

"Thanks, Jack."

The silence that fell back over us felt more natural than it had before, questions pinging around my head daring me to ask them. There was so much I wanted to ask about his life, his struggle, what happened our last night together. I needed to know. *I could ask him. He's being responsive right now. Maybe he'll bend.*

"Can we talk about that night?" I asked.

Immediately, he stiffened. "Why?"

"Because I want to know what happened. If we're going to be spending a considerable amount of time together, *fiancé,* then I don't want questions hanging in the air," I explained, my nerves already starting to bubble in my gut.

"You want to know why I left." It wasn't a question. It was more of a statement.

"Yes."

Slowly, he took a deep breath, raising his coffee to his lips. His hands shook, just a little, and for a tiny fraction of a second, I genuinely thought he was going to tell me what happened.

But the words out of his mouth froze me in place.

"If you don't trust me when I say what I did was best for you, then I don't know what to tell you, Mandy. You weren't the only one who was in love."

# Chapter 17

## *Jackson*

The harsh winter air and snow beneath my skis were exactly the kinds of things I needed after the intensity of my week.

I'd flown into the Colchester Resort this morning by helicopter after deciding that I'd had enough time away from my closest friend. He ran the resort and skiing had always been his deepest passion, but he had an accident that unfortunately caused him to stop competing. Owning and running a resort was the next best thing in his eyes and luckily I got first dibs on the freshly snow-ridden mountains with him.

"I need to know every single in and out of what the hell is going on with you," he laughed as he greeted me, clunking his way up to my side while we waited for the ski lift seat to scoop us up. "I know you've been texting me but man, I know that isn't telling the full story. How's Mandy?"

I grunted as metal hit the back of my knee, forcing it to buckle. I fell back onto the seat, the swaying throwing me off kilter. "Uh, yeah, she's good. I mean, she's changed a lot since NYU."

Wade boarded much more gracefully, unsurprisingly. He pulled the bar above us down over our heads, locking us in place. "That's not surprising. You have, too, Jack."

The ground below moved farther and farther away as the lift ascended up the mountain. I'd never been one to be afraid of heights, but every time I got on a damn ski lift with Wade and he moved around rocking the damn thing, I thought I might die. "Jesus, can you stop moving?" I snapped, my knuckles tightening around the bar. "I might have changed but not nearly as drastically. She's become a stubborn, angry shell of herself. It's frustrating trying to dig her back out."

"It's been ten years," he sighed, one gloved hand clasping my shoulder. "She's not going to just naturally open back up to you. She's not the same bubbly, pinball-obsessed girl she was and that's okay, man. That shit takes time. She was really hurt when you left."

My goddamn balls felt like they were in my stomach as we lifted even higher, the chair creaking under our asses. "Is this thing safe?"

"Yeah, man."

I gave him a skeptical look. "Okay. I know she was hurt, but I'm trying to make up for that now. She has to see that and assuming she does, she could open up at least a little. There have been moments where I'm like, oh my God, there she is. But then she withdraws within the blink of a fucking eye."

The wind howled around us as we climbed ever higher toward the top of the mountain. As I noticed the fresh air, the cloudy sky, the dense and snow-covered forest beyond the resort, I could understand why Mandy loved this state so much. It made me miss the only trip we'd had here together, the one where I'd finally worked up the nerve to kiss her. My palms had been so sweaty in the frigid winter air and I'd worried about touching her skin, about whether she'd think I was gross for sweating so badly from my nerves.

She didn't, though.

"You really broke her by leaving, Jack. I don't think you realize how much," Wade said, his voice quiet. "You weren't there, man. She called me almost every day. I don't know if she knew for sure that I knew where you were, but she at least had an inkling. She cried over the phone; daily turned into weekly and weekly turned into monthly until it slowly fizzled out, but that took almost a year."

Wade knew where I was. In fact, I think he might have been one of the only people that did. My family knew I was gone and that I was safe, but Wade was the only person I kept in contact with. But it was infrequent. He'd been sworn to secrecy even to this day. "I didn't have a choice," I muttered through a steeled jaw, the words hurting as they left my mouth.

The hump of snow hitting my skis warned me that it was time to get off. Wade lifted the bar, sliding effortlessly into a standing position, poles on either side of him. I, on the other hand, barely managed to stay on my feet.

I followed him to where the course began, little yellow flags lining the basic route and red ones lining the harder track. I already knew which one Wade would be going down on. "Jack."

I turned, my poles stuck firmly in the ground, my skis slipping a little under me. "Yeah?"

"You should tell her what happened," he said, his eyes solid as they stared at me, not a hint of joking around in his expression. "It's the only thing that will help her to trust you again."

*No.* It was the only word that ran through my head, echoed over and over again. Revisiting that time of my life, having to explain it, having to *feel* it again... I wasn't sure I could do that. "I don't think it'd change anything," I replied. "She's determined to hate me no matter what."

"She'll always wonder about it, man. It'll hang over her head until you tell her." He placed his ski goggles on his face, twisting into his starting position and holding himself in place with the poles. "Just think about it."

Within a second he was gone, expertly skiing down the hard lane. Clumsily, I pulled my own goggles down, pushing off the top of the mountain and aiming straight toward Wade. I knew my chances of catching up with him were slim to none but I had to try. I had to prove to myself that I wasn't so far removed from skiing as well as with Mandy. I needed one thing I could latch on to.

Turns out that trying to keep up with an ex-professional skier is harder than I thought. He was flying down the mountain, deep between turns in the trees, avoiding every obstacle that popped up along the route. That left me alone, soloing down the mountain with nothing but my thoughts, trying not to fall.

*"Jack."*

I turned my head, the sound of my name echoing in my mind catching me off guard. There wasn't anybody around me.

*"Jack. Fuck, oh my God, Jack, yes."*

Mandy. I could hear her voice as clear as if she were standing right next to me but it was only in my head. Ten years ago back to that night.

*"I think you're going to make me come. Holy shit. Holy fucking shit, Jackson."*

*Mandy's eyes rolled back as her fingers dug into my*

*shoulders, her nails biting, and one by one, her muscles tensed as she cried out. Her body shook, little aftershocks rolling through her. I coached her through every single one.*

*"Fuck, princess," I chuckled, kissing her lips, her cheeks, her chin. "You handled this like a champ."*

*She giggled as she caught her breath. I'd already found my release inside of her, buried so deep that I thought I'd never come out. She deserved to get hers, too. "Thank you," she breathed. Her unruly hair was fanned out across the pillow, and I swept it to one side as I laid down beside her, careful not to lay on a single strand.*

*"You're welcome." I tucked myself in closer to her, the sheets pooling around her waist as she breathed heavily on her back. I traced little circles with my fingertips in the center of her chest, over and over, my eyes growing heavy.* I could tell her, I thought, the idea of confessing even more of my wants with her pinging around in my head. I wanted her, I loved her, and I could keep her forever.

*Before a word was able to cross my lips I was too far gone into sleep, too calm with her next to me.*

*When my eyes opened again, they were trained on the soft glow of my phone screen. It buzzed softly, a number that I recognized far too well. Against my back, Mandy's warmth clung to me, her soft breaths telling me she was still fast asleep. Hesitantly, I lifted the phone to my ear.*

*"What? It's three in the fucking morning," I whispered harshly. Phone calls from them were never good, and I'd never received one this untimely.*

*"Ten-twelve-eighteen-two," the person recited. It was a passcode, a notifier that this was an important call, indeed from the people I suspected.*

*"Eight-six-fourteen-twenty," I said quietly, irritation dripping off every word. "Now what the fuck do you want?"*

*"Stay where you are."*

*Goosebumps prickled my skin.*

*"We will be there soon to collect you."*

"How long?" I dug my fingers into the pillow as Mandy breathed against my back, her warmth spreading.

*"Five minutes."*

I hung up the phone and set it gently on the bedside table. The temptation to slam it instead was raw and unhinged, but I didn't want to scare her.

Slowly, I rolled, pulling her into my arms as softly as I could. I wanted to wake her, wanted to tell her I had to leave but that I'd be back soon. I didn't want her to wake up alone, not after what we'd done tonight. She was mine, my girlfriend, my everything, and I didn't want her to doubt that for a moment.

But at the same time, she was exhausted and she had class in the morning. I likely wouldn't be gone more than a day; I could text her that something had come up and that I'd be back as soon as possible. I would make up an excuse, one that would be believable. I knew if I told her that I was leaving she'd want to come with me.

I planted a kiss on her forehead, just above her brow line before gently moving her arms and crawling from the bed. I found my clothes in the mess of her floor—scattered textbooks and sketchpads strewn everywhere. I wanted to kiss her, to fall back asleep holding her, to tell them to fuck off and let me have one night. But I knew I couldn't.

A small knock at the bedroom door nearly sent me flying to the floor out of sheer fright. They could move silently, I knew that, but getting in the dorm without a single sound was impressive. The door opened as I pulled on my second sock.

*Four of them. They'd sent four men, armed to the teeth.*

*"What's happening?"* I hissed, my eyes going wide as I watched them form a line between me and Mandy. Thankfully, she slept. *"What's with the fucking guns?"*

*"We don't have time for questions,"* one of them whispered, his finger resting on the trigger. This wasn't normal. This wasn't what usually happened—it had always been just one guy that came to collect me. Not four and definitely not with assault rifles. *"Get your shoes on, Jackson."*

*"Where are you taking me?"* I breathed, slipping my shoes on one after the other. *"How long will I be gone?"*

*"We can't say. You're going somewhere secure. It'll be for a while,"* the one on the far right answered. *"We need to go now."*

*"Can I leave a note?"* I asked, my panic rising as I realized this wasn't going to be like all the other times. I wouldn't be gone for just a couple of hours, a day at most. This was serious. Something had happened. *"Can I text her? I can't just leave—"*

*"There's no time."* He replied before grabbing my phone from the bedside table and cracking it in half in his gloved hands. *"You can't be tracked."*

I was going to be fucking sick. I could buy a new phone, no problem, but what the fuck did that mean? *"What about my family?"*

*"Your family is being informed now and are being taken to separate locations."*

*"I don't want to do this."* I stood my ground, my gaze caught on Mandy still sleeping soundly behind them, her hands resting where I had been. *"I don't want to go. Tell them to go fuck themselves."*

*"That's not an option, Jackson. We leave now."*

A face full of snow and an aching on my side brought me back to reality, the harsh glow of the sun reflecting off the white powder ground and blinding me temporarily. My goggles were somewhere off behind me, likely buried in my little crash site.

Pulling myself out of the trench I'd unintentionally made for myself, I shook my head, trying to forget. I hated that night. I hated it so much that I wished it had never happened, even with all of the good. I wished I'd woken her up. I wished I'd told her I loved her. At least then it would have been out in the open before my life changed for the worse.

My heart belonged to her. It always had, it always would. I had to win her back. I had to fight for this.

I had nothing without her.

# Chapter 18

## *Mandy*

Bitter air flowed between the high-rises on either side of us, whipping my hair about my face. Chicago was only a smidge warmer than the temps back in Boulder, but I couldn't complain—we arrived here on a private jet.

Quincy, a native architect Jackson had reached out to, approached us. He was fairly quiet until I got him going on architecture. I kept the conversation going, even though he seemed to be speaking to me as if I were a student. Just because this was my first large-scale project didn't make me any less of an interior designer, but he seemed to think it did.

Jackson's hand rested at the small of my back, overtop of the wool coat that he'd given me. Absentmindedly, I spun the ring on my finger. I was getting used to it being there, no longer constantly aware of its presence.

I knew this wasn't just a work trip, that it was PR as well. I didn't have an issue with that, not when I was getting so much out of it. Not only was I getting inspiration, I was also getting advice and priceless knowledge from a seasoned architect. It was well worth it.

Quincy led us into The Rookery, an office building with a handful of shops in the lobby. It was number one on my list of places I wanted to go—Frank Lloyd Wright had designed the lobby back in the early 1900s. After several renovations, it had finally been restored to his original designs.

"Wow," I breathed, coming to a stop in the center of the lobby. Shoppers and business men and women dodged their way around me but I didn't care, I could stand here for hours, taking in every last little detail. "This is incredible."

"It is." Quincy grinned. "They restored it back to its original design—"

"Back in the eighties and nineties," I finished for him. I wasn't able to contain my growing smile, even with Jackson's arm so casually wrapped around my shoulders. "It's Frank Lloyd Wright's only work in the downtown area. I've done my research."

Quincy chuckled, nodding to himself. "Well then. How much can I reasonably teach you if you've learned all you need to know?"

"I can definitely learn more," I responded, leaning back into Jack just a hair. His warmth flooded my back as he pulled me in closer, his arm moving to hold me in place against his chest. I could feel his chin against the top of my head, just before he placed a little kiss. "I want you to show me. And talk to me, tell me everything you know. It's nice to actually chat with someone knowledgeable about this stuff."

"Don't you get that with Harry?" Jack mumbled against my head.

"Not to this extent. Harry knows his stuff, but I still know more than he does." I snorted at the admission, but it was true. I'd excelled in university, and Harry... well, he'd passed. "How do you feel about the light fixtures?"

"I like them," Jack said quietly.

"Are they original?" I asked Quincy, my stomach beginning to churn with nerves from being so close to Jack.

"Yeah, they were put in back in 1905. If you wanted something similar, you'd have to get them custom-made."

I nodded as I pulled out my notebook, making a quick note to remind myself of that later. It was already half full of ideas from the other places we'd stopped at so far. "The tile is gorgeous. Is that original?"

Quincy nodded.

"I don't know how well that would work in the central offices, but for the lobby, something with this kind of design but more in your colors, Jack, could look really interesting," I tacked on, jotting down another note.

Jack nodded against my head as he adjusted his arm, knocking into mine on accident. My notebook fell, the pen following after it, echoing through the already noisy lobby as both hit the cold tile.

"Sorry," Jack said, releasing me in an instant. Before I could even bend to pick them up, he was down on one knee on the dirty ground, collecting them for me. I watched him, my breath frozen in my lungs, and he gave me a little smirk as he tucked the pen neatly back into the fold of the pad. He stood too close to my short skirt for my liking. I jumped as I felt something against my ankle, just a single finger trailing up the back of my leg over my stockings, so light I almost didn't notice.

A shiver ran down my spine as he reached my skirt, lifting it just slightly at the back. He only pulled away once he'd reached the swell of my ass, a smug little grin plastered to his face as he looked down at me. "Are you alright, Mandy?"

My cheeks warmed as I felt the blood rush not only to my face but down between my thighs as well. Already, I could feel the smallest pool of heat form beneath the tights. *Bad day to not wear fucking underwear, Miranda.*

I cleared my throat. "F-fine."

He'd been very touchy-feely today, always holding my hand or resting his somewhere on me, and now this. I wasn't sure if it was just because of the cameras and occasional paparazzi or if it was more to do with what he'd let slip days ago at his campus. I still wasn't sure if I believed it.

"Should we move into the library?" Quincy asked, gesturing with his hand toward the stairwell.

"Yes, please."

---

Jackson's hand rested firmly on my knee as we sat in the Tesla that he'd rented for the day. I was tired, my feet hurt, and all my mind could think about was getting back on the plane and flying home, getting to sleep in my own bed, and...

My stomach growled audibly.

*Food.* I was starving. I'd spent so much of today engrossed in architecture and interior design that I'd completely forgotten to have lunch, let alone dinner.

Immediately, Jackson turned a corner, cutting across two lanes of traffic and turning off the main road, no longer following the signs to O'Hare International. "Jack?"

"Yeah?"

"Where are you going? The signs said—"

"Don't worry about it, princess."

He turned down a side street, and then another, stopping in front of a small building with a plain black exterior and a little sign next to the door that simply said *Oriole*.

"Come on," he grinned as he pushed the driver's side door open. "Let's eat. I'm starving."

He opened my door for me before I even had the chance. "Is this place fancy?" I asked, already worried about my casual attire consisting of a black skirt, white button-up blouse and flats, easy clothing to walk and stand in all day. The nicest part of my outfit was the wool jacket that Jack had given me. He had worn black slacks and a black button-up. At least he'd look the part.

"Maybe a little," he grinned, offering me a hand. I took it.

"I'm not exactly dressed for fancy," I mumbled, my face paling as I realized this place wasn't just fancy—it was exclusive.

"You look beautiful." He pushed a stray strand of hair out of my face, tucked it behind my ear, and lit a fucking fire in my veins all at the same time. "You never need to worry about that."

―――

The place was exclusive plus.

Jackson sat close to me, his body occasionally rubbing up against mine as we ate course after course of absurdly

*Big & Bossy*

expensive and delicious food. Crab, tartar, wagyu, foie gras, caviar. He'd bought an entire bottle of wine but only had one glass because he was driving. By the time dessert arrived, I'd downed at least three. It was delicious.

The thing that threw me off wasn't the fancy food, the gorgeous restaurant, or the expensive wine. It was Jack. His attention was focused entirely on me as I babbled on about all the things we'd seen today and the ideas I was coming up with from all of the inspiration. As much as I hated to admit it, his initiative of visiting places instead of just looking at them online had done a lot of good for my mind and my muse. It had genuinely helped the process, and he seemed more keen than ever to hear me talk about it.

"I think we could get someone local to recreate something similar to those light fixtures in the Rookery," I said around a mouthful of creme Brulé. "We could do them in black and white instead of dark brown and cream. I think it would take the lobby of your campus to the next level."

"I would love that," Jack grinned, his plate empty and pushed to the side. He leaned on one elbow, his gaze trained on me. "You know that big mural we saw at the Chase Tower? I was thinking of hiring another local to create something like that in one of the hallways. We could have it be an homage to tech featuring all the important figures that have gotten us where we are today."

I blinked up at him. "That's... yes. Yes, absolutely. We can do that." The idea was genius but I couldn't tell him that. I didn't want his ego to blow up even more. But just knowing that idea had come from his mind was surprising and downright attractive.

Jack's free hand rested on my thigh, too close to the bottom hem of my skirt. "You were like a magnet today, Mandy," he said, that little cocky grin drawing me in. "Listening to you talk about your passions, seeing those walls breaking down..."

"Thanks," I whispered.

"I just..." He took a deep breath, trying to find his words. "It was amazing to see you like that. That's all."

"Thank you." "I wish I could see you like that more often."

I chuckled under my breath as I pushed my hair behind my ears. "Be nicer to me more often, then."

His lips twitched upward as he leaned a little closer, his face just an inch from mine. I could smell the glass of wine he'd had and every delectable note from the food we'd eaten on his breath. "Don't tempt me, Mandy. I'd be a fucking saint to you forever to see that every day."

My breath hitched as my pulse quickened. He couldn't say stuff like that to me. It wasn't fair.

His lips brushed against mine, likely for any journalists observing this moment. I leaned against him as his hand slid along my neck, pressing our lips more firmly together, and *God yes* this is what I wanted.

He pulled me closer, his lips parting, his tongue coasting across my lower lip. I opened my mouth wider for him , breathing him in, tasting him as my heart pounded against my rib cage. I hated how much he tasted like desire, like passion, like home. *It's just his familiarity, that's all,* I reminded myself, letting my hand fall to his cheek, his jaw.

His touch turned desperate once again, just like it had in my office. He wanted more. I could tell from the way his fingers caressed my skin, from how intensely he pulled me closer, from the deepening of his kiss. This was raw, passionate, and obviously just a show for any cameras trained on us.

Right? It had to be just for show.

When he finally pulled himself away, he gathered up a small amount of creme Brulé on my fork, holding it out for me. His eyes were dilated, his lips parted and puffy, his breathing just a little too heavy.

Maybe it wasn't all for show. It certainly felt real enough, but I also knew him. I knew how well he could pretend. Was it so bad if I let myself pretend, too?

## Chapter 19

## *Jackson*

The idea that I needed to tell her hung heavy over me as I watched her. The soft hum of the plane was the only sound between us as she stared out the window into the night, watching the stars move at their glacial pace. She looked tired, and I couldn't place whether that was because of everything going on or the sheer amount of exploring we'd done today.

I could do this, I *had* to do this. We were alone in the cabin, the door to the cockpit closed.

"Mandy," I began, leaning forward on the couch I was seated on across from her. She turned, her expression unreadable as she wrapped her arms tight around her knees. I wouldn't tell her that I could see the dark patch where the cotton of her tights came together between her thighs. "Can I talk to you?"

She nodded, her gaze wary as she watched me.

She deserved to know the truth. The whole reason I'd moved my company to Boulder was because of her. If what had happened between us all those years ago was the only thing holding her back from being able to let herself go with me, then Wade was right—I needed to tell her.

Wade was always right.

"I..." I took a deep breath, my palms already beginning to sweat. I wiped them on my slacks. "It's..."

"You okay?" She asked, her brows creasing as she watched me.

"Yeah, fine," I lied. "I'm just... I'm trying to figure out how to word this."

"I can get you a dictionary," she joked, her eyes softening.

I breathed out a laugh. "It's about that night."

Her brows rose, her breath going silent. "Okay."

"I don't even know where to start," I admitted, pushing my hands through my hair to calm myself. I hated talking about it. I hated thinking about it, but I had to do this for her. " I guess I should start with the military."

"The military...?" She asked, clearly confused.

I nodded. "So, while I was studying, I was working on the side within the intelligence section of the military. My family has ties going back generations, so I was a shoo-in," I explained, forcing my voice to be calm. I didn't want to scare her, I just wanted to explain. "I've always been good with tech, Mandy. I didn't need a degree to further that. But it was useful in the meantime."

"I don't really understand," she sighed.

"That's okay. I'm not done yet." I flexed my hands, wringing out the tension. "Do you remember when you'd call me and I'd be too busy to see you for a few days? It wasn't because I was too busy studying for a test or had a project to complete. I whipped those out easily. It was because I had been called in to dig into something or someone. I didn't really get to choose when or where I was needed, and I wasn't allowed to tell anyone about what I was doing. Only my family and Wade knew."

She narrowed her eyes at me, her finger playing with a hole she'd ripped in the stockings she wore. "So Wade *did* know."

"Yeah. He did. But he wasn't allowed to speak about it."

"I knew it."

"You did," I nodded, giving her the smallest smile I could muster. "That night, I got a call around three in the morning. I can still remember how warm you felt pressed up against my back, your arms holding me as tight as they could. They told me I had five minutes until someone would be there to collect me."

"I don't remember that," she said.

"Thankfully you slept through all of it. I thought about waking you up, but you had class in the morning and I knew you were stressed out of your mind because of midterms. I didn't want to ruin your sleep and besides, I didn't think it was going to be anything different than what I was used to," I explained, my voice cracking at the end. I cleared my throat again, forcing my hands to grip my thighs to calm down. "I had no idea what was actually happening."

"And what was that?"

"Three of my colleagues' family members had been kidnapped. And a fourth had been taken about an hour before they came to get me. Wives, kids, partners. They'd followed them, held them at gunpoint, and took them. I needed to be secured because apparently, they were actually after me. And that put you at risk," I said. The backs of my eyes were burning, the memories too much. I refused to allow the tears to escape, though. I needed to get through this. "They came into your dorm. There were four of them, armed with assault rifles, there to escort me somewhere safe. Nothing like that had ever happened before."

Mandy's face was pale as she lowered her legs to the floor. "There were four armed men in my bedroom?"

I nodded. "Thank God you never woke up. They broke my phone and told me I'd be gone for a while. I asked if I could leave you a note and they said there wasn't time." My voice had dropped to a whisper, little cracks breaking through. "I wanted to wake you up. I wanted to tell you I was sorry that I had to leave. I wanted to explain everything. I wanted to tell you I loved you. I just kept seeing you lying there, your hands resting where I'd been, the sheets turning fucking cold—"

"It's okay," Mandy said quickly, her body shuffling out of the chair. She crossed the aisle, sitting down on the couch next to me, her knees bumping against mine as she took my hands in hers. "Breathe, Jack."

I nodded as I took in a shaky breath. "They kept me away from the world for a year," I sighed, directing my gaze at the floor. I couldn't look at her. Didn't want her to see the wetness building in my eyes, didn't want her to think I was weak. "An entire year, Mandy. I couldn't speak to anyone outside the program apart from Wade and my family. Everyone was told to act as if I didn't fucking exist. I tried so many times to sneak a message to you, to get onto Facebook or anything where I could reach out, but they blocked it all in ways even I didn't know how to get around. Wade kept me updated on your studies, how you were doing. He told me when you graduated. Even showed me a photo of you in your cap and gown."

Her hands squeezed mine. Just as I'd taken care of her and calmed her when she was overwhelmed, she was now doing . the same for me.

"When I was finally released, they told me that I'd have to be extremely careful. That security would always need to be at top of mind and although I was used to that in my family, I wasn't used to having armed men around me twenty-four-seven. It was a lot. I wanted to come to you, to explain everything, but at the same time... fuck," I gasped, wiping the dampness from my eyes with the back of my hand. "I didn't want that for you. A life of secrecy, a life of always looking over your shoulder. Wade said you'd moved on, and even though it hurt like a fucking bitch, I stayed away, keeping tabs on you through social media. I couldn't bring myself to cross that line and bring you in on my shit. Just the thought of you getting hurt because of it was too much to bear."

"Jack." she whispered, her own voice cracking.

"I left the program. I started my own business. I still have security, but I'm not a massive target anymore. And so when I was presented with the opportunity to move my campus, my team..."

She nodded, one hand coming to rest on my cheek. She gently turned my head, forcing me to look at her, and damn I wished I knew how to read minds. Her face was unreadable, her eyes glassy. She was too beautiful, too good for me but I needed her. I would always need her.

Without a moment's hesitation, I pressed my lips to hers, too much emotion churning in my mind to know how to deal with all of it. I just wanted her, and I hoped beyond hope she wanted me too.

Her body reacted in my favor. Within a second, she climbed into my lap, kissing me hungrily, her fingers burying themselves in my hair. It felt like I could breathe again, it felt like home.

I dug my fingers into the small of her back, gripping her

blouse, twisting it in my palm. She sighed against my lips, and I took my chance to delve into her mouth, to taste her, to claim her. If I only had this for the rest of my life, I'd be happy. "Mandy," I breathed, moving my lips across hers, down to her chin, her neck. I kissed, nipped, licked at that spot beneath her ear, the one I remembered so fondly. It always set her on fire.

She groaned, the sound so soft, so sweet. Leaning into me, she trailed her hands up and down my chest, hesitating at the belt buckle beneath her hips before making their way back up to my collarbone. She was overwhelmed, fighting with herself for what she wanted.

"Do you want this?" I asked, dragging my fingertips up along her stocking-covered thigh, beneath the hem of her skirt. I dug my fingers in her flesh, my thumb so close but so far from what I already knew was a little damp patch. Her back arched into me. "Do you want me to touch you?"

"Yes," she whispered, her hands springing back to life and unbuttoning the top of my shirt. I stopped her. I wasn't ready for her to see the tattoo. "Please, Jack."

*Please, Jack.* It echoed in my mind as I let my fingers explore more of her, reacquainting themselves with her body. I grabbed the gusset of her stockings with my nails, pulled, and ripped it. Fucking nothing underneath.

Blood pooled in my cock immediately. She hadn't worn underwear. Was she expecting this? Was she hoping for it? Whatever the reason, it excited me that much more, and I knew damn well that when the time was right, I'd tease her about it.

I slid my fingers in through the tear, brushing them against her. She was slick already, eager, wanting. "Fuck," I sighed, finding her clit and brushing my thumb against it gently. She shivered. "You're perfect. So goddamn perfect."

She ground her hips forward, pushing my thumb harder against her. "More," she begged. She buried her face in the crook of my neck, her breath fanning out against my flesh. "More, Jack."

She moaned as I slid two fingers inside of her, so easily, like slicing through butter. She ground against me again, and I circled my thumb over her clit, taking in every sound she made and memorizing it. If this moment was all I'd be getting, I wanted to keep it forever.

My cock pressed painfully against my zipper. She had to have felt it beneath her, but I wasn't going to push. This was enough. "Please," she begged again, her dampness pooling in the palm of my hand. "Fuck me. I need you to fuck me."

*Holy shit.* I paused, every part of me going stiff, the words lingering between us. "Do you mean that?"

"Yes," she whispered without any hesitation.

"Look at me, Mandy." I grabbed her gently by the back of the neck, forcing her to make eye contact with me. "Do you mean that?" I repeated, emphasizing every word.

She breathed heavily, her breasts sliding against my chest with every rise and fall. "Yes," she said again, giving me a little nod. "I mean it." *Yes. Yes. Yes. Yes. Yes.*

She was going to fucking break me.

I groaned a sigh of relief as I pressed my lips back to hers, more demanding this time. She was giving herself to me on a silver platter and I would take every bite she would allow me.

I stood, picking her up with me, gripping her by her thighs. Her stockings ripped more as I carried her, little holes with lines spreading down her legs, and without giving myself a moment to chicken out, I sat her down on the table in front of the seat she'd occupied only moments ago.

She hooked her legs around my waist as I fumbled with my belt, releasing it as quickly as my shaking hands would allow. I kissed her lips, her neck, her jaw. I wanted more of her body, but I wasn't going to let this slip away. It was now or never.

My cock sprang out as I pulled my slacks down, the freedom of it making me gasp. The tip rested gently on her entrance, the warmth of it feeling like heaven, and I hooked my fingers into the top of the hole in her stockings, ripping it just a little bit more, giving myself further access.

I'd slept with women since her. I'd been in relationships since her, but nothing, absolutely fucking nothing, would compare to this.

She laid back on the table, her back arching, her moans growing louder as I slid myself inside of her. She fit around me like a fucking glove. "Yes," I grunted, leaning over her, the sense of rightness almost too much to bear. "Yes. We fit together so fucking perfectly."

Heat flooded her cheeks as she watched me, a little smile tugging at her lips. I found her clit again, my fingers slowly beginning to circle as she shivered, little ripples from her muscles massaging my cock before I even started to move.

But then I did.

"Jack," she gasped, her hands flying to my collar, my neck. She pulled me down further toward her, her eyes wild, her body wriggling frantically beneath me.

My hips met hers, moving slowly at first, but soon picking up speed. I couldn't hold back my grunts, my moans, not with her. It was too much.

Her eyes glanced down to where our bodies joined, her

skirt flipped up against her stomach. "Oh my God," she whispered, as I buried every inch of myself inside of her, the feeling of her walls gripping me tighter driving me insane. "Harder. Please. I want to see you fuck me harder."

How could I *not* give her what she wanted?

I picked up my speed, slamming into her with more force, my own release building. I could hold out for her, but it had to happen soon.

"Is this what you wanted?" I asked, pushing her legs further up, opening her more to me. I kept my pace on her clit, knew damn well that if she wanted something different she would ask, but just looking at her like this made me want more from her. "Tell me, princess."

"Yes," she moaned, her head falling back against the table with an audible *thud*. Her muscles squeezed me tighter, her little groans growing more desperate, more frequent. "It's what I wanted. *Fuck*. You're gonna make me—"

She cried out, a guttural, frenzied noise ripping from her throat as her body seized and then released. She gasped for air, her orgasm ripping through her, her walls pulsing. My own orgasm chased hers and she shook gently beneath me as it hit me like a wave, pulling me under the surface, drowning me in her. I'd gladly go out like that.

I kissed her and held her as our climaxes subsided. "Jack," she muttered, still catching her breath as our movements stilled. Every part of me was blinded by piercing satisfaction, pleasure rolling through my veins like ecstasy. I struggled to focus. "Jackson."

"Hmm?"

Her hands rested gently on my cheeks as I lowered her legs, minimizing the space between us. "Did you mean what you said before? That I wasn't the only one in love back then?" She asked, her voice small, words a little broken between breaths.

Her question pulled me back to the present. I slid an arm under her waist and lifted her so she was sitting up. I kissed her forehead, her eyelids, her lips. It hurt that she still didn't quite believe me, but it was something I was willing to keep reinforcing until she did.

"Jack," she whispered. A quiet request for an answer.

I rested my forehead against hers, unwilling to let this moment be ruined but knowing damn well she wouldn't appreciate my silence.

"I don't think I ever stopped loving you, Mandy."

# Chapter 20

## *Mandy*

I hadn't been able to stop thinking about what happened on the flight for the last week. It consumed every waking thought, every dream. Jackson, emotional, vulnerable, nearly in tears as I held his hands, as he told me what happened. Jackson, strong, looming, sexy, buried deep inside of me.

I hadn't come that hard in a long, fucking time.

"Mandy?"

I turned, hitting my ear with the curling iron, sucking in a breath through my teeth as it burned the tender flesh. "Yeah?"

"You okay?" Amanda asked, sitting down next to me at the table in her pink robe. She plonked her massive case of makeup in front of us. "You seem a bit out of it."

"Mmm-hmm," I nodded, catching Harry out of the corner of my eye as he came around the corner. He'd insisted on hanging out with us as we all got ready for Tiana's bachelorette party, citing the fact that I clearly never told him anything anymore. He was still giving me crap about the fake engagement, stating it was a cruel joke allowing him to believe it was real. "Just thinking about, you know," I whispered, low enough for only her to hear. She nodded.

Harry didn't need to know about what happened on the plane. He was so fiercely protective, so adamant that I needed to keep my distance from Jackson for my mental well-being, and although I appreciated that, I didn't want the inevitable lecture I'd get if he heard that I'd let my guard down and slept with him.

I still wasn't sure if I regretted it or not.

"So where are we going that requires this much prep?" Harry asked, adjusting his tie in the mirror.

"Some place called Suite 200. Jack said to dress fancy, so that's what I'm going off of." I searched through the litany of shades of foundation in Amanda's bag. You'd think she was a makeup artist with all this shit instead of a chef.

"Do you do everything Jack asks of you?" Harry snorted, pushing his hair back from his face and spraying a bit of hairspray on it.

"No, but his sister is an angel. Don't take your annoyance with him out on her. I'm not."

I slid the ring from my finger as I started on my makeup. I didn't want to ruin that, especially not tonight. The press would likely be all over us, they'd been following me for the past week, including today to Denver. Jackson assigned some of his personal security to follow me around to ensure they didn't hassle me too much.

Harry saddled up beside us, picking up the ring off the table and inspecting it between his fingers. My stomach sank as he twirled it around. I didn't want him touching it, I didn't want anyone touching it. "This thing is so tacky," he said, his face crinkling with disgust. "It's not even a diamond. Does he even know how to propose correctly?"

"I didn't want a diamond," I snapped, plucking it from his hands and pocketing it in my robe.

Harry glared down at me, blinking in confusion. "I'm sorry, did you design it together?"

"No, but the point remains. I didn't want a diamond."

"So it was a lucky guess," Harry surmised.

I shrugged. "Maybe. We might have talked about it back in the day."

He huffed as he stepped away. "Didn't realize you guys were ever quite that serious," he chuckled, double checking himself in the mirror. "I'm going downstairs to get a coffee. You guys want anything?"

"Mocha!" Amanda chimed, aiming a big smile directly at him. "I'll Venmo you for it."

I waited until the door shut behind him to let out my groan of frustration. "I don't know what to fucking do, Amanda. My mind is swimming. He's going to break my heart again. I know it. I'm—"

"Hey, hey, calm down," Amanda said, her hand resting on my shoulder as she looked at me with a gentle gaze. "You're not going to let him do that because you're not going to let it get that far."

"I know that. But I'm having a really hard time keeping my heart out of this," I sighed, trying to distract myself by looking for a blush. "I can't even talk about it with Harry because he'll just get angry. I already know what he'd say —'You're being stupid, he's an asshole, you're doing this to yourself.' Yeah, I know all that. It already fucking hurts."

"It's okay if those feelings from ten years ago are starting to resurface. You were really into him and he broke your heart. It's okay, Mandy. It's natural to be feeling what you're feeling."

"I don't know if I can do this," I whispered, the backs of

my eyes already beginning to burn. "Every time I'm with him, it gets easier and I just want more. It shouldn't be like that. I should hate him."

"But you don't." She stated, grabbing a tissue and dabbing it under my eyes.

"No," I squeaked, my voice breaking. "I don't think I do anymore."

---

Music poured from the speakers as the three of us entered the club. At the back stood a security guard outside of a curtained, roped-off section and I knew that had to be where our party was situated.

We gave our names to the guard and he let us through, parting the curtains to a second room. Tiana stood in the center, a white, floor-length gown clinging to her body, a massive slit up the thigh. She wore a pink sash around her torso with the words 'Bride to Be' written in big white letters across it, and a little tiara sat atop her head.

She beamed when she saw me.

"Mandy!" She shouted, running over clumsily in her heels, throwing her arms around my neck and meeting me with nearly enough force to knock me over. I laughed as I hugged her, ten years of her absence in my life hitting me at once. "I'm so, so happy you're here! Jack said you were coming but I didn't believe him."

"Of course I'm here," I grinned, pulling back from her. "God, look at you! So grown up. You were, what, sixteen last time I saw you?"

She nodded, her broad smile so different from her usual sour demeanor. She was always happy to see me, though, and I loved that it hadn't changed. "Yeah, sixteen. And now I'm getting married!" She squealed, releasing me to hold my hands instead. "And so are you," she giggled, winking at me.

She was already tipsy.

"Who are your friends?" She asked, peeking over my shoulder at Amanda and Harry.

"This is Amanda," I said as I gestured toward her. "You may have met her when you and your parents came to visit at NYU. And this is Harry, he's my business partner. Guys, this is Tiana."

She gave them both a hug, her smile never fading. Definitely tipsy. "It's so nice to meet you guys," she chimed, adjusting her tiara as it fell. "Jack told me he finally came clean to you. I've been telling him to do it for years but he's still technically not allowed to talk about the whole military project thing."

"Yeah, he told me," I nodded, following her across the dance floor and toward the private bar.

"If he wasn't so worried that getting back together with you would have put you in danger, he would have come for you the second he got out. He was terrified that the same thing that happened to his coworkers could happen to you," she carried on, tacking on a quick order for three cocktails to the bartender without even asking what we wanted. "That's why he pulled back, buried his feelings. He was so scared of putting you in harm's way he'd rather be without you than risk you getting hurt. Even if it fucking killed him."

Harry stiffened by my side, changing his drink order with the bartender.

"I'm so happy that he found you again, though. Even if it's different now."

I spun the ring on my finger, my stomach churning. Hearing her talk about it solidified things in my mind. I knew he wasn't lying, but a part of me had wanted to believe that he was. It still didn't excuse the fact that he should have found a way to tell me after he was released. All of it was beginning to break me again, tearing down every little wall I'd built to keep him out.

"Let me introduce you to my friends!" Tiana exclaimed, knocking me out of my torrid thoughts.

---

As the night progressed and drinks were consumed, Tiana's party devolved into slight chaos.

Pin-the-penis had ended up with one of Tiana's friends getting poked in the forehead with a tack, resulting in screaming and tears when a single drop of blood ran down the girl's face. Truth or dare had one of the girls pole dancing without a pole on top of the bar, giving everyone an eyeful when she bent over and wasn't wearing underwear. And, of course, beer pong had thrown the bride-to-be into overdrive. Tiana drunkenly argued with two different people about whether it counts if a ball bounces off a cup, which led to a mess of tears and streaked mascara.

It was eventful, to say the least.

Tiana had been in my corner most of the night. Once the alcohol really started flowing, some of her friends started opening their mouths and becoming too loose with their words. One girl she'd introduced to me as Penelope, had inspected my ring with a face of disgust.

"Is that musgravite?" She asked, turning the band to get a better look at the leaves and branches. "Can't believe he'd give something this valuable to someone so... you."

"What's that supposed to mean?" I challenged. My inhibitions were far too low and I couldn't conceal the scowl on my face.

"Haven't you read what the press has been saying about you?" Penelope giggled. "Jackson's engaged to a *nobody*. I wonder how long that'll last."

Tiana shoved her shoulder into mine, her lower lip jutting out as she struggled to hold her balance. "My brother loves her. It doesn't matter if she doesn't come from money."

"I... thanks, Tiana, but I have enough to support myself," I grumbled, taking a long sip through my straw. Harry and Amanda had already abandoned me, both of them far too drunk to hold themselves up. I made a mental note to not have an open bar if I ever got married and those two were in attendance. "I don't really care what the press has been saying about me. I didn't invite them into my life."

Penelope snorted, one hand wrapping around the arm of one of her friends. She pulled her into the conversation, the poor girl stumbling over her own heels. If I remembered correctly, her name was April, but things were beginning to get hazy. "Look at her ring," Penelope instructed, placing my outstretched hand into April's. "Musgravite."

April squinted, getting her face far too close to my hand for my liking. "What is that?"

"An absurdly precious gemstone," Penelope explained. "More expensive than the finest diamond. It's ridiculous. He must have spent an absolute fortune on this, for someone like *her*."

April's face contorted before saying, "Eww."

"You guys are so annoying," Tiana groaned. She leaned onto me, her dress catching on one of the little sequins on mine, and I held her up as best I could but my balance was starting to go too. "Just be nice to her. I like her. That's all that matters."

"I just don't understand why you never set any of us up with your brother. I'm pretty sure we all asked at some point," Penelope continued, her drink sloshing over the edge of her cup and dripping down her hand. I yanked my hand back from April as she tried to take my ring off. "You always said he didn't want to date. Obviously, that was a fucking lie."

"It wasn't a lie," Tiana hissed. "He was waiting for her." She leaned into me even more, her weight hitting me and knocking me backward into a chair, Tiana landing square on my lap with a little gasp.

"So fucking drunk she can't even stand," Penelope said, her eyes rolling dramatically. "You should be happy the press is not around now to photograph you." The two of them laughed as they walked away, the alcohol bringing out their worst qualities.

I sighed as I readjusted Tiana on my lap. No point in forcing her to her feet now. "They're assholes. Why do you hang out with them?"

"Same circles," she slurred. She tugged at the sash around her shoulders, the hem of it leaving a little red line against her neck. "They've been trying to get with Jack for years. Sorry about them."

"It's fine," I lied, the irritation still bubbling in me. What had she meant when she said he was waiting for me? It gnawed at the back of my mind and I wanted to know. The alcohol forced me to ask the question. "Jack was waiting for me, huh?"

She giggled as she turned in my lap, laying back against my chest dramatically as she put one hand to her forehead. A fake swoon. "Mmm-hmm. Very romantic. That ring you've got on was always meant to be..." she hiccupped, then another giggle, "...it was always meant to be yours."

My stomach churned at her words, my skin losing its color. "What does that mean?"

"He asked Mom for it ten years ago," she grinned, tilting her head back to look at me upside down. "I was there."

## Chapter 21
## *Jackson*

Sweat poured down my back in droplets, the heat up far too high in my personal gym. The stair master was kicking my ass because I hadn't exercised in nearly a week and it showed.

I clicked through article after article on my phone, most of them about me, my 'fiancée', or our engagement. I needed some form of entertainment to get me through my workout and laughing about the fake gossip spreading about us was ideal, even if it irritated me.

*Jackson Big and his new fiancée Miranda Littleson planning a wedding in Egypt?*

Uh, no. Absolutely not.

*Miranda Littleson: everything we know about the former child star.*

Where on earth did they come up with that?

*Jackson Big's new fiancée is pregnant!*

Nope. Unless she has something to tell me. But I highly doubt she'd tell the press before telling me.

My phone buzzed in my hand as I swiped, lighting up

the screen with Samantha's face and name, a little PR symbol next to it. I answered.

"What's up?" I wheezed, hitting the stop button on the stair master and following it down, my aching legs hitting the ground.

"I just wanted to check something with you. Do you have a minute?" The sound of papers shuffling in the background echoed through the phone.

"Yeah, shoot."

"Great. So, you're probably not too aware of this yet, but your inboxes are, well, overflowing," she explained. "It's too much for us to handle with you being in the media like you are right now. There's a lot of spam that we have to sort through in order to find legitimate requests from reporters and journalists. Well, spam and a few death threats."

*It's fine. It's not related.*

I chuckled. "Yeah, that's not unusual."

"I know that. But we're struggling to keep up. Would it be okay if I hired another secretary to help us sort through all of it? Otherwise, stuff is going to get missed, and I doubt you want that. Ideally, we need to be on top of this shit in order to get the media off your backs."

I scratched the little bit of scruff growing under my chin, making a mental note to shave before bed. "Uh, yeah. That's fine. We definitely don't want to miss any important bits."

"Amazing. Thanks, Jack. I'll let you know when we've got someone, but I'm going to shift one of the HR reps over to cover in the meantime, they're not too busy right now."

"No problem—"

Another call made my phone buzz against my ear.

"Hold on, Sam."

I pulled it away, checking the screen, and my stomach dropped. *Why are you calling me?*

"Same, I've got to go. Thanks again," I blurted, hitting the end call button and answering the other.

"Hello? What's up?"

Giggles. So many giggles.

"Mandy?"

"Hi, Jack," she slurred, her voice far too loud. *Drunk.* "How are you?"

Grabbing the towel from the stair master, I wiped down the back of my neck as I made my way toward the door. "Well, I'm sober, for one. How are you?"

She hiccupped, the sound bleeding through the speaker. "I'm amazing. So good. A little lost, but good."

"Lost?"

"Mmm-hmm. Amanda and Harry already went back to the hotel."

The sound of people mingling, chatting, and singing started pouring through the phone as I made my way through my living room, down the stairs, and toward the door. "What about Tiana?"

"She left with her friends."

"For fucks sake, Mandy." I held the phone between my ear and shoulder as I slid my jacket over my arms. The closest shoes were slippers, and they were going to have to do. "Where are you?"

"Don't really know," she slurred. She shouted something behind the phone, something that sounded suspiciously like an order for a rum and coke. "I found a bar so I'm just kind of hanging out here."

"Great," I mumbled, pulling open the front door. Bitter air hit me like a wave, leaving my shorts covered legs exposed to the freezing air. "Listen. Send me your location and I'll be there as soon as I can."

She giggled again, the unmistakable lilt to her voice that told me she had a straw between her teeth. "Don't be silly, Jackson. I'm all the way out in Denver. That's, like, almost forty minutes away."

"Not with me behind the wheel."

"You're so dramatic. I'm fine, Jack. I'll find someone nice enough to drive me to the hotel—"

"Absolutely fucking not. You're staying exactly where you are and you're going to send me your location. *Now*." I ripped the driver's side door of my Ferrari open, wishing I'd had a spare five minutes to pre-warm the car, but it would warm up soon enough. She was silly drunk and a fucking target.

"And if I don't?"

"Then I will check every single fucking bar in Denver until I find you."

"Can I tell you a secret, Jack?" She asked, her voice fading into the background noise.

I took a deep breath as I started the engine, switching the phone to Bluetooth, her voice coming out of my car speakers instead. "If you send me your location."

She was silent for a moment, just a few faint noises making their way through. I could hear Shania Twain in the background, so I was guessing she was in a southern-themed bar. My phone lit up with a text from her with her exact location. The Grizzly Rose. I sighed a breath of relief.

"Okay, you can tell me your secret now."

"Wait, there's one of those electric bull riding things here—"

"Mandy, no. Tell me your secret."

She hiccupped. "I miss you."

*She's just drunk. She doesn't mean it.*

"And I kind of wanted you to come get me tonight."

My fingers gripped the steering wheel, my knuckles going white. "Well, it's a good thing that I'm on my way, princess."

---

I waded through the sea of people crowding the bar, men in cowboy hats line dancing and women in their daisy dukes bouncing along with them. I glanced at the electric bull as I passed, half expecting her to be on it, but thankfully, it was empty.

I spotted her bun first, loose and nearly falling out. She was wearing the sequined black dress I'd bought her, one strap was falling off, and her heels were resting on the floor beneath her. Her head rested heavily against the likely sticky counter, a half-drunk glass of rum and coke next to her. Even drunk off her ass and half-dead on the counter of a random bar, she still looked beautiful. She was lucky that the press hadn't found her.

I came up behind her, my hand landing on her bare shoulder blades, her body jumping beneath my fingertips. "There you are, princess," I drawled, leaning over her as she lifted her head toward me. A little trail of drool hung from her red lips, far too enticing for my own good and hers considering how absolutely plastered she was.

"Jack," she whispered, her voice barely audible over the blare of Toby Keith. Her gaze met mine, eyes wide as saucers as I dragged my thumb under her lip and wiped away the saliva. "You came."

I couldn't help but chuckle. "Of course I did. Did you think I was going to let you wander around Denver at the start of winter, alone, in the middle of the goddamn night?"

"What time is it?" She asked. The glare of the spinning lights overhead landed on her, lighting every inch of her beautiful face, every spot of her flawless makeup that had somehow stood the test of whatever had gone down throughout the evening.

"About three in the morning."

"Shit," she mumbled, scooting her butt to the edge of the barstool and stretching her feet down to reach the floor. She slid her shoes on one at a time, her fingers fumbling with the little straps until I reached down to help her. We needed to get out of there and into the privacy of my car as quickly as we could before anyone noticed who we were. The last thing either of us needed was more publicity, drunken at that. "Thanks, panda bear."

The breath left my lungs as the words crossed her lips.

She was just drunk. *Yeah, but it's been ten years.* It didn't mean anything. *You know it meant something.* She didn't know what she was saying. She couldn't control her mouth. *Isn't that exactly what you wanted? The truth from her?*

I released a breath as I stood straight, my leather jacket crinkling uncomfortably against her sequined dress as I wrapped one arm around her waist, hoisting her up and onto her feet. "Can you walk?"

She snorted as she took one wobbly step. "Obviously. I'm not a baby."

One more step and her heel snapped to the side, her

foot going out from under her, my arm sweeping her back to her feet. "So that was a lie, then."

"No. It was a stretch," she clarified, her giggles breaking through the sober mask she so desperately tried to cling to.

I held her around her waist, taking the brunt of her weight as I practically carried her out the front of the bar, leaving Toby Keith and his far-too-excited fans behind. The bitter air whipped around us in an instant, sending the little curls hanging loose about her face flying, her eyes widening at the sheer sharpness of it.

I made a mental note to make a complaint about The Grizzly Rose when I had the chance as I opened up the passenger side door, depositing her in her rightful spot beside mine. They shouldn't have served her more alcohol, not when she was as drunk as she was. And they definitely should have done more to help.

Though I guess I was thankful they hadn't called the police. Her mugshot would paint the tabloids for weeks.

"Jack," she mumbled again. Those fucking red lips, those half-lidded eyes. *Absolutely not.*

Taking a shaky breath and urging my blood flow away from my pelvis, I shut her door, going around to the driver's side and slotting myself in beside her.

---

I got distracted and spotted a classic, old-school style diner halfway back to Boulder. Food would sober her up and make her feel less like she was dying in the morning.

She sat back into the red vinyl of the booth, her droopy

eyes on mine, a coy little smile on her mouth as she stole a slice of bacon from my plate. It made me think far too much about the times we had back at NYU, the late-night study sessions or dates we'd have in the diner by campus, that last night when I'd finally found enough courage to ask her to be mine officially.

"Thank you for this," she cooed, biting down on the fatty strip that ran along the edge of the slice. "It's definitely helping."

"I can tell." The edge of my lip twitched as I reached across the table, stabbing my fork straight into the top of her stack of pancakes. I plopped it back onto my plate, my conquest feeling far too laughable as she glared at me. "You wore the ring tonight."

She nodded as she swallowed. "I wasn't sure if there'd be press. You would've been surprised if you'd seen the way some of Tiana's friends reacted to it, though."

"Tiana's friends are assholes," I grunted, shoving a massive bite of pancake into my mouth. "I don't think I would've been surprised at all."

She looked down at the ring as she spun it around on her finger, her lids still heavy from alcohol and lack of sleep. "Tiana told me something about it," Mandy said softly. "Is it true? Was it supposed to be mine?"

My hand froze, a solid bite of pancake stuck to the end of my fork. *Of fucking course Tiana opened her mouth.* "Would you prefer a yes or a no?"

"I'd prefer the truth."

I gathered myself, forcing the anxiety brewing in my gut to calm. I could do this. "Then yes, it was. I asked my mom for it a few nights before the final night we were together. I wasn't planning on doing it right away, but I knew what I wanted."

She nodded, almost to herself, as she tore her gaze away from her ring and tried to focus on her food once again. "Did you graduate?"

"Yeah, technically. I finished my degree after my hiatus, but most of it was online at that point. I set up J.B. Tech about a year after. You moved home after you graduated, right?"

She chuckled as she swallowed a bite of pancake. "Such a stalker. Yeah, I did. Met Harry. Started planning to open up L&V, and a few years later we got it up and running. I did a few internships in the meantime while living with Mom."

This was the stuff I knew very little about. I'd kept tabs on her through the years, trying to figure out where she was, who she was with, where she was living. I knew bits and pieces from what I could gather online, but her passions, her motivations, her life in general was still a mystery. I wanted to know more. I needed to know more, I'd lost ten years of her.

"And then it's been pretty much the same ever since. I do miss New York sometimes, though. I've gone back a couple of times over the years but it no longer feels like home the way it used to."

"Because I wasn't there," I joked, the words falling from my tongue too easily.

"Yeah. Because you weren't there."

———

Getting her back to the car after she ate was a lot easier than the experience at the bar. I didn't need to hold her up this time, only a little bit of sway to her step. Her words were less slurred, the bit of brain fog dissipating, but it was clear that her inhibitions were still a little too low. I wouldn't try anything. I couldn't.

"Jack," she said softly, her back leaning against the curved roof of the car. She clung tightly to my jacket around her shoulders, my only source of warmth the NYU hoodie I wore over my tank top and shorts. "Can I ask you something?"

"Anything," I replied, leaning closer to her for extra heat but also because I just couldn't keep myself away.

"Did you think I'd say yes?" She lifted her left hand, the ring glinting off the low light of the street lamps. She tilted her chin up, a little bit defiant, a little bit needy.

"I hoped you would. I wasn't sure what your answer would be, but I knew what mine was."

She breathed out, a little cloud of fog filling the small gap between us, and before I could react she stretched upward. Her lips met mine, gentle, soft, her red lipstick staining me the instant they touched. *She's drunk. She's drunk. She's drunk.*

*She's sobering up.*

I parted my lips, kissing her eagerly, every part of my body being set on fire, chasing away the chill. She wanted this. Her hands on my neck, my hoodie, she pulled me closer, pressing her body to mine as she let me explore her mouth and the heat that came with it. I could kiss her forever—I wanted to devour her, have her, claim her.

The hand that clutched the front of my hoodie moved, her nails raking down my chest then lower, down to the waistband of my gym shorts. *She's drunk. She's sober. She's drunk. She's drunk.* "Fuck," I grunted as her hand broached the elastic band, dipping behind my boxers. My cock was already hard from kissing her. "Mandy."

"I want you," she breathed, her fingers wrapping around my hard shaft. "Please."

"We can't," I bit out. Every part of me screamed to continue, to let this happen, but I wasn't that guy. If she wanted me, she could have me when she was sober. "You're still drunk."

"Yes but it's okay—"

She retreated within a second, her eyes going wide, her body freezing up. Her breath came quicker, her chest rising and falling a little too fast, a little too panicked. "Mandy?"

"I'm..."

She breathed in a shaky breath, one foot stepping away, then a second later her arm painfully clutched mine as she spewed every single drop of pancakes down the front of my NYU hoodie.

# Chapter 22

## *Mandy*

My head felt like it was going to explode—literally.

I grunted as I rolled over, a pillow clutched between my arms and legs, and squinted my eyes open the moment I felt something warm against my hand. Wherever I was it wasn't my room. There was a hint of blue light coming from Jackson's phone as he scrolled aimlessly through social media...

*Jack.*

Despite the pounding in my head, I suddenly felt wide awake. *Where's my dress?* I had on shorts and a big T-shirt. *Where am I?* Jack's house. *How?* He picked me up. Slowly the events from the night before began filtering in, memories assaulting me one after the other. On one hand, I was thankful that I'd never been the type of person to forget anything that happened on a drunken night out, but on the other, I wished I didn't remember throwing up down the front of his hoodie.

"Oh my God," I mumbled, burying my face in the pillow beneath my head as I clung to the one in my arms.

Jackson chuckled as he laid his phone facedown against his bare chest. "Good morning, princess. How are we feeling?"

"Morning?" I breathed, peeking out at him over the crest of the sheets. It was so dark I could barely make out the features of his face, could only see the small amount of light in the room reflecting off his eyes. "It's the middle of the night."

"It's eleven in the morning, Mandy," Jack drawled, his body shifting beneath the covers. "It's just the blackout blinds."

I groaned as I rubbed at my eyes, my headache annoyingly localized behind only one of them. It made me want to gouge it out of my skull. "I feel like I want to die."

"Do you not want me to open the blinds, then?"

I shook my head, the sheets rustling beneath me and filling my ears painfully. "You can open them."

He rolled to his left, his hand reaching out toward the bedside table. One click of a button and light began to filter in from behind me, his upper body coming into view much clearer than before.

"I'm sorry I threw up on you." He turned back, every muscle in his chest rippling as he fought to get the covers over him before I saw the tattoo.

But it was too late.

My hand reached out instinctually, stopping him from covering the little bit of ink on his left pectoral. My fingers on his bare skin, his breathing shuddered as I traced the lines, any existing thought evacuating my mind. A tiny panda, fairly simplistic. The view was from the side as it sat on its butt, his face peering down at the little crown in front of him, lying limply on the ground. I couldn't breathe.

"Please don't," he whispered, his Adam's apple bobbing as he swallowed. "It's nothing."

It wasn't nothing. It was something, it was *everything*.

Gently, he wrapped his fingers around mine, removing my hand. "I'll run you a bath, okay? We should get you cleaned up."

I watched as he shuffled out from under the sheets, his boxers clinging far too tightly to his ass, his bulge. He disappeared around the frame of a door, leaving me alone in his massive bedroom, the sound of the faucet turning on and water running filtering through.

Two of the four walls in his room were glass, the blackout blinds sitting on electric wheels at the top of them. What I assumed was usually greenery filled the view, a few auburn leaves left from the change of the season, most of the trees bare and stiff from the cold. Little specks of snow fell between them, coating the already white ground below. It was peaceful and calm. I couldn't remember the drive here, I'd likely fallen asleep, but based on the view I assumed we were about halfway up one of the mountains just outside of Boulder's main center.

It was a completely different environment than my plain ol' neighborhood.

I tried not to let my eyes wander back to the ink on his chest as Jack came back in, his jaw steeled as he walked over to my side of the bed. "Come on, princess," he said, offering me a hand.

I winced as I sat up, the pain filtering back in and slamming against my left eyeball. I took his offer as I covered my eye with my free hand, planting my feet on the ground, slowly lifting myself out of bed. The world turned on its axis, the wobble of last night still ever-present. I almost lost my footing entirely as Jack wrapped an arm around me to keep me steady, and it definitely wasn't because of the hangover.

He ushered me into the bathroom, the tile beneath my feet warm to the touch. *Of course he has heated floors.* The room was grand, about half the size of his bedroom. A large garden tub sat separate from the fully-tiled, glass-walled shower that looked like it could easily fit a basketball team. "I'll find some decent clothes for you while you relax. I doubt you'll want to go home in your dress."

I turned, catching another quick glimpse of the tattoo as Jack walked back to the door. "Wait," I breathed. He paused. Nerves bubbled in my stomach, my chest aching, my head throbbing. "Stay."

He blew out a breath, the muscles in his arms flexing as he clenched his hands into fists. "You don't want that."

"I do."

"Mandy..."

"Please," I added, my fingers grasping at the hem of the oversized shirt covering me. I didn't have the energy to fight him on it. I couldn't hate him right now. Not after last night and how he'd taken care of me, and definitely not after I'd seen what marked his chest. I couldn't even try to pretend.

I lifted the shirt up and over my head, baring my upper body to him. Somehow, despite the glaringly obvious fact that I'd had sex with him recently, this felt more intimate. Maybe because in our haste we'd been too turned on to even get undressed. He hadn't seen me fully naked in ten years, and I could tell that just the sight was enough to fluster him.

The tub, nearly full, was big enough for both of us. "Help me get cleaned up?" I asked quietly.

A beat of silence passed, his eyes hooked on me. But then he moved, feet padding across the floor one slow step at a time. His chest met mine as he pushed me back into the counter, one hand on my cheek. His eyes were wide, his pupils massive as they flicked between my own, his lips parted just barely. "This is a line we haven't crossed," he breathed. "If you want this, there's no going back."

A knot formed in my throat, big enough to choke me. I nodded.

So slowly, so softly, I felt like I could have imagined it. He placed a little kiss on my forehead as he hooked his fingers in the waistband of the shorts I had on. I could feel his heart hammering against his chest, and with one breath, he pushed the garment down, letting it pool at my feet. He placed his hands under the slope of my rear, lifting me up onto the ledge, and I immediately wished his heated floors had been extended to include the counter too.

I made a move to remove the ring, not entirely sure if I should wear it in water or not, but his hand stopped me. "Leave it on."

His boxers fell, joining the shorts, and when he slotted himself back between my parted thighs I thought I might pass out. "Jack."

He lifted me again, forcing my legs to wrap around his waist and my pussy to rest just above his cock. He was hard, but he paid it no mind as he carried us over to the tub and climbed the steps to the bath, stepping into the warm water. Slowly, he crouched down, submerging my lower half, and stretched out his legs in front of him so could sit.

The water was perfect. Not boiling, but enough to warm my body, my bones. He didn't need to say a word as he tipped me backward, my back arching, my breasts rising and falling with my breath as I soaked my hair thoroughly. I could feel his gaze on them, could feel the heat from his hand as he gripped my waist to give me leverage.

I righted myself, his hands doing every bit of the work

for me. I couldn't choose what I wanted to watch more—his eyes, his mouth, his hands or the panda bear tattoo. My hand found its way back to it, tracing each little individual, simplistic line as he covered my hair in shampoo, working it into every single strand.

"Do you like it?"

I couldn't decide. A part of me felt so fucking swollen with emotion that I wanted to cherish it forever, stare at it forever, but then another part of me, the more sensible and reasonable side, wanted to scream at him for marking himself as permanently mine. But even that made the butterflies take off in my gut. "Yeah," I breathed.

"I was worried you'd hate me even more if you saw it," he sighed. His fingers ran the shampoo through to the ends until he coaxed me back again, my spine curving, my breasts up. He rinsed every drop from my hair.

"I almost did," I admitted, my voice small, strained from the position. I stared up at the ceiling, trying to calm down, forcing myself to focus on the feel of his body against mine, his hands on me. It felt too right, too perfect. "A part of me still wants to scream at you for it."

"You can if you want to." He lifted me back up, my soaked-through hair clinging to my breasts, my back. "I deserve it."

"You don't." I wasn't sure if I believed the words that came out, but I didn't give myself the chance to take them back. I didn't want to.

"You called me it last night," he whispered. I leaned into him as his fingers traced my jaw, my lips. "Do you remember?"

*Thanks, panda bear.* It had slipped out in my inebriated state, the nickname so easily finding its home again. I blushed, my lips twitching upward in the smallest smile imaginable.

"It's okay. It was nice to hear it again."

His fingers slid beneath my ear, behind my neck, holding me. Too nice. Too much. I didn't resist as he pulled me closer. His lips met mine, tentative and soft. I didn't want to fight him anymore, I didn't want to pull away from him. I wanted him, and that was okay. It had to be.

My heartbeat kicked into overdrive as I let myself feel what I wanted to. I kissed him back, eagerly and needy, bringing my bare and wet body flush against his. His free hand slid around my waist, holding me tight to him, not giving me an inch of space as he met my urgency and desperation. Lips against lips, teeth, and tongues; it was too much to put into words. We let our bodies do the talking instead.

Sex with him on his jet was nothing compared to how this felt. This was ten years of lost time. This was two people who should never have been separated. This was bleeding nails against a brick wall, trying to get to one another.

His lips moved, nipping and kissing my jaw, my neck as he rotated us. He lifted me up, out of the water, my ass landing solidly on the hard edge of the tub where it met solid marble. He slotted himself between my legs, the hard length of him laying flush against my wetness as his hands explored the rest of me.

His fingers cupped my breasts, his tongue soothing the little nip he'd left below my ear. "I want this, Mandy," he breathed, his grip against my breasts turning just a little rougher, pulling a little moan from me. "I need it."

My legs dangled in the water as he leaned me back enough to kiss his way down my chest, his lips locking around my left nipple. His tongue dragged across it, slowly, then quickly, causing more sounds to escape from my throat. "Take it, then," I replied, my shoulders hitting marble, the biting cold of it making me gasp.

"This is more than last time—"

"I know." I gripped the back of his neck, forcing him to look at me.

He held my gaze as his fingers trailed down my body, slipping between my parted thighs. Featherlight, he ghosted across my bundle of nerves, slick already from too much passion and need. "Can I ask you something?"

"Anything," I breathed. His touch grew stronger, little circles around my clit as he positioned the tip of his cock at my entrance.

"Would you have said yes? If I'd asked you to marry me, if I'd never left, would you have said yes?"

My breath halted and he slid in halfway, my grip tightening on him as my body adjusted to his width. The knot in my throat returned with a vengeance, his question throwing me for a loop. *I don't know. I don't—*

"Mandy." He said sternly, drawing my attention back to him, back to his body, his cock inside of me. He slid in further, slowly, achingly, until his hips were flush against my own. "Answer the question, princess."

"I..." Heat flushed my cheeks as he pushed my thighs up, giving himself a bit more room to sink even deeper. The sensation was unreal, better than before, too much and not enough. I needed more. I needed him. Always had, always would. "Yes. I would have said yes."

He breathed out shakily as he lifted his mouth from my breast, eagerly finding my lips instead. His hips began to move, slowly at first, gentle little thrusts. My mind fogged as he kissed me, everything else falling to the wayside. The hangover, me chucking up on him, his question, my own questions. Ten years disappeared in the blink of an eye, and it was just us, nothing else but the water sloshing in the tub around his thighs as he made love to me.

I absolutely would have said yes. Had he not disappeared and we'd carried on the way we were, I would have said yes in a heartbeat. He was the closest thing I'd ever found to happiness, to a fulfilling relationship that didn't end in violence or screaming. He was the only one I'd ever let get close enough.

"Fuck," he grunted, his thrusting picking up the pace as his free hand interlocked with one of mine. "You're perfect. So goddamn perfect."

I could feel the pleasure building in my gut already, tempting me, baiting me. It was as if he remembered every curve of my body, every movement I liked. As if he'd stored it in his mind for ten years in some kind of time capsule, ready to go the moment he needed it. Perfect little movements with his fingers, the exact angle I needed for him to hit that spot inside of me that made me want to scream out in unabashed pleasure, exactly how I wanted to be touched and spoken to. It was too intense. Everything with him was.

His fingers squeezed my own. "Tell me what else you want," he growled, his face contorting with pleasure with every thrust. "Anything, princess. I'll give it to you."

"Nothing." I dragged my free hand down from his neck, right on top of the panda tattoo. I gripped him, digging my nails into his skin. "Just you."

His eyes flared as they met mine, his thrusts harder, his fingers working faster. His pupils were wide enough that I could see myself reflected in them. "You already have me."

My orgasm snuck up on me far too rapidly, my moans escalating with every touch, every thrust. I crashed over the edge, ecstasy ripping through my veins like a wildfire, nails in flesh and back arched. A cry tore from my throat, loud enough to hurt as my body locked and released, holding onto him, refusing to let him go.

He kissed me, coaxed me through it, his hips still moving, faster and more wanting. He groaned against my lips as he took my hands in his, holding them above my head. Sputtered grunts and desperation left him as he found his release, filling me so completely, warm liquid spilling down into the water below.

Our breathing ragged and strained, he held me as he kissed me. Wet flesh against wet flesh. The height of our orgasms still coursing through us, I'd lost any filter I had on my words, my thoughts. "I still love you." My voice cracked, my eyes burned. I didn't want this to end. I was giving him myself on a silver fucking platter again.

He pulled back, just an inch. He searched my eyes for any hint of deceit, any glimmer of the part of me that still hated him for everything. She wasn't here. "And I still love you," he muttered, his fingers squeezing mine.

# Chapter 23

## *Jackson*

"Mandy, please," I begged, my eyes glued to her as she dragged the wand from her lipstick across her lower lip. Dark maroon, a bold choice to go with her fairly muted eye makeup. "We're going to be late."

"And whose fault is that?"

"Yours," I laughed, coming up behind her and shifting the long locks of curls over her shoulders. "We were on schedule until you fucking tempted me with that mouth of yours in the shower."

"Don't you dare complain about that," she giggled. I wasn't complaining—I enjoyed every fucking second of her lips around my cock, but we couldn't be late for my sister's wedding because of it.

The dark green, floor-length satin gown that she wore was nearly too much to handle. I had no idea how I was going to make it through the evening without ripping it off her body. I couldn't get enough of her during this entire week we'd spent together, and I wasn't about to make an exception tonight.

We'd agreed that we wouldn't talk about the fake engagement, at least not yet. We'd kept our mouths shut unless something absurd had dropped in the press, only bringing it up if it was necessary. She'd gone to work throughout the week then came straight home to my house. She'd slept with me every night. She'd been mine for seven whole days, and I was unable to see spending any more weeks by myself.

"Come on, princess," I drawled, dragging her from the mirror as she checked herself over one last time. "You look perfect. We need to go."

---

As we neared the church, I couldn't help but look at Mandy. She looked unreal, like something out of a dream. Her hair, half-up and half-down, her flawless makeup, her body, her *everything*. She was wearing the ring I'd given her as she had for the last week, the green in it complementing the green of her dress, and I found myself wondering what the fuck I'd done to deserve this.

Because things always went wrong for me. They never seemed to work out. This was too perfect and I almost didn't trust myself with it, with her.

"What?" She asked, catching me looking at her, her eyes searching mine.

"Nothing," I said, forcing a smile.

I pulled the car up to the front of the church. In the distance, I spotted my sister walking toward the entrance. *Fuck.*

I pushed the car door open, grabbing my jacket and throwing it over my shoulder as I rushed to the other side to get Mandy. "Let's go, princess, we're later than I thought," I said, holding out my hand for her.

"Oh shit," she replied, her gaze snagging on Tiana in the distance. She grabbed my hand, holding on for dear life as I pulled her from the car, her heels struggling to find their balance on the pebbled ground. "Tell her to wait!"

"She's the bride," I laughed, dragging her toward the front door of the church. "She's going to run on her schedule, no one else's."

Mandy gripped her dress in one hand as I pulled her along, narrowly sliding in the front door around a bridesmaid as she made her way down the aisle. "Jack," she breathed, her cheeks reddening as we made our way toward the front. "We're like, crashing the wedding right now."

"It's okay, just don't look at the people staring," I chuckled, slotting her into the pew beside my parents.

"You're late," Mom hissed at me. Her brows shot up as she locked eyes with Mandy, her irritation slipping away instantly. "Miranda!"

"Katherine, hush," Dad said.

"But Miranda's here!"

"So is your daughter."

The crowd stood at once as the pianist began to play The Wedding March. We followed suit, Mandy's back flush against my chest, and watched as my sister made her way down the aisle alone.

Post vows and Mom's incessant badgering of Mandy, asking how she's been for the last ten years, we all slowly made our way out of the church and back into the gravel area that stretched the expanse of the walkway.

As the guests began to make their way to the reception venue down the hill, the photographer held the bridal party and family back, insisting we do a photo shoot in front of the church. I knew it was standard practice, but after so many years of being in the public eye, posing for a photo always seemed to make me nauseous.

"Should I stay?" Mandy asked quietly, her gaze flicking between me and the guests as they walked down the road. "I feel like I'm intruding."

I blinked at her, my brows furrowing at her absurd question. "You're staying. You're family."

"I... I'm not Jack," she whispered, lifting her left hand toward me. "This is fake, remember? I mean, I know we're not supposed to talk about it, but I doubt Tiana would want me in her family wedding photos."

"She wants you here. *I* want you here," I told her, wrapping one arm around the small of her waist and pulling her in for a kiss. "There's a long list of reasons you should stay and a very short list of reasons why you shouldn't. Stay for me, at least."

She nodded, her fingers absentmindedly spinning the ring on her finger. "Okay."

"Jack! Mandy!" Tiana shouted, one hand in the air, the other desperately clinging to her bouquet. "Come on!"

Mandy's hand in mine, we walked down the hill behind the rest of the family and bridal party. It had taken a bit of work to get Mom to leave her alone after the photos, but I wanted her all to myself. I wanted to focus on just us for a little bit, even if it was only a few minutes. I couldn't help but want that with her.

"Can I ask you a question?" I said, grinning as I watched her.

"Anything."

"Say I didn't get taken away ten years ago, proposed, and you said yes," I drawled, shifting so I was in front of her, walking backward. "What do you think our wedding day would have looked like?"

"Oh..." she chuckled, biting her lower lip as her eyes locked with mine. "I don't know. Big white dress, lots of people, probably too much money thrown at the whole thing."

"I'm serious," I said, slowing my steps one by one until we came to a halt. "What kind of wedding would you have wanted, princess?"

She looked up to the sky for a moment, her dark red lips opening and closing without any words. Too many thoughts running through her head. "I don't know, Jack," she answered. "I mean, I've dreamed about my wedding day like every other little girl in existence, but that kind of stopped when my dad died. It felt too weird to think about without him there."

I squeezed her hand in mine. "I understand."

"But if I had to pick something, right now, on the spot," she continued, drawing her gaze away from the sky and back to me, "I'd probably have gone for something in the woods, or maybe Rocky Mountain National Park. Autumn, so it wouldn't have been too hot or too cold, and the leaves would be changing colors. You'd have been in an all-black suit, and I'd probably have worn some kind of color other than white since the whole thing is nontraditional anyway."

I could see the light filtering back into her eyes as she imagined it.

"I'd walk down the aisle to some folk cover of a classic song. But there wouldn't be very many people there—Amanda, Harry, my mom. Tiana. Your parents. You and me. Wade, if he's around. That's all I'd need. And instead of some massive, crazy reception with everyone drinking and making speeches and lots of crazy food, we could just rent some cabin in the middle of the mountains and have a cookout with everyone then later light a bonfire. Tell stories, listen to good music."

"Is that what twenty-one-year-old Mandy would have wanted?" I asked, drawing her a little bit closer as she slowly filtered back to reality. I couldn't stop my heart from pounding, my mind spiraling and thinking of every single way I could make that happen for her. I'd do anything to give her what she wanted, no matter what that was.

She shrugged. "I don't know. It sounds nice." I planted a little kiss on her forehead, trying to shrug off the intensity of what I was feeling. "What? Why are you being so nice?" She giggled, pushing back on my chest.

"No reason. You're just cute when you stare off into space."

But there was a reason and she had to know that, in her gut. I wanted every second of that day for her—for us—and the more I thought about it, the more I idealized it. I knew we were moving fast, making up for lost time, but god fucking dammit I wanted that with her. I wanted it all.

I wanted to marry her more now than I did when I was twenty-one.

# Chapter 24

## *Mandy*

The reception kicked off with a bang. Everyone was on the dance floor, spinning around to some upbeat song, Jackson and I included.

When they introduced the bride and groom, they did it by their first names only. Jack had told me that Tiana was keeping her maiden name, and I liked the rejection of traditional values in that. Instead of a first dance, they joined the rest of us. Tiana had swapped her long, form-fitting white dress for a shorter, more casual one. It hung from her thin frame, white crisp satin, down to her calves with a slit up one thigh. Comfortable enough to dance in, yet still bridal. She looked incredible.

Fred shared Tiana with everyone on the dance floor. Together, they spun, danced, and held hands with every single person who had come to the wedding—all two-hundred-something of them.

"I'm so glad you came!" Tiana shouted at me over the music, her hands interlocked with mine as I spun her on the spot. "I thought maybe you wouldn't."

"Why?" I laughed as she tripped over herself, nearly falling over into the crowd.

"Because my bridesmaids weren't very nice to you."

I shrugged, spinning her again, catching her before she could misplace her feet. She was never very coordinated.

"It's nice to see you and Jack together," she said, giggling at her own words. She knew the engagement was fake, but she, along with everyone else in her family it seemed, didn't care. "It's been a long time since I've seen him like this."

"Like what?"

"Happy."

Off she spun a second later, landing in the arms of someone else, leaving mine empty as Jack danced with his mom across the floor.

I took the moment to catch my breath, making my way through the sea of people and toward where apparently everyone had jointly decided to place their shoes. I wasn't used to wearing heels for so long, and my feet were screaming at me to take them off.

"Mandy."

I turned toward the deep voice as I kicked off one of my shoes into the pile. Jack's dad loomed over me, nearly as tall as his son, the smallest smile on his face as he held out one hand toward me. "Hi, Paul."

"Would you like to dance? Tiana seems a little too busy and Jack's taken Kate from me."

My eyes went wide as I realized what he was asking. It almost felt like I was somewhere I didn't belong, yet was being overly welcomed, nonetheless. "Uh," I hesitated, kicking my other shoe into the pile and righting myself. "Yes. Of course."

He took my hand in his as he led me out to the dance floor, my break far too short, feet still screaming. Paul was an awkward man, always had been, and his dancing was absolutely no different as he tried to slow dance with me in the middle of another upbeat song.

It felt strange dancing with him. He was so similar to Jack in all the weird ways, but also different at the same time. It was odd to think how Jack wouldn't exist without him, how he had physically made him, brought him into this world, turned him into the man I loved and was still falling for.

He let out a light little laugh as his eyes met mine. "I know this is all for publicity and what-have-you," he started, spinning me in place slowly, "but I see the way he looks at you. The way you look at him. It was always you. Always has been."

A knot formed in my throat as I watched him. I didn't know what to say, was it really that obvious?

"Every other girl he's been with over the years... none of them ever made him light up like you did. Like you do. I know he and I aren't close, and I know he avoids us, but he can't hide how he feels about you. He's never been good at covering it up," he chuckled, his eyes landing on Jack across the floor as he passed his mom off to someone else. "I've just been patiently waiting for both of you to end up back together."

He made a move to let me go, but I pulled him back. "Do you mean that?" It felt too good to be true, too much like an overblown fib.

"Of course I do. I just wish it hadn't taken ten years."

His words hung heavy in my head as he let me go, my bare feet padding across the dance floor toward Jack. I wanted him, needed him to calm me down because damn, that was heavy.

Jackson plucked me from the crowd, spinning me into

his arms and planting a kiss on my cheek. These were the arms I belonged in, the ones that felt like home, and the idea that I'd been blind to that made me want to cry for being so stubborn. "Looking a little lost, princess," he smirked, his thumb dragging across my stained lower lip. "Penny for your thoughts?"

I breathed a laugh as the music slowed. "Just... your dad."

"Not like that, I hope."

"God, no," I giggled, kissing the inside of his palm as I looked up at him. "He uh, he said to me, 'it was always you,' and then a few other things about how he'd wished we'd fall back together someday."

He tried to cover up the humor he found in my words with a little confused grin. "Really? Dad said that?"

I nodded. "Yeah. He said he wished it hadn't taken us ten years," I continued, my cheeks warming. It felt overwhelming to say it out loud myself. "I wish it hadn't taken us ten years, too. I should have reached out. I shouldn't have been so angry when you showed back up. I should have given you the benefit of the doubt, instead of assuming—"

"Hey, hey," he interrupted, pulling me flush against his chest and kissing my lips, my cheeks, my forehead. "We can't change that. There's no use in wishing it was different, okay? But what we *can* do," he started walking us back off the dance floor, "is not waste another second."

"What do you mean?" I asked, stumbling over my feet and nearly falling on my ass. He caught me, lifted me, and planted my feet on top of his.

"Let's get some fresh air. You and me," he grinned, taking us through the sea of people, off the dance floor, and over to the pile of shoes. "We can cool off, have a breather. Get away from all the people."

"Why'd she invite so many?" I asked, slipping my shoes back onto my sore feet.

---

The venue itself sat on the side of a mountain, with incredible gardens overlooking the small bit of Rocky Mountain National Park that covered this area. We walked hand in hand down the slope in the brisk air, the sun setting as the music faded in the distance. It really did feel like we were all alone out here.

Although we had been together almost nonstop for the last week, this felt different. Things were becoming real much faster than I thought they would. I'd meant it when I told him that I loved him, but I wasn't sure if I was expecting the reality of what would come from that, the position it would put us in. The temptation to talk about the fake engagement was becoming overwhelming and I needed clarity.

A bench sat at the end of the slope, perfectly set up for a view of the river that ran between the mountains below. It was drying up, too little of the snow atop the peaks melting for it to run as quickly as it normally did. Jack led me over to the bench as he shucked his jacket from his arms and wrapped it around my shoulders.

"You're quiet," he said, motioning for me to sit before he did. He sat beside me, immediately putting his arm around me, pulling me close. I didn't want to say that this all seemed too good to be true, that I was wondering when things would start to go wrong. It seemed everything was fitting together too easily and I wasn't used to that.

"What's wrong?"

"Nothing," I said. "Can I ask you something?"

He chuckled. "Is this our new thing?"

"Maybe."

"Then yes. Anything."

"Say you hadn't left, and you'd proposed, and I'd said yes, and we'd gotten married," I said, snuggling in closer to the side of his chest. "Where do you think we'd be now?"

One of his fingers wrapped itself in a curl of my hair, spinning it in his hand. "Boulder. I'd have still moved for you," he said. "Two kids, a dog or two. A cat. Maybe we'd even be in the house I have now. I never wanted anything as tacky and big as my parents have."

My lips twitched at the mention of two kids. I'd told him back in the day that I wanted two—a boy and a girl.

"We'd have named our daughter Jess. She'd probably end up a bit of a tomboy like her mom. And our son…" he hesitated only briefly, his chin resting on the top of my head… "We'd have named him Arthur."

The backs of my eyes burned as he said it. Arthur, after my dad.

"We'd have filled one of the rooms with pinball machines," he continued, a little smile to his voice that I wished I could see. "And you'd be running your business, I'd be running mine. I would have opened my headquarters in Boulder instead of back in Chicago. You would have helped me design every inch of it, from the ground up. I'd work from home most days so I could be with the kids while you went off to your meetings and consultations."

I wanted that. I wanted that more than I could say.

"We'd spend Christmas with your mom. Tiana would

fly in. Then we'd do New Year's with my parents, and alternate Thanksgiving. You'd probably start a garden and everything would die," he laughed, "but I'd sneak out there in the middle of the night and replant everything, make you think they'd come back to life. I'd take you on trips while your mom watched the kids, anywhere you wanted to go."

"We'd be happy," I choked, my voice cracking as a tear broke free.

"Yes, princess. We'd be happy."

The silence we fell into was more comfortable than any I'd ever experienced. Just him, his breathing, the cold air, the low hum of the music. The setting sun and the mountains. The buzzing in my purse. The quiet whisper of the wind through the aspen trees, the slow trickle in the stream below. The buzzing against my breast in the pocket of Jack's blazer.

*The buzzing.*

I sat up as it clicked, fishing my phone from my bag as I handed him his. Text after text from Amanda littered my screen and Jackson's, and as I went to swipe it open, a call came through.

"Hello?" I asked warily, turning to Jack and watching his face pale as he scrolled through the texts.

"Fucking finally," Amanda rasped. The sound of sirens filtered in through the phone, accompanied by the wonderful arrangement of flash photography. My stomach dropped. "You need to come home."

"What's happened?"

"Your house. It's trashed, Mands."

And there it was, the other shoe that had to drop.

# Chapter 25

## *Jackson*

"I just... I don't understand."

"How can I help you understand?" Mandy asked, her sigh palpable as she leaned back against the passenger seat. "I mean, I know we're a thing, now. But I'm also used to living on my own."

"You lived with Amanda in college," I pointed out. I twisted in the driver's seat at a red light, locking my eyes on her. "I'm not tryingto make you move any faster through this than you're ready. I'm coming at this from a safety perspective, that's all."

"And I appreciate that."

"Then move in with me. At least for the time being."

We'd spent the last five days together since the wedding. She'd stayed at my house as the police gathered what they needed from hers, but the second they'd finished, she'd said she wanted to go home. It was confounding. She was safer with me, even if I littered her house with security, and somehow that didn't sway her. Although nothing was stolen and all she had to do was replace a few windows and clean up, I found my thoughts wandering to putting bars on the windows or replacing them with bulletproof glass. Someone as special as her needed to be kept safe, and even though our presence in the news cycle was waning, she was clearly still a target for someone.

"Please, princess. For my own peace of mind."

She grunted as she pushed her door open, kicking her feet out and planting her fur-lined boots in the snow. "I'll think about it, okay?" She said over her shoulder, her lips pursed, her fingers tightening around the frame of the door.

I left the car on as I got out, keeping the heat blasting so it wouldn't be freezing when I got back in. Winter had hit hard, bringing a lot of snow and ice. There was something magical about seeing Boulder from the angle of her office, and if I wasn't so damn stressed out of my mind with keeping her safe after the break-in, I would have insisted we take a moment to appreciate the white mountaintops and the glittering snowfall surrounding us.

"What are you doing?" She asked, turning to me as she grabbed her bag from the car.

"Walking you in."

"Oh."

My brows furrowed as I shut my door. I'd been walking her in every day that I'd dropped her off at work recently. I padded across the wet ground to the passenger side and took her hand in mine as I led her toward the glass entryway of her building. Not a single photographer stood outside, no one there to snap photos of us or beg us for an interview, trying to obtain any comment they could get their hands on. The plan was working— we were slowly but surely being left alone.

"I guess you don't have to kiss me at the door anymore," she chuckled, pushing the loose curls that hung from her bun back behind her ears.

I sighed, the frown forming almost painful. I didn't like this, any of it. Not her nonchalant attitude, not her wanting to go back home, not whatever *this* was.

I wrapped one arm around her waist, hating the way her woolen coat separated her skin from mine, and pulled her into my chest. I pressed my lips to hers as I cupped her cheek, a little rough at first and thinking far too much with my cock, but turning softer as she melted into me, welcoming me in. I could spend an eternity kissing her, kissing her and nothing else and be happy.

I pulled my mouth from hers just far enough to speak, our foreheads pressed together, the winter wind whipping around us and coating her jacket in little specks of snow. "I don't need a reason to kiss you, princess. Never forget that."

The fog of her breath hung thick between us for a moment before I let her go, her lips a little swollen and her cheeks pink, a small smile on her face.

---

I floored it as I made my way across town to the offices we were still, annoyingly, renting. I was desperate for Mandy and Harry to finish up at the new campus, I fucking hated coming to work here.

"Good morning, Jackson," Angela deadpanned from behind her desk before glancing back to her computer screen. "Public Relations is waiting for you in meeting room two."

"Perfect." I set a takeout coffee on the top of her desk,

the words vanilla bean written across the top in block letters. "Thanks for getting them set up."

She glared at the coffee, her nose sniffing the air. "What is that?"

"Read the lid."

She picked it up, her face contorting in disgust. *You can't be serious Angela.*

"Vanilla bean? Eww."

"My God, Angela, just be appreciative," I snapped, reaching out toward the coffee to snatch it back before she had the chance to pull it closer, missing by an inch.

"I don't like vanilla bean. I'll drink it, though."

"You liked vanilla bean, what, a month ago? You can't just change flavors on me and not tell me."

"I like caramel now," she grumbled, setting the coffee down in front of her as she turned back to her computer. "You could have checked."

I opened my mouth to spit out a retort but closed it as I realized it was pointless. Doing something nice for Angela would never be appreciated, and that was okay. She just wasn't that person.

I made my way through the dark and dreary hall, the ceiling too low, the windows practically nonexistent. I almost wished I'd asked them to meet me at my home, but I needed to be in the office today, needed to check on how things were going with Infinius, and to deal with the situations at hand concerning coding and getting it all off the ground. We were so close.

But I'd still rather be at home with Mandy.

Pushing my way in through the door and rattling the blinds, I nodded at the room full of people already seated and ready to go. They'd asked Mandy to be in attendance as well, but seeing as she had her own work to do I'd scheduled myself alone.

"Good morning, Mr. Big," Samantha chirped as she slid a small stack of papers out from her binder.

"Please don't call me that," I said. I sat down in the chair at the head of the table, my briefcase slapping against the wood. "When have you ever called me that?"

She shrugged as she twisted in her chair, rocking side to side. "Just don't want to be on your bad side this morning. Angela said you were in a mood."

"Angela always thinks I'm in a mood."

"Then I guess we can just get straight to business, Jack," she chuckled. She pressed a clicker in her hand, lighting up the far wall with a projector, a few scattered pictures of me and Mandy littering the poorly painted drywall. "Here's the thing, bud. The plan's working."

I nodded as I stared at the photo hovering in the top right, the one of Mandy feigning excitement in her black dress as I held the ring in front of her. *I want that. I want that to be real excitement.* "I figured as much. There weren't any reporters outside her office this morning and I've not seen many articles about us recently, either."

She nodded as she clicked to the next slide in her presentation. A few emails littered the screen. "We're mostly being contacted specifically about J.B. Tech now. Media houses want to know about Infinius, the new campus, and its grand opening." Another click, another slide. A few well-known actors and actresses popped up on the wall. "There have been quite a few new relationships and engagements coming out of Hollywood that have broadly taken over the spot you two were filling."

"That's great news." *No, it isn't. I don't have an excuse to be close to her anymore unless she wants me to be.* I booted up my laptop, my mind too full of emails and worry to really focus. "The break-in hasn't made the news, right?" I asked absentmindedly, logging in to the server.

"No, we bought every photo off of the press that was taken. No one has the rights to the story but us, and if they try to publish it, we can get it taken down fairly easily," Jason said.

"Perfect." I scrolled through email after email, trying my best to look as though I was paying attention. The new secretary had done a good job of filtering through the bullshit, but some of it still made its way through to me. Clear threats against Mandy for being 'engaged' to me and stake claims on either of us were being sent straight through to security as requested, but the juvenile ones that were nothing more than empty threats or silly statements, were still slipping through. "Any updates from security?"

"Uh, we don't really handle that," Jason said.

"Can you get one anyway?" I pressed, trying not to let the irritation seep into my voice. An email less than twenty-four hours old caught my eye. *READ ME, JACKSON BIG.*

"Online security will let us know if anything comes in that is particularly worrisome, Jack. The moment anything comes through about the new campus or a direct threat toward you or Mandy, it will be investigated." Samantha slid her stack of papers across the table toward me, but I ignored them. "That's everything they've found so far, but none of it has been worth speaking to the police about."

Temptation and sheer curiosity made me open the email. I'd avoided my inbox for days, leaving it up to those I'd hired to sort through the mess, but this one felt like it was something worth reading, and it had slipped through undetected.

My breath left my lungs as I started to read.

*You would think that a billionaire like you would hire someone specifically to keep your 'fiancée' safe. But you haven't done that, have you, Jackson? At least not well enough. Not secure enough to keep me out of her house.*

*I laid in her bed. I showered in her bathroom. I know the layout of her house by memory now. Don't worry, I was smart. They won't find a trace of me left behind, and really, I have you to thank for that.*

*Didn't you learn anything from your past? Or was all that military protection enough to make you forget? Or, better yet, do you just not care because of all that money you're making?*

*I would care if I were you, Jackson.*

# Chapter 26

## *Mandy*

Twenty minutes. That was all the time I had until Jack would arrive to get me and then head to the airport. I was a bit uneasy about going back to where everything had been set in motion for us, but I hammered it home to myself that this was just a networking event, an opportunity for me to meet new people, create new connections, and to get more ideas. It wouldn't hurt.

"I don't understand why you even need to go in the first place," Harry grumbled, his back against the doorway of my private office. "We have plenty of clients. We're good."

"We'll need more after we finish up with J.B. Tech if we want to stay afloat. You know that." I grabbed my stack of business cards and shoved them in my purse, along with a folder full of examples of L&V Interior's work. Harry had been short with me ever since I told him that I was going with Jack to the conference. In truth, I was genuinely excited to talk shop with new people, but he was souring the mood.

"If this is such an important thing, surely I should be coming along," he snapped.

"Yeah, sitting on a plane with you and Jackson bickering for four hours sounds like a great idea," I mumbled as I zipped up my bag.

"It would be if Jack wasn't going."

I glared at him as I grabbed my coat off the back of my chair. "Jack is the entire reason I even get to go in the first place. He deserves to tag along."

"Hasn't all the media attention you've been getting enough to draw clients in?" Harry asked, his eyes fixed on me as I pulled my jacket over my arms. He'd been out of the office pretty frequently lately, working from home, and I could tell from the dark circles under his eyes that he wasn't getting much sleep.

It almost made me not want to argue with him, almost. "The attention is dying down. We've gotten a few new clients from it, but it's not enough."

"It's dying down?" He asked, his brows raising, his body more alert. I knew what he was thinking already—I could stop being around Jack so much. He could stop worrying about it. "Does that mean the fake engagement is over?"

I shook my head and checked the time on my phone. Nothing from Jackson yet. "No, not yet."

"Ugh," he groaned, crossing the few steps between us and picking up my left hand. He inspected the ring again, his face contorting. "Can't you just ask him to call it off? I just want to get back to normal, Mandy. It's concerning, you being with him all the time."

"I'm not his boss. I don't get to make those calls, and I'm fine being around him," I snapped, pulling my hand back. "You don't need to worry."

"I do," he insisted. His wild, sleepless eyes met mine, and despite how irritating he could be, I could see the worry behind them. "I can tell your heart is already in it. Your priorities are getting all crisscrossed."

"My priorities are fine. I'm doing what's best for *our* business and you need to be okay with that," I pressed, thinning my lips. I knew he just wanted what was best for me, but god, why did he have to be so intense about it?

"No, you're doing whatever you damn well please," he countered. He ran his fingers through his dusty blonde hair, the little curls rippling in the wave of warm air coming through the vent above him. I could feel the tension between us building the way it always did when we got into these... *conversations*. He felt like a powder keg about to explode with the way his jaw tightened, the way his hands flexed. He just needed to cool off.

Harry was starting to piss me off, and I really didn't want to have to deal with this, not before my trip. I didn't want to spend the next twenty-four hours wondering whether or not he was going to meetings with our clients or if he was avoiding work entirely because of this.

"You've slept with him, haven't you?"

I froze. "What the fuck does that have to do with anything?"

He took a step back, his eyes going wide, his mouth opening in a shocked grin. "Oh my God, you have." He rubbed his jaw, an angry chuckle seeping out from between his lips. "I honestly thought you were better than that."

"I'm not talking about this with you," I breathed, the anger beginning to boil in my blood. I snatched my bag from my desk and took a wide step around him to give myself space. "Who I sleep with is my business, not yours."

"No, *this* business is your business, Miranda. You're going to end up getting your heart broken by him again and I'm going to be left to pick up the pieces, aren't I?" Harry glared at me, his dark circles appearing more prevalent with the fluorescent lighting coming down from above. "I'm going to have to show up for all these new clients you're going to be bringing in, while you're at home crying in your shower, drowning yourself in sad music and wine, pretending that you couldn't see it fucking coming."

My lower lip quivered. I bit it to keep him from seeing, to keep myself from overthinking about why his words bothered me so much. He could have said a million other things to me, but he chose to say that, knowing damn well it would hurt.

"I'm sorry. I... I shouldn't have said that. I just don't want you to get your fucking heart shattered by him again," he said, the words clashing against the tone he'd used only seconds before. It was almost like whiplash. "You're too good for him. You know that, I know that, the whole world knows that."

The burning in the back of my throat spread to my eyes, making them water a little too much to keep under control. I turned my head from him, trying to hide that, too, but I knew it wasn't enough.

"Please don't cry," he breathed. "Please. I'm sorry."

I nodded. I knew what he'd meant, knew why he was so angry, knew that he only had my best interest at heart. But for the love of all things holy, he could learn to speak those words clearer and less like they were a dagger being shoved into my chest.

"I just worry about you. That's all."

"I know," I croaked, swiping my eyes with the back of my hand and throwing a passing glance at the ticking clock. "But you're wrong if you think I haven't considered any of that."

A crease formed between his brows as he let out a huff.

"All right. I... I'll drop it, for now. Just please, Mands, be careful. Protect yourself."

---

Jackson wasn't in the car that arrived for me. Instead, an older man named Steve, graying and bearded, had shown up in an unmarked, tinted Range Rover. I didn't like that Jack wasn't there. I had hoped that his presence would make me feel better about the argument with Harry.

"Are we still going to the airport?" I asked, our eyes meeting in the rearview mirror.

"Of course, Ms. Littleson."

"Without Jack?"

"Jackson will be joining you at the airport, I believe," he explained as he put the car into drive. Harry stared down at me from behind the glass window of our office block, his arms across his chest, his jaw locked. His eyes never left the car as we pulled away.

I filled the bitter silence by distracting myself with my phone. I couldn't help but look up any remaining articles about Jack and me, what had once filled the news cycle now only took up one or two slots. We weren't even trending anymore. The plan had worked.

So why wasn't I happy about that?

My heart jumped as my phone started vibrating in my hand. As much as I wanted it to be Jack, I was instead met with a cute photo of Mom and me at the beach in New York nine years ago, my curls swept up into a bun just like hers. "Do you mind if I take a call, Steve?"

"No, ma'am. That's fine. Would you like some privacy?"

"Yes, please," I nodded, watching as he pressed a button on the console, a dark, glass divider going up between the front and back seat.

I swiped to answer the call.

"Hey, Mom."

"Hi, sweetie," she cooed. I could hear her loudly cutting vegetables in the background, way louder than usual. *She has me on speaker*. "I haven't heard from you in a bit. How are you doing?"

I glanced at the divider. "I'm doing okay," I sighed.

"That doesn't sound very convincing. What's going on? Is it Jack?"

"Yeah, I guess," I said quietly, settling into the leather seat. "It's a bit complicated, Mom."

"Do you want to talk about it?" She asked, her voice going soft as she put down the knife.

"I don't have enough time to unpack it all," I chuckled. "I don't know. Feelings are there. I don't think they ever left. And then on top of it, we're falling out of the news cycle, so our fake engagement will probably end soon and we're about halfway done with the campus, so I guess... I don't know. I'm preparing myself for the inevitable."

"Oh, honey."

"I told him I still loved him."

Silence overtook the line for a moment before she breathed out. "Did he say it back?"

"Yeah," I croaked, that same quiver in my lip making a reappearance. "He did. It's never been like that with anyone but him, Mom. I don't know how to handle it. I don't know what to do. I don't want it to end but I feel like it's going to have to."

"Oh, sweetie, I'm sorry. That's so tough. You went to his

sister's wedding, though, right? I saw some of the photos online. Surely he wouldn't want to break it off if he included you in the family photos."

I sniffled as I sank further into the leather, hoping that Steve couldn't hear. "But I don't know if that was for publicity or not. It's all so confusing. We spent most of the reception outside just watching the sunset and talking about where we'd be if he hadn't disappeared on me ten years ago. That was enough to make me want to cry."

"You should talk to him about it, Mandy. Get your answers. Don't overcomplicate things by putting it all on him and getting yourself twisted up over it, okay?"

I nodded before realizing she couldn't see that through a telephone call. "Yeah," I sniffled.

A knock came on the divider before it lowered down enough so Steve could peek at me through the rearview mirror. "We've arrived, Ms. Littleson. Time to board."

"I've got to go, Mom. I'll call you later."

Steve opened up my door and helped me get my bag from the car. Jackson's plane sat on the tarmac before me, the pilot and copilot standing by the steps leading inside. One of them grabbed my bag from Steve and carried it into the cabin. *Jack must already be inside.*

"Thanks, Steve," I called over my shoulder as I walked up the steps, one pilot behind me and one in front. Aside from the humming engine, it was silent, and as I entered the body of the plane, Jack was nowhere to be found.

I whipped around in an instant.

"Where's Jack?" I demanded, catching the door to the cockpit before they could close it behind them.

"He'll be joining you in a few hours. We've been given the go-ahead to get you out to New York."

*What?*

Uneasiness bloomed in my gut. I let the door close as I pulled out my phone, finding his name in an instant. Still *Jackson Pig*. Four rings, voicemail. Again. Four rings, voicemail. He never avoided my calls.

*Four rings, voicemail.*

*Four rings, voicemail.*

I stared dumbfounded at the call log, blinking until I couldn't help but flick it away. Was he even joining me at all? *Did he stand me up?*

The knot in the back of my throat felt more like a fucking log as I pulled up my texts and fired two off to Harry, shock and anger driving every movement of my thumbs against the too-bright screen.

*Me: I think he's stood me up.*

*Me: Maybe you were right.*

# Chapter 27

## *Jackson*

I felt bad leaving Mandy in the dark on this. I really did. But this was my problem, my issue to fix. I couldn't handle a threat against her and I wouldn't stop until no stone had been unturned, until I knew exactly who was behind it and made sure they were behind bars, unable to touch her.

I'd worked through the night with security trying to track the IP address the email had come from. Angela had sent Mandy what was originally meant to be a hotel reservation for the two of us, and although I hadn't had time to call her back, I got the vague idea from Angela that Mandy wasn't happy that the situation had become a reservation for one . But I'd rather she be alone in New York and booked under a fake name than alone in Boulder.

Landing in New York went smoothly. I'd gotten approximately two minutes of sleep in thirty-six hours, and even though I was desperate to fall asleep and try to forget about the threat, I was desperate to see Mandy more.

The event was already in full swing as I made my way through the crowd. I'd called ahead to ensure Mandy was able to get in on her own even though the tickets were bought in my name, and although it caused a bit of confusion when I arrived separately, it was worth it to see her in her element.

Short skirt, high heels, hair down. I could pick her out in a crowd from her hair alone, but the trio made me confident it was her.

I took my time approaching as she spoke to three different people at once, one woman, two men. She laughed, talked shop, handed out her business cards. She commanded the space so easily, dropping names of people I'd never heard of and picking up on tidbits of their work. She was thriving.

"Hello, princess," I said softly into her ear as I leaned over her from behind. "Sorry I'm late."

She turned her head, locking eyes with me for a moment and giving me a small smile. "It's fine." She pursed her lips together as she handed out another business card.

"How's it been going?" I asked, coming around to her side. "Have you seen anything that would add any nice final touches to the campus?"

She nodded, her gaze absent as she looked up at me. "Yeah. It's been good."

I knew she wasn't happy that I was late. I knew a part of her was irritated and guarded. It wasn't unreasonable, but damn, it still stung like a bitch. Like we'd gone forward ten steps and jumped back one hundred.

I took her hand in mine and gave her a soft peck on the cheek.

"Show me what you've seen and loved," I said, giving her the most apologetic grin I could muster.

She nodded as she led me through the maze of people toward the back of the room. I could feel the ring on her finger—as good a sign as I was going to get from her. It made my chest swell, even if she only wore it because this was a public event. "Where were you?" She asked, not a hint of enthusiasm in her voice.

I didn't want to tell her, not until I'd figured out who the email came from and if she was truly in danger. No use in scaring her if it was harmless, but I knew in my gut it might not be. "I was busy with PR," I lied, squeezing her hand.

"And that took all night?"

"Unfortunately."

She gave me a knowing glance, that one look that sent shivers going up my spine. I was never good at lying to her.

"If it makes you feel better, I would have much rather spent the night with you in the hotel instead of back in Boulder. I didn't sleep," I added.

"That does make me feel better."

"That I'd have rather been with you?"

"That you didn't sleep."

---

The rest of the networking event went by in a daze, half because I was so exhausted and half because I spent the majority of it staring at Mandy instead of the things she wanted me to look at. It was hard when all I wanted was her, not interior design and architecture.

A couple of guys she'd said she'd spoken to earlier approached her as we made our way to the door. I did my best to try to concentrate on her and the way she conducted herself, but with the way that the man on the left kept staring at her and the ring on her finger, I found it difficult to wrap my head around a single word coming out of her mouth.

He mumbled something about losing her business card, and the giggle that seeped from her rubbed me the wrong way.

I placed my hand on her lower back, drawing her an inch closer to me. I wasn't sure if it was the exhaustion or the threat that made jealousy boil in my blood, I'd never been an overly jealous person, at least not with others that I'd dated. But then again, everything was different with her. *Everything.*

"We should get going, princess," I said, making sure he heard me and took note of my proximity to her. He locked eyes with me, his brows furrowing.

"Got plans or something?" He asked.

"We've got to catch our flight home."

"And where is home, then?" He grinned, taking a look at the business card she'd handed him. "Boulder?"

Mandy nodded. "Yes. Have you been?"

"I go out to Colorado every year for skiing." I hated the smirk he gave her, hated that he even thought he might have a chance. Hated that she was giving him the time of day. *Why?* "I don't normally go to Boulder but... maybe I'll stop by in January."

"That would be amazing!" Mandy exclaimed, her grin too wide, her excitement too palpable. "I can show you around the office, and Jack's campus should be open by then too so I can show you firsthand the work my company's done on that."

I couldn't help but dig my fingers into her back just a little bit. It felt like she was doing this to prove some kind of point because I was late. I knew I was spiraling. I was exhausted, stressed, and I just wanted to bury myself in her and fall asleep, never leave her side again. I needed to calm down. I blanked out the rest of their conversation, unable to listen to a second more of it without getting angry, and I didn't want to be angry with her. I just wanted peace, and I wanted to go back to how things had been last week, back to how we were ten years ago before any of this was a problem.

"Mands," I said softly. I pushed the hair from the side of her face behind her ear as I leaned closer. "Let's go for a late lunch, yeah? Just us. I know a spot."

She glanced up at me, her expression tight, reserved. "Alright."

Our hands were locked as we made our way to the exit. I knew exactly where I wanted to take her, the flight could wait.

## Chapter 28

## *Mandy*

Things between us didn't feel right. Recently it had felt like we'd slotted together easily, like two puzzle pieces coming together in a perfect match with no seam, but now it felt like someone had put the wrong ends of us together. Close, but not quite. But as I got out of the car, the bright winter sun boring down on us and making me squint, I felt a little closer to that feeling we'd had before.

"I thought you might want to beat your old high score," Jack drawled as he shut the car door behind me.

The front of the arcade had definitely taken a turn for the worse. Cobwebs littered the corners of the sign, half the neon letters flickering or out completely. The area was quiet even in the middle of the day. Granted it wasn't in the center of New York City, but it used to be busy with college kids at all hours of the day.

"Come on, princess," he grinned, turning and walking backward to the front door, one hand stretched out to me. I took it.

"I doubt my old score is still on top," I chuckled, the stale, musty air hitting me as we stepped through the door.

"You got the highest score I'd ever seen. The real question, though, is if they still have your favorite machine," Jack said, planting a little kiss on my cheek before turning his attention to the quarter exchange.

Two minutes later he had a purple Crown Royal bag in his fist, filled to the brim with quarters, way more than we needed. I doubted he was planning on staying here through the night like we had a few times in the past, but even if we did, it would still be far too many quarters.

Jack took my hand and led me toward the back, the bag of change jingling as he walked. They hadn't moved the pinball machines from where they'd been ten years ago, they were still around the corner in their same little spot, still flashing even though some of the bulbs had burst.

I lost count of the number of times I'd leaned over the Addams Family one with Jackson watching over my shoulder or leaning against the wall next to it, making me feel like he was genuinely interested in my constant attempt to beat my own high score. The nostalgia of it flooded in as I stood there, eyes fixed on Morticia and Gomez as they clung to each other above the now thirty-something-year-old table.

"I can't believe they still have it," Jack chuckled as he took up his usual spot beside the machine, his back against the wall. "Go on, then, princess. Are you still the highest scorer?"

I rolled my eyes as I walked up to the machine. "It's so unlikely."

He held out the bag of quarters for me, the top open. I plucked a couple out and slid them into the slot, the table lighting up immediately, two sets of initials and their high scores popping up on the screen.

MEL - 698,000,000
MEL - 696,000,000

"Holy shit," Jack laughed, his brows raised as he looked at the chunky block letters. "Ten years and no one's beat you."

"MEL is such a common set of initials," I replied, not quite believing it myself. "It's probably not mine."

"I'm pretty sure I watched you get that second score." His lips twitched up on one side, a devilish little smirk. "I guess you got the other after I left."

I tried not to allow the intrusive thoughts back in. Tried not to remember the countless hours I spent here after he'd gone, filling my time playing this machine just to break up the monotony of tears and exams. "I had to do something to keep myself from constantly crying," I snapped, regretting the words the instant they left my mouth. I couldn't hold them back, though. Not when the memories were hitting me left and right. I pulled back the plunger, took in a deep breath, and released, sending the first ball flying.

Jack blew out a breath. "Is this where you spent most of your time?"

"Yeah," I said, pinging the ball up, around the staircase, down the metal slide. "When Amanda needed space, I'd come here. When I felt like screaming and tearing my hair out, I'd come here. When I wanted to call Wade but knew I shouldn't, I'd come here."

First ball down already. I was rusty.

"Fuck," I snapped, taking a step back from the machine.

"Don't stop."

"It's fine, I'll just sink the rest. I'll start over." I pulled the plunger again and again, sinking each of my balls until the big red letters on the screen read LOSER.

Jack handed me another two quarters.

# Mia Mara

. . .

---

NEW HIGH SCORE.

I stepped back from the machine, my eyes wide, my hands tired. "How the fuck...?"

Jack sat on the floor beside the machine, his suit wrinkling on the dirty arcade floor that likely hadn't been cleaned once in the last ten years. His eyes blinked open as he lifted his head from where it rested against the wall. "What happened?"

"I beat it," I laughed, the adrenaline starting to kick in. "I fucking beat it, Jack!"

He was on his feet in a second, wide eyes glued to the big red letters on the old screen. "Holy shit. Have you been practicing?"

"No. I haven't played this one since college," I grinned, bouncing on the soles of my feet. I had too much energy, too much excitement. All the months I'd spent grinding to beat that second-highest score, and I beat it after ten years of not touching the Addams Family.

"Put your initials in," he said, a sleepy grin spreading across his cheeks. "Don't want anyone to forget you're still on top."

I giggled as I pressed the little buttons, sorting through the letters until I got MEL back on the screen. Miranda Eleanor Littleson. I'd done it with him by my side, even if he was half asleep. Somehow, that made me feel better, made me feel closer to him.

"Mands?"

I turned, my hair whipping about my face. Blonde hair, tied up in a ponytail. A polo shirt with the arcade's logo on it. Tight black jeans, combat boots. Hayley Moretti. She'd worked at the arcade during the last two years of my degree, always cheering me on from the sidelines, waving at me when she'd pass me on campus between classes. She was a smart girl. She'd studied physics.

So what the hell was she doing still working here?

"Hayley?" Jack asked, turning on the spot. The back of his suit was wrinkled from sitting on the floor, a little bit of gum stuck to the flap of his jacket.

"Oh my God, Jack," Hayley laughed, her fingers covering her lips as she set down the broom. *No wonder the carpets are so dirty.* "I can't believe you guys are here. What a small world."

"We're only here for the day," Jack grinned, stepping a little closer to me. "Came into town for a networking event for Mandy."

"Oh. You guys living out in Boulder?"

I nodded. "Yeah. Jack just recently moved out there."

"Nice. Congrats, by the way," she chirped, taking a step toward me. Her hand met my left one, lifting it gently to inspect the ring. "I saw the announcement in the papers. Always knew you two would end up back together."

Why did everyone else seem to know or hope for this except for me?

Jack placed a kiss against my temple as he struck up conversation, filling in the gap I'd left behind so easily. Hearing that from her was bittersweet. I'd been hurt by him. Destroyed, really, if I was being honest with myself. But I knew damn well that he was what I wanted now, even with his erratic behavior lately. Had I known all along? And if everyone was right and we were meant to be together again, then why the hell did it feel like he was pulling away?

---

Jack's lips against mine nearly stole the breath from my lungs.

He pressed me down against the back seat in the rented Escalade, his jacket gone, his hands on my bare thighs. He slotted himself between them, pushing them up toward my chest as his mouth moved ferociously against my own.

The adrenaline peaked when we left the arcade. Hayley's words had echoed in my head over and over until we left and paired with the sheer excitement of beating my old high score, I couldn't help but celebrate in the one way I knew how with Jack.

I kissed him. And he'd kissed me back harder.

I grabbed him by the tie, holding him close to me, forcing him to stay against my lips as I dragged my fingers down his chest. I could feel every ripple of muscle beneath the cotton, could feel his heartbeat against my hand. He was tired, but this was more important.

He wanted this more than sleep. I could feel it in the way he touched me, in the way his lips hungrily tasted my own, in the way he unbuckled his belt with one hand, freeing the hardening length of him beneath. I could feel it in the way his fingers raked against my flesh as he pulled my underwear down my legs, in the way he sighed a breath of relief as he sank himself inside of me, filling me so fully I wished he'd never leave.

"Godammit, Mandy," he breathed, tugging his tie loose as he came up for air. "You're too tempting. I can't seem to stay away."

I chuckled and wrapped my hand around the loose scrap of fabric, pulling him back down. "Then don't."

He hummed his approval against my lips. Slowly, painfully slowly, he pulled himself out to the tip, hesitated, then plunged back in. It made my head swim, made every drop of adrenaline in my system kick into overdrive. *Damn that felt so fucking good.*

His fingers wrapped around my throat gently, flesh against flesh, and that was too much. I loved it. I fucking loved it, could feel the way my muscles down below clenched around him at just the hint of something darker. I wanted to breathe, but the thrill of knowing he could squeeze at any point was enough to set my skin on fire.

"Touch yourself for me, princess," he grunted. He pulled back out, plunged back in. Back out, back in. Slowly building up his pace. "Touch yourself so I can keep my hand like this, since you like it so much."

I nodded and slid my hand between our bodies, over clothes and buttons, over the flap of my skirt, down where our skin met. I touched myself in just the way I liked, alternating pressure, little circles. "Fuck," I breathed, pleasure blooming, spreading. "Don't you dare pull out again."

"Not going to," he laughed. His fingers flexed against my neck, keeping the pressure off as he placed a kiss on the tip of my chin. "I'm never fucking leaving."

I laughed out a moan and tugged his tie harder. "You can't say things like that," I breathed, my smile too wide to contain. "It's not fair."

"Does it turn you on?" He asked, his shit-eating grin too

wide, too evil. "Do you like when I threaten to never take my cock out of you?"

I bit my lip as I felt myself dampen further, the slickness spreading to my fingertips. I quickened my circles, nodding a tiny, defeated yes to him.

"So dirty for me," he drawled. His finger inched its way up my neck, hooked my lip, and forced it from the clasp of my teeth. "Don't hide those. I want to see that smile when I make you come, princess."

He adjusted his angle, hitting that sweet spot inside of me. I could feel myself building already, too soon, too quick. I didn't want this to end. I never wanted it to end, especially not now. "You're clenching for me," he grunted, his voice breaking with pleasure halfway through. "Fuck, that feels so good. You're close."

"Yeah," I squeaked. I struggled to breathe, struggled to focus on anything other than him and the growing ecstasy in my body. I was rapidly approaching the cliff's edge, seconds from hurtling myself off it willingly.

"Come for me," he commanded, his eyes wide. "Let me see you come, princess. Let me watch how easily I make you come undone."

My fingers spasmed as my orgasm wrenched its way through me, a barely contained scream tearing from my throat. He fucked me through it, every hit an extra beat of pleasure, every groan he made sending shivers down my spine. *Breathe. Breathe. Breathe.*

"Breathe," Jack whispered, his hips stuttering. "Breathe for me, princess."

I gasped in air as my fingers found their way to the back of his neck, keeping him close. Each little wave from my dwindling orgasm was like heaven with his cock twitching inside of me, so close, about to break—

He moaned out his release as his hips collided with mine harshly, burying every drop inside of me. I could feel its warmth, could feel it spreading around his length. "Thank you," he sighed, pressing a kiss to my lips, my cheeks, my temples, anywhere he could reach. "I needed this."

"Of course," I giggled. My high was fading, my hips were aching. As much as I didn't want to call it quits, we had a plane waiting on the tarmac for us, and we were still in the Escalade outside the arcade. "I'm not ready to be empty."

He chuckled, his hips slowly pulling backward, leaving me leaking on the rental car's leather seats. "I'm sorry, Mands. We gotta get going."

"I know." I pulled his lips to mine briefly, a quick little peck. "Thank you, too. I love you."

"You're welcome," he said.

And nothing else.

# Chapter 29

## *Jackson*

The view from the back balcony of my parent's house was unmatched and always had been. As a kid I'd played in the gardens, chasing my baby sister around the pruned hedges and the fountains, the staff screaming at me to keep her away from the water. Now, she showed it off to Fred, the ground coated heavily in snow, their boots leaving a trail of footprints. Most of it the greenery was bare, but even in the winter, Mom insisted on decorating it with lights and decorations.

I clutched my cup of coffee as if it was my saving grace, the steam wafting upward and assaulting my nostrils. It had been two weeks since I didn't say, "I love you" back to Mandy, and with every passing second, it weighed heavier on my mind. I did love her. Of course I did. But I couldn't say it when even uttering the words could put her in danger.

So instead, I distracted myself. Sleepless night after sleepless night spent pouring over information, trying to get to the bottom of the threat. My team was great, but even so, they were struggling. When I'd run out of new information to distract myself with, I tried to see Mandy, or I'd surround myself with the woodlands by my house. But here, at my parents, there was little to distract myself with.

I'd been summoned home for a post-honeymoon family gathering. They'd managed to talk me into staying an extra night.

The sliding glass door behind me squealed before shutting again, three heavy footsteps telling me very clearly that Dad had come to join us. Either that or our house was infested with very smart bears.

"You leaving in the morning?"

I didn't bother turning, just clutched my coffee tighter. "Yeah. I'll probably be gone by the time you guys wake up."

"Nothing out of the ordinary then," he snorted, his breath fogging around us as he stepped up to the railing next to me. "You seem distant."

"I'm always distant, Dad."

"More distant than usual," he explained. He watched Tiana and Fred as they started gathering snow to make a snowman, something she and I had done countless times growing up. It was nice to see her giggling and smiling instead of scowling. "How are things with Miranda?"

*Yep. Should've guessed he wanted to talk about my love life.* "Fine," I lied, my jaw steeling.

"Is it serious?" He asked, tearing his gaze from my sister for once and looking at me. "Or are you still convinced it's all for show?"

"I don't know," I admitted. "I'm not sure what's happening anymore."

"I've had a few friends pull the same stunt you did," he chuckled, plucking the coffee cup from my hand and stealing a sip. "I'd say about half of them are happily married now to their faux-fiancée."

The words swam around in my brain. "What are you saying?"

He sighed exasperatedly as he stared me down, my mug of coffee swirling steam up around his wrinkled face. "Look, Jackson," he started, his bushy brows furrowing. "I know we've never been exactly close. But I'm going to say to you the exact same thing I said to Miranda at the wedding—you're different with her. More alive. More yourself. It's like you never got taken away in the first place, and that's really fucking saying something, son."

"Dad—"

"No, listen. You lock her down. She loves you, I can see it, and I know damn well you love her too. You always did. You wouldn't have asked for that ring if you didn't. You may be doing this to save your asses but there was nothing fake between you two at the wedding."

I sighed, forcing myself to look away from him. I knew he was right, knew it in my very soul, but being right came with consequences, consequences I wasn't prepared to make her face. I wouldn't put her in danger, not again, not ever.

I would break myself in two before I let it come to that.

I sucked in a breath and watched the little pieces of snow that floated down in the moonlight, infrequent and delicate, trying to distract myself from what I knew was inevitable. "I don't think any of that matters."

Dad released a long breath, his mouth opening then quickly closing as he shook his head. He slipped my mug of coffee back into my hands, turned, and headed for the house. "I don't understand why you won't let yourself be happy."

The glass door opened and slammed shut, nearly hard enough to shatter it.

He couldn't understand. He never would. As far as I knew, Mom had never been under threat, at least not one as serious as this. I knew they loved each other and if Mom was under the same kind of life-altering or life-ending threat as Mandy could be, he would do whatever it took to keep her safe. I had to believe that.

I looked back to Tiana and Fred as they popped a carrot into the snowman's face. Fred stepped to the side, breaking a couple of branches off the hedges for arms. *Would Fred pick up and leave for Tiana's safety? Would he be as devastated as I was slowly becoming with no leads, no information, to put the threat to rest?*

I pulled my phone from my pocket with nearly frozen and numb fingers. I could at least call the security team, check for any new updates. They were supposed to call me, but—

My phone buzzed before I could make the call, the screen lighting up with wouldn't you know it. *Speak of the fucking devil.*

I answered it without waiting a single second. "Any leads?" I asked, the chill beginning to sink into my bones. I sipped my coffee, warming my throat and coating my insides.

"Hi, Jackson, how are you? I'm great, thanks for asking." Marsha, head of security. Always so snippy.

"I'm sorry. Hi. I'm shitty. Again, any leads?"

"Well, since you asked so nicely, it is my absolute honor to inform you that we found the original IP address. As I'm sure you're aware, the sender was using a VPN, but we managed to get a hold of the VPN company and they agreed to work with us."

The breath left my lungs in a thick cloud of air. "You found it."

"We did, indeed," she chirped. I could hear the faint clicking of a mouse in the background, fading into near nonexistence as my sister squealed from being hit with a snowball. "It was sent from the Boulder Public Library."

I lost my grip on the mug. It fell forward, off the edge of the railing and down one story, shattering against the cement floor of the back porch and making Tiana scream. "Surveillance video. We need the surveillance video, Marsha."

"I know. We're on it, but you know how government moves, they're slow as shit. If it was a private business we could have it by tomorrow, but unfortunately, we just have to wait," she sighed. "But we will get to the bottom of this, Jackson. We'll find them. There's a lot more hope now than there was yesterday."

I simultaneously wanted to scream in frustration and celebrate the breakthrough. Adrenaline coursed through my veins, finding nowhere to run, snaking up my spine instead and making me feel jittery. An overload of nerves and panic mixed with excitement. "Thank you."

"Of course. We'll be in touch as soon as we get the video footage."

She hung up before I did, leaving me in the silent snow, half frozen , and on my way to a panic attack. We would figure this out. We had to. If we couldn't, if we hit a brick wall, it would all be for nothing. The move to Boulder, getting Mandy back, loving her...all for nothing.

I couldn't let that happen.

Tiana shouted something up at me as I pulled my phone from my freezing skin, the brightness nearly blinding in the low light. A text from a number I hadn't saved but still recognized filled my screen, and I stared at it, my eyes barely agreeing to focus through the haze of endorphins.

*Unknown Number: You know she deserves better than this.*

*Unknown Number: You can't just hurt her again and again and expect it to be okay. I'm not going to let you. Leave her alone for her own sake.*

Fucking Harry.

Anger rippled through and joined the goddamn party of stressful emotions tearing me up inside. *What authority does he think he has?*

I shoved my phone into my pocket, huffing out one final puff of fog. I could put him on the back burner for now.

## Chapter 30

## *Mandy*

The builders, painters, and installers I'd hired had started their work a couple of weeks ago, and as I walked through the massive entry hall that smelled of fresh paint, I could tell that things were coming together slower than I wanted.

The tile was laid down, but the grout hadn't gone in. Some of the so-called finished walls only had one coat of paint. Art was stored alongside used paintbrushes, rollers, and open tins. Everyone was in overdrive, but nothing was finished. The grand opening was three weeks away, and in just *two* weeks, Jackson's board of directors would be doing a walk-through. This had to quicken up.

"Can we get guys on caulking, please?" I shouted over the sound of a jackhammer somewhere in the distance. *Why the fuck is a jackhammer being used two weeks before the walk-through?* "And some on paint? These walls are atrocious."

"Everyone is busy right now." Nathan pulled his hard hat down over his brows as another worker walked past, a handful of lumber tucked under his arm, and I genuinely had no idea where he was heading.

"Then get more guys in," I hissed, grabbing the clipboard from his hand and looking it over. A list of names with duties assigned next to them, each one booked solid. "The budget is whatever you want. Hire more."

"Yes ma'am," he grunted.

"At least twenty more," I insisted, handing him back the clipboard.

I let out a stressful groan as he walked off, wishing Harry had gotten off his damn ass and showed up on time so I wasn't in this alone, also wishing Jackson had agreed to come with me. He'd been so busy lately that I'd hardly seen him, barely spoken to him. Meeting after meeting, he'd said. I was trying not to let it bother me, but he'd been there before when things were busy. Something was clearly going on behind the scenes, something he didn't want to talk to me about.

I at least had something to look forward to, though. Jack was taking me out for dinner tonight—an apology for his absence. He was picking me up at seven, and taking me somewhere new; hopefully, if things went well, we'd end up at his house after. I'd get to the bottom of whatever was going on with him. It was all I could think about.

That and the fucking paint.

---

As I walked into the massive room toward the back of the campus that Jack had allocated for shared offices, a familiar face struggled into the room from the opposite set of doors. What I thought was going to be my saving grace morphed into yet another disappointment.

"Where the fuck have you been?" I hissed, taking in every inch of the food-stained clothes and oversized hoodie Harry wore. He looked like a goddamn mess, and with every step I took toward him, he looked even worse. Massive dark circles, unkempt hair, unshaven. He wasn't even wearing a hard hat or a safety vest.

"Sorry," he grumbled. He rubbed his eyes, scratched his jaw. "I've not been feeling well. I know I'm late."

"Have you seen a doctor?"

"Not yet. I've got an appointment tomorrow," he said, his eyes raking across my body and landing far too solidly on my left hand. "Why are you still wearing the ring? Surely you can take it off while you're in a construction zone."

"I don't want anyone asking questions if they notice." I spun the ring on my finger with my thumb. That was a lie—I didn't always wear it when I was here, but knowing I was going to see Jack tonight was enough to make me want to. "Why do you care?"

"I thought you were breaking it off," he snapped. He stepped out of the way as a man carried cans of paint past him and toward the opposite wall. Across the room, people began to bring in piece by piece of the hanging art that Jack and I had commissioned, and if I was smart, I would go over there and help instead of staying with Harry. "You were supposed to end the fake engagement."

"He didn't stand me up. He was late. I didn't get the chance to explain—"

"So you're defending him now?" he asked, his lips pursing as he looked from me to the ring and back again, as if it was offending him just by being on my hand. "Do you understand why I'm worried about this, Mandy?"

Dragging my tongue along my teeth, I sighed. "Look," I started, clutching my clipboard to take out my frustrations on something that wasn't him. "Miscommunications happen. I'm not *defending* it. I'm just not as upset as I was on the plane. Things are fine, he's fine, we're fine."

"I don't think you're seeing things the way they are."

The cheap wood of my clipboard nearly snapped. "And I don't think you're giving him an ounce of grace. Both of us can still be somewhat correct."

"You're looking from the inside out, not the outside in. Of course you're going to feel like things are going well, but for fucks sake, just take one look at what the press has said about his past relationships. He doesn't give a shit about the women he fucks."

I blinked at him, my mind going blank with rage, my jaw stiffening, my eyes struggling to focus. "You have no right to tell me if he does or doesn't give a shit about me."

"I'm not saying he definitely doesn't. But you *have* to understand that there is a chance. You *have* to see where I'm coming from."

In all honesty, I didn't want to.

"I'm sorry, I know I said I'd chill out on this, but I can't just stand by as he breaks you and mends you and then starts again. I know there are feelings involved, I know you have history, but it's clouding your vision." His hand pushed through the grease in his hair, slicking the curls back far too easily. "I'm terrified for you."

Of course I'd considered it. In every passing moment where I wasn't all for Jack, those were the exact thoughts swirling in my head. But there were too many green flags, too many positives to this, and the goddamn tattoo... I couldn't imagine he was getting a tattoo for every other woman he wanted to sleep with.

But I also knew that Harry's worries weren't unfounded. I'd been broken by him so wholly before that I thought I'd never recover. I was worried it would happen again, too, but maybe not quite as much as Harry was. He didn't want to see me hurt.

"I'm not clutching at straws here, Harry. I've got... reasons to be in this, to feel the way I do. He's not just going to drop me."

"Well, where is he, then? He's certainly not here. I haven't seen him around the office. If he cared so much, Mandy, wouldn't he be here with you?" He snickered, stepping closer. He was making a scene now, drawing attention from the men and women at work around us. If I was unlucky enough, one of them would video it and sell it to the press.

"He's busy." I swallowed. I hated how he was able to use this to his advantage. I didn't like the fact that I hadn't seen much of Jackson lately, but the fact that Harry was starting to notice wasn't a good sign. "He's taking me out to dinner tonight. We're fine."

"Are you? When was the last time you even saw him, Mands?"

My hesitation was enough to answer that question.

"Fucks sake," he hissed, taking a deep breath as he forced himself to stare at the ceiling instead of me. "Please, for me, just try to keep your head above water. You've been broken once. There's only so many times we can put the pieces back together and still have a functional person."

I flinched at his words and took a step back. I'd lost count of how many times Harry had voiced his distaste for my situation, and every time, it hit me like a javelin to the gut.

I wanted to tell him to go fuck himself. Wanted to tell him to keep his nose out of my business, wanted to tell him that I could handle myself. But his points were valid — I *was* questioning what was going on in Jack's mind. There were occasional red flags. I couldn't say it out loud, couldn't accept it when this was everything to me, but they existed. And I knew he was only desperate to keep me intact.

"I know you're trying to help," I breathed, my voice calmer than I felt. "But you're not the one in this situation. I am. And I can take care of myself."

"You thought that last time—"

"I was twenty-one." I cut him off, pointing out the one thing he'd failed to consider. "I didn't have much back then. I had him, and I had class, a few friends, and an addiction to pinball. I wasn't nearly as strong then. I'm older, now. Wiser. Stronger."

His eyes locked to mine. Everything about him had softened slightly, the crease between his brows ironing out, but his lips were pressed into a hard, thin line. "I don't know if that's enough with him, Mandy."

I didn't want to be doing this. Not here, not anywhere, and especially not with him in whatever state this was. Unwell or not, it wasn't fair to me. Not when we had enough on our plates with the walk through in two weeks. "Please let the dead dog lie. For now, at least. I can handle myself."

## Chapter 31

## *Jackson*

The echo of my footsteps in the stairwell was the only sound loud enough to cover the pounding in my ears. I was *barely* on time if that meant being ten minutes late, and although Mandy had given me far more grace than I deserved lately, I didn't want her to have to.

Sucking in air through my teeth as I set foot on flat concrete, I tugged the knot of my tie, giving myself just an inch of breathing room. Fuck, I hated these offices. Freezing cold or boiling hot — but somehow, the stairwell was *always* humid.

The door out into the parking garage squeaked violently as I slipped through the gap. The harshness of the biting wind was enough to kick me into overdrive, beating away every little drop of sweat I'd accumulated or drying it into my skin. I just needed to get to my car in — I checked my watch — ten seconds.

God, I was so screwed.

The taillights of my BMW flashed twice from across the

lot. Thankfully I hadn't been enough of an idiot to ride my Harley in this morning.

I shuffled my laptop case into the hand that held my keys as I slipped my phone from my pocket with the other, pulling up Mandy's contact details in a flash. If I could just text her, give her a heads up that I knew I was being a piece of shit but I was on my way, maybe it would take a little bit of the sting away.

She'd already been kind enough to agree to meet me there so we could be somewhat on time for our reservation, anyway.

"So your phone *does* work."

My head snapped up.

How the *fuck*?

In the five seconds it had taken for me to look away from my car and pull out my phone, stained sweatpants and a far too baggy hoodie had come between me and my BMW far too silently for my liking. Messy, short blonde hair and dark-circle-laden grayish eyes stared me down.

"Why are you...?" I asked, words failing me as I checked over my shoulder. Part of me wanted to imagine that maybe, just maybe, in some weird and helpful way, Harry had driven Mandy to me instead. But there was no one there — just a handful of cars, most of them ones I recognized, but there, in the corner, idling...

Was I that sleep deprived that I missed it entirely?

Harry's ass leaned onto my car. I couldn't help but dread whatever stain he'd leave on it. "Heard you had a date tonight," he said. His gaze drifted from me and out toward the opening between floors of the garage, the sun long set and the moon just slightly out of view. "I thought I'd made myself clear with my texts. But apparently, I hadn't."

*Made himself clear?*

His jaw steeled as his hands came to rest on the curve of my BMW's trunk, his nails pushing into it. The little scratching noise it made was almost as bad as nails on a chalkboard.

"So... I'm sorry, what? You're here because you sent me a couple of texts?" I said, the words falling from me and not even making sense out loud. I didn't understand—couldn't—and in my spiraling thoughts surrounding him, one thing came out clear.

I still needed to get to fucking dinner.

"You didn't even bother to respond." Another crunch of the paint on my car. "You didn't even consider it, did you?"

"Honestly, Harry, I can't deal with this right now." I pressed down on the little button on my keys and the engine roared to life behind him. I couldn't imagine dealing with this at *any* point, let alone now, but I'd say whatever I needed to get him out of here and get me to Mandy. "I'll, uh, call you later or something. Okay?"

"No."

Adrenaline rocketed through my veins as he pushed himself upright, abandoning the scratched paint of my paint and turning to look directly at me.

"I'm not letting you see her." The words dripped from him like venom, his chest broadening, his chin stealing. He was only a few inches shorter than me, but *god*, he looked like a fucking pipsqueak, like a seething chipmunk.

I looked him up and down, took in his disheveled state and the hint of booze on his scent. If any part of him wanted a fight, he would lose. "Look, respectfully, you don't want to do this."

"I'll do what I damn well please," he snapped, spittle flying from his mouth and smacking me in the face. I wiped it with the back of my hand and leaned forward over him, crowding him, not giving him the space to breathe that he wanted. He didn't shy away, but I could *hear* the quickening of his breaths, could see how easily I made him uncomfortable. "Hey—"

"What do you want out of this?" I asked, letting the words drip from me like venom. "What do you gain from coming here? Do you realize how much training I've had, how easily I could put you in the goddamn ground?"

His Adam's apple bobbed as he swallowed, his gaze flicking between my hardened stare and the ceiling. He didn't even do me the justice of answering my question — just held his position, stupidly bold.

"You're making me late," I hissed. "I'd suggest running back to whatever hole you crawled from if you don't want to get run over by my fucking car." Another press of a button, and the driver's side door popped open.

His lips pressed into a thin line, the breath from his nose fogging the air between us. "You know what you're doing."

I blinked down at him as my brows knitted together.

"And you don't give a shit."

My phone buzzed in my pocket and I took a step back, keeping my eyes locked on his. "Don't tell me what I do and don't give a shit about," I snarled.

The wind whistled through the garage as I turned. I needed to get to dinner, needed to get to *her*, and all I was doing was allowing this to make me even later. *Fuck it*, I thought, and headed straight to the goddamn drivers side.

"You're actively hurting her!"

I turned on my heel, my hands curling into fists. "And you're not?"

His eyes widened, the little red veins almost darkening. "I'm not the one who fucked her and tore her into pieces."

Anger burned the back of my throat in an instant.

"Don't talk about things you know absolutely nothing about," I spat, throwing my bag and keys onto the passenger seat and slamming the door shut without getting in. If this is what he wanted, then *fine*. "You want to sit there and act all high and mighty, act like you have everything figured out, act like you know who she is and what happened between us — but you have no goddamn clue the shit we've been through. You don't know where I've been. You don't know who I *am*."

He crossed his arms over his chest, his sneer forcing my hand, forcing me to move. My vision tunneled, my mind overriding every normal thought. "I know enough about you to know you're a piece of shit, sorry excuse for a man. I know enough to know that you don't deserve her. I know enough to know that you don't have her best interests at heart, that you're just going to break her *again*, that you're going to chew her up and spit her out for *fun*—"

Pain exploded through my knuckles as a *thwack* echoed against the concrete around us.

Blinking through the haze, my vision slowly came back, revealing a bloodied-nosed Harry on the ground, his upper half held up by his elbows. Wild eyes met mine, the same shit-eating grin stapled to his cheeks, and — yeah, his nose was broken.

But he *laughed*.

"God, she's going to *love* this."

My body moved again of its own accord, reaching down to fist the front of his hoodie and haul him to his feet. I walked him back, shoving him against the concrete pillar two spaces down my car, and spat in his blood-covered face. "You knew better, didn't you?" I sneered, pulling him forward before slamming him back into the concrete. "You wanted this. You practically *begged* me."

Blood coated his teeth as he spoke. "I have no idea what you're talking about," he laughed. "You're just digging your own grave, Jack."

"Do you want to fucking join me in it?"

My hand left his shirt, only to bloom with pain again as it collided with his jaw.

He caught himself against the pillar, spitting blood and saliva out of his clenched teeth. "Fucker," he rasped, wiping his face with the back of his arm and hissing from the pain. "You probably would have done *this* to her, too."

Nope. No, no, no.

I saw *red*.

Taking the front of his hoodie in my hand again, I acted on instinct. I fisted it, held on for dear life, and wrenched him from the pillar before releasing at the last second, sending him skidding across the concrete ground beneath us. The distance closed as I followed, one booted foot hitting him square in his ribcage with an audible *crack*.

And another.

And *another*.

It took everything in me to stop. Every ounce of control I had after sleepless nights and endless work. I left him there as he spat blood and cackled, clinging to his ribs. I must have broken at least two, if not three. Must have done enough damage to keep him down.

"You're fucked up, man," he yelled to me as I opened my car door. Red coated the front of him as he slowly, achingly, pushed himself up to a seated position.

"Yeah, well, I warned you and you still made me late." I flexed the fingers on my right hand as I slid into the driver's seat, the smallest droplets of blood leaking from the broken skin.

# Chapter 32

## *Mandy*

*Me: Where are you?*

I stared at the unanswered message between us as my phone lay silently on the dining table. The people around me hummed and spoke in low voices, each enjoying their own meal with whomever they'd come with that had actually shown up. Lingering glances from the waitstaff burned at the edges of my vision, and all I could do as I sat there alone with a glass of wine and a basket of bread was feel like I was only cheating myself.

Thirty minutes had passed since the time our reservation was booked. He'd warned me he was running a few minutes behind, but this long? He wasn't even answering his phone.

Weeks of pushed-back dates, weeks of barely hearing from him, weeks of feeling like I'd been placed on the goddamn back burner and forgotten about, left to sizzle and evaporate on my own. I just didn't have the patience anymore.

I didn't think about it. I just acted.

Flagging down a waiter, I apologized for the inconvenience and asked for the bill. "You'll have to pay for the bread," he said, and I agreed because *what else was I supposed to do?*

I downed my glass of wine and set the company card down on the receipt, marking down a hefty tip and making a mental note to add it to J.B Tech's bill. I waited anxiously as they took it, charged me, and thanked me.

And then I left.

I didn't hold back the angry tears on the drive home. I needed to let them out, needed to feel the way I felt, and needed to rethink *everything*.

I didn't bother with taking off my makeup in the bathroom of my empty apartment. I didn't bother trying to preserve the expensive red dress he'd bought me, didn't care if I stained it with dripping mascara. No. I wanted a bath, and I wanted a glass of wine, and I wanted to rid him from my thoughts for the evening so I could decide if being with him, going through this again with him, was worth the pain it was causing me.

Too long had passed since he'd said he loved me.

Too long had passed since I'd been able to enjoy his presence.

The faucet spewed hot water into the tub as I stared at myself in the mirror, and took in the train wreck on the outside instead of soothing the one on the inside. I smeared the black from my waterline, leaving streaks in my wake. I wiped the snot from my nose, smearing my foundation and lipstick. I let the burn and the ache fill the back of my throat, quelled it with sip after sip of wine. Poured another glass, and then another.

# Mia Mara

At nine o'clock, my phone lit up on the counter, just as I'd removed my dress and stared at my naked form in the mirror.

I could see in the reflection who it was. Could see his image and *Jackson Pig* in reverse.

I ignored it.

With my third glass of wine sitting on the edge of the tub and my phone in my hand, I sunk into the steaming water. My mind rapidly switched over and over between endless, racing thoughts of *what am I doing to myself?* and utter silence. I stared at the ceiling, letting whatever happened happen, letting myself fall into some of the same thoughts I'd had ten years ago. There wasn't a part of me that had the energy to fight it.

My phone buzzed once.

I almost didn't look. I almost let it lie there, ignored, unwanted. But I couldn't do that, either.

With wet hands, I scrambled for it on the side of the tub, nearly dropping it and my wine into the water below. Jackson's name wasn't the one that lit my screen — no, it was Harry.

*Harry: Three photos Received.*

I flicked it open.

*Oh my god.*

There, in the blue light of my phone screen, was Harry's blood-covered face. The first image, one taken straight on, showed a crooked nose and blood smeared across his jawline, his mouth, his teeth. The second image, one taken from below his face and pointing up, showed a massive red patch of skin just to the right of his chin, one that would likely turn into a bruise — and also showed just how badly his nose was broken. And the third image, one of his chest, showed red patches along his slightly misshapen ribcage. Each one had a background that I knew fairly well — the local ER.

I felt sick.

My phone buzzed again, and below the images, a text came through from Harry.

*Harry: In case you were wondering why your "fiancé" was late tonight.*

Screw feeling sick. I was *going* to be sick.

I felt the bile rise in my throat as I scrambled from the tub, chucked myself over the side of it, and lifted the lid of the toilet before spewing the few scraps of bread I'd eaten and the glasses of wine I'd guzzled. I wretched, shivering from the water on my skin and the temperature difference.

As if my night couldn't have gotten worse.

I clicked his name at the top of my messages as I desperately tried to control the acid trying to leave my esophagus and tapped the *call* button.

He picked up on the first ring. "Hey, Mands."

"Please tell me you're okay." The words came out in a rush, in a choked sob as another wretch hit me.

"Yeah, I'm all right. Couple of broken ribs and a broken nose," Harry chuckled, the sound almost hollow. "Fucking hurts, though. And the bill I'm going to get isn't something I'm looking forward to."

"I'll cover it. Whatever it is, I'll cover it," I breathed. In through my nose, out through my mouth, over and over until I finally regained control of the muscles trying to fill my mouth with vomit. "What happened?"

Still shivering, I pulled myself back to the bath and up and over the edge, sinking back into the warm water as Harry spoke. "You don't want to know," he sighed. I could hear the echo of his car unlocking in the background of the call. "It'll just muddy the waters."

"I don't care. I need to know."

I could hear the hesitation in his voice, could practically feel the air leaving his lungs. "All right," he murmured. "I was still at the campus, going over a few things with Nathan about the new hires. I went to leave and I ran into Jack in the lot. He looked... angry? I don't even know if I can call it that. Different, I guess. Like he hadn't slept."

I downed my glass of wine before he could say something that would make me shatter the glass.

"I went over to give him the rundown on how things were going, y'know? Just wanted to keep him in the loop since you'd left early. He just... snapped. Something about hiring more workers, the budget creeping up. I told him I'd asked for more 'cause I didn't want him to take that out on you."

*Oh, god.*

"I guess that set him off even worse. He yelled at me. Has he ever screamed at you? That man is fucking terrifying when he's yelling," he said.

"No, he hasn't," I answered, my voice feeling far too small.

"I guess that's a positive." His engine roared to life down the phone. "I mentioned you'd said you had a date tonight and that he should probably get going 'cause I was trying to de-escalate or just get him away from me, I don't know. And he just exploded. Broke my nose on the first punch. Almost broke my jaw with the second. I freaked out and tried to crawl away but he just started fucking kicking me."

My hands shook as I pushed the free one under the water. "Oh my god."

"It's okay. I'm... mostly fine," he laughed, the sound cutting short as he sucked in air. "Fucking hurts to laugh."

I didn't even notice the tears had escaped until I felt the coolness of them hitting my chest. Sniffling, I wiped them with the back of my damp hand, only making things worse. "I'm so sorry," I croaked. "I'm in fucking shock."

"It's not your fault."

"It *is*."

"It's not. I would've taken the fall for that any day, even if it ended like that each time," he said, his voice a little quieter, a little more vulnerable. "I didn't want to have to tell you. I even considered *not* telling you. But I couldn't just let you, y'know, be around him without knowing what he's... uh, capable of."

"No, I appreciate it." I took in a shaky breath and let it out through a tiny hole between my lips. "I'll add whatever your bill comes to onto his invoice."

The laugh that choked from him was wretched, hurt, but full of genuine happiness. "Attagirl."

"Please don't worry about coming in the next few days," I added.

"Thanks, Mands. I'll call you tomorrow, okay? I'll try to do some work from home."

As the call came to its natural end and we each hung up, I could feel myself slipping down the back of the tub. Inch by inch, I let myself submerge, covering my abdomen, my breasts, my throat, my mouth — sunk until I was under the water entirely, my hair floating behind me, my knees curled up and poking from the surface. I pushed the back of my head against the bottom of the porcelain.

And I screamed.

I screamed until I ran out of air, forced myself to the surface, sucked in air, and back down I went. I screamed again, feeling the bubbles form around my mouth, piercing my eardrums with the sound of it. More air, and another. More air, and another. More air, and I screamed until my throat went raw, until I couldn't take it anymore, until my diaphragm ached and my stomach tried to empty itself, until my lungs nearly dared to fill themselves with water.

Oxygen felt like swallowing knives when I came back to the surface for good.

Another buzz from my phone and all I wanted to do was throw it at the wall and watch it break into a thousand tiny pieces, but I didn't. I checked it just in case it was from Harry.

*Jackson Pig: Should I go home?*

Why did this have to happen now?

*Jackson Pig: I'm so sorry, princess. I know I should have been here sooner. I just got caught up with something at work. They said you'd left but I was kind of hoping you'd come back.*

*Jackson Pig: Are you at home?*

*Jackson Pig: Can I come to you?*

*Jackson Pig: We should probably talk about what happened tonight but I don't want to do it over the phone.*

I waited until the messages stopped coming through, waited until he gave up and the little indication of him typing had gone away. I didn't want him here. Didn't want him anywhere near me.

But there was the networking event tomorrow. The one I needed to go to, the one he held my ticket for, the one he had managed to get me into. I was caught between two options: run from him and let it end like that, or tough it out until we got through the opening of his new building.

I couldn't fucking decide.

*Me: I don't want you to come over.*
*Me: I need space.*
*Jackson Pig: I know I messed up. But please.*
*Me: Stop. Just stop. I'm going to bed.*

# Chapter 33

## *Jackson*

The only sound in my office was that of my incessantly tapping foot as I stared at the three screens in front of me, filled corner to corner with coding software and programs. Through the glass wall on the opposite side of the room, the snow fell silently, a gentle blanket on top of the massive piles outside. The floodlight bore down on the driveway, and the two armed security officers by the gate. It was enough for now.

I'd barely had a moment to actually focus on work for the last few weeks. Every ounce of energy had gone into the threat against Mandy, and every leftover drop had trickled into making sure the campus was ready for rollout in three weeks. And because of that, I'd fallen seriously behind, my work for Infinius building up to an overwhelming amount.

It felt good to shut off from the world overnight after everything that happened. I'd needed it, craved it, and although a part of me still screamed from the back of my head and longed for Mandy, it was comforting to focus on the one thing I knew I was good at. The thing I knew I could do, could fix. It was like a breath of fresh air after being on a plane for too long. Not exactly a saving grace, but enough to keep me going.

The growl from my stomach pulled me out of my thoughts.

I stood from the desk, stretching my arms over my head. I'd been sitting here for *hours* at this point, long enough for the sun to go down and rear its angry head again in the early hours. I wasn't sure exactly what time it was, but somewhere *had* to be serving breakfast by now.

I grabbed my phone from where it rested face-down on my desk. I must have been insane to think that maybe, just maybe, my screen would be littered with texts from her, but it hurt regardless to see nothing but a handful of notifications from my emails and a reminder of the imminence of our grand opening.

My fingers ached as I gripped my phone, almost willing Mandy to text me, call me, scream at me if she wanted. The blisters on my knuckles had stopped burning hours ago, and maybe it was the adrenaline still pumping through my system or the countless cups of coffee I'd drank overnight, but the pain was rearing its angry head again.

Part of me wanted to set it down, go back to work, and try to drown it out. Overriding government systems was insanely difficult but not *impossible*. I could crack it eventually if I had enough willpower, enough steam, but my stomach was growling and my chest ached from finally allowing myself to think about her for more than two seconds.

There was only so much grace she'd give me. I knew that too well, knew it deep in my bones, knew it in that stupid ache in my chest and the knot in my throat.

*Fuck it.* I knew she was avoiding me. It was evident

from her lack of responses last night. But that didn't mean that I couldn't try.

I pressed the little picture of her on my screen and tapped *call* for what felt like the millionth time since I drove off last night.

*Ring.*
*Ring.*
*Ring.*
*Ring.*
*The person you are trying to reach is not avail—*

Gritting my teeth, I ended the call and flipped across to our texts instead. The ones I'd sent last night still sat there, a horrible, gut-punching reminder that I was barely able to contain my feelings for her even when they put her in danger. I didn't want to have to keep looking at them, didn't want to see how desperate my *I'm sorry*'s read.

I lifted the phone closer to my mouth and hit the little microphone.

"Princess. Please."

*Delete. Start again.*

"I'm sorry. I know you're mad. I know I don't deserve an ounce of grace right now, but I swear, I did everything I fucking could to get to you as quickly as possible."

*Liar. You could have left earlier. You could have walked away from him.*

*Delete.*

"I'm a piece of shit. I get it."

*Delete.*

"Please, just talk to me. I know I don't deserve it, but please, Mandy, I'll take you screaming at me over silence."

*Send.*

*Keep going.*

I leaned forward onto my desk, my mind racing. "I'll

make it up to you. I'll do anything. Just don't block me out. I can't — I can't handle another ten years."

*Send.*

"I love you. I love you so fucking much and I know I'm screwing everything up. I know. I just... I wish I could tell you everything. I wish I could tell you how I'm doing all of this for you, how I can't get a moment's sleep because I'm spending every goddamn second trying to figure this out. I wish I could tell you that I'm worried things are bad again, that I have cause to believe you're under threat by the same people who were so horrible that I had to hide. I wish I could tell you that I love you more than you will ever fucking know. I wish..."

My fingers dug into the wood, scratching the varnish and veins.

"I wish we'd have had what you imagined for us, back at the wedding. That I'd asked you to marry me when I wanted to, that we'd fucked off into the national park with just the people you wanted and married you in that goddamn all-black tux and you in whatever color you wanted, that we'd rented a chateau, that we'd had a bonfire, that we'd celebrated you and me the way you imagined it."

Even without her on the other end, I could feel it all slipping through my fingers. Why did this have to hurt so much?

"And I wish we'd had two dogs and cat and kids and a house full of a shit ton of pinball machines, wish we spent Christmases with your mom and New Years with my parents, wish you had a fucking garden full of dead plants that I could replace, wish we had a life that we *wanted*. If I had a time machine... shit, I'd make everything happen the way you wanted. I'd take away every second of suffering that I could and replant each one with happy memories and *us*."

My nail chipped and splintered, and I hissed from the pain.

"But more than fucking anything, princess, I wish I could just tell you all of this. I wish I could lay everything out there for you. But I can't, at least not yet. So... I'm sorry. And I love you. I love you more than I can ever put into words."

My thumb hesitated over the send button, too many thoughts and emotions racing through my brain. *I could do it. I could send it, clue her in, let her know.*

But I couldn't. She wouldn't care about the risk to herself, and I knew that too well.

*Delete.*

Collapsing back into my chair, breakfast no longer sounded like a good idea despite the growling of my stomach. The thought of it made me feel sick, like I'd end up throwing up all over my desk and computers and ruining everything even more than I already had.

I stared at my phone, almost contemplating replaying the two voice notes I'd sent just to hear how positively desperate I sounded and cringe at myself, but for a brief second, almost so quickly I didn't see it, the little *typing* bubble appeared from her end before disappearing again.

I shot her another text too quick, too rash.

*Me: Let me explain what happened last night. I'm sure you've already heard, but please.*

The bubble reappeared for a moment before vanishing.

*Me: I don't want to do this over text. Let me come over. I can explain everything, princess. Just let me see you.*

The bubble returned and stayed, and each passing

second felt like an hour, like my racing heart was about to beat its way out of my chest and flop onto the desk.

*Mandy: Are we still on for the networking event this morning?*

I blinked at the screen, my mind caught between elation from a response and absolute horror that she was focusing entirely on that.

*Me: Uh, yeah, I'll be there.*
*Mandy: Okay. If you say so.*
*Me: Mandy. Come on.*

The seconds ticked by again, pushing the acid up my esophagus.

*Mandy: See you in a bit.*

---

I didn't bother with trying to fit in a quick nap.

I'd hopped from the home office to the shower, from the shower to the kitchen, barely stomached my breakfast, got my shit together, and headed out early. I didn't want to risk missing another thing — not when she was already upset with me, not when I didn't want to fuck this up any further. I'd been distant, yes, but if I ended this it would be because I *had* to, not because I'd fucked up.

The event was in Denver this time, close to home. Mandy had insisted on driving herself instead of riding with me, and although it grated on me, I would overlook it for her. Stubborn and independent.

I pushed my way through the doors on the other side of check-in, my eyes scanning the crowd of the main room. It wasn't too packed yet. These things rarely were this early in the morning, and if she wasn't here yet, I was more than willing to wait.

It didn't take long.

Less than thirty minutes later, as I sipped a cup of black coffee and one of the spare seats in the room, Mandy came through the doors. Her wild hair was up in a bun, her wool jacket covering the slacks and button-up shirt she wore. Boots on the bottom.

Not dressing for me, then.

Her sullen eyes met mine, barely-covered dark circles beneath them. She huffed out a breath before looking away, bee-lining for the coffee cart.

*I have to talk to her.*

I lifted myself up out of the chair, pushing through the growing crowd of people until I stood behind her as she ordered her coffee. I knew she could feel my presence — could see the way she stiffened from the heat of my body, the way her breath shallowed as the man behind the cart told her the total.

I tapped my phone on the card reader before she could protest.

"Is that necessary?" She hissed, grabbing my arm and pulling me to the side and out of the line. "I'm perfectly capable of buying my own coffee."

"I know that. I was just trying to be nice."

"It's rude either way. I don't need you throwing your money at me," she snapped. She threw a quick thank-you to the man as he handed over her coffee.

"I wasn't trying to be rude."

I slid my hand along her back, ushering her away from the coffee cart and back toward the stalls that were beginning to open up. She walked silently beside me, her left hand clutching the paper cup. I tried to keep my eyes trained on hers, trying to pick up the things she was interested in and pulling her towards them, but instead, I couldn't keep myself from looking at the lack of a ring on her fucking finger.

I didn't want to think about the why. I had to believe she'd just taken it off for something and forgot to put it back on, but the idea of her taking it off in the first place was enough to make my stomach sink and my blood boil.

Even if I desperately tried to avoid the thoughts, they filed in anyway.

*She doesn't love you.*
*It's all a lie.*
*You've read too much into this.*
*You're nothing to her.*

I wanted to throw up.

I spent the majority of the event in a daze, hardly able to participate in a single conversation with her or the people she connected with, half because I was so wrapped in my own thoughts of her and half because I was running on three hours of sleep over the last forty-eight hours. Not only were there others in the business here, but potential clientele for her as well. As much as I loved to listen to her speak about the thing she cared the most about— including pinball —I couldn't focus. I couldn't bring myself to actively listen, only random numbers and giggles filtering in through the haze.

Until a potential client asked the question I'd been unable to stop thinking about.

"Congratulations on your engagement, by the way," the man said, his height nearly meeting mine. He smirked at her as his eyes went to her left hand. "No ring today?"

"Oh," she chuckled, flexing her fingers as she looked at

the indent that hadn't faded. "I must have forgotten to put it on this morning."

"You don't wear it to sleep?" I asked. There was more than a hint of irritation in my voice — I was too tired to conceal it, too stressed to try.

Her eyes narrowed as a blush spread across her cheeks. "I wouldn't want to risk damaging something so expensive."

"Are you sure that's the reason?"

"We can talk about this later," she hissed, turning back to the too-tall, too-attractive man in front of her. "I'm sorry. Let me get you my business card."

"That's, uh, that's okay. It was nice to speak to you. I'll see you around," he said, giving her a tight smile as he stepped back into the crowd, disappearing in an instant. I knew it was wrong of me to feel relief but that didn't stop the feeling of a breath of fresh air.

"Great. Thanks. You made me lose a client," she grumbled. Her eyes scanned the crowd, already leaving me in the dust in her mind as she went silent again.

But I didn't want to fucking deal with this anymore.

I grabbed her by the arm, her wide, angry eyes meeting mine in a second. "What are you doing?"

"We need to talk." I gently pulled her toward me as I walked back toward the edge of the conference room. She went without question, thankfully not fighting me even though I fully expected her to. It felt like every second of silence as we found somewhere quiet and calm was stabbing me in every soft spot on my body, dragging its claws along the cuts and widening them. The little huff she gave as we settled against the wall only drove that home. "I know I fucked up. I'm fully aware. But the way you're acting is like I did something unforgivable—"

"Oh, I'm sorry, am I just supposed to brush off the fact

that you beat the ever-living shit out of my friend?" she sneered, her teeth bared in a way I hadn't seen from her in a *long* time. Her eyes went glassy as my stomach sank.

It hadn't been *that* bad, had it?

"I can't—I can't speak to you about this, not here. This isn't okay. This will never be okay," she said. I could hear the venom in her voice, could feel it coating me, painting me in permanent ink. "You think this can be settled with text messages and voice notes? You think you can make things okay by paying for my coffee and showing up to a networking event?"

"No, of course not, but—"

"But nothing," she snapped, her voice rising just a little too loud before she brought it back down. "You can't just do what you want, Jack. You can't. He had to go to the hospital. I mean, he's fine, but still. It's not okay. We aren't okay."

*We aren't okay.*

She turned, and without giving it a second thought, I grabbed her by the forearm, spinning her back to me. Her brows knit as she looked down at my hand, took in the scabs and the bruises along my knuckles.

"Mandy," I breathed, trying to pull her just that single inch closer to me, but she stood her ground. "I'm sorry. I'm so fucking sorry. I'll get on my goddamn knees, okay? I'll beg. I'll grovel. I don't care. Just please, *please* see it from my side. You have to understand — he came at *me*. He invaded *my* space, he tried to stop me from leaving, he—"

"It doesn't *matter*," she whispered, each word emphasized with anger.

"It does." I pulled again, and she slipped from my grasp.

"Stop, Jackson."

"I can't. I don't want to lose—"

"You need to get yourself together and support me

through this fucking event," she said. *No, no, no, no, this isn't what I wanted.* "You shouldn't be so worked up over this."

"How...?"

The grin that spread across her cheeks was less than reassuring. It was all teeth and brick walls, all anger and apathy. I felt like I could hardly breathe.

"Mandy—"

"It's all fake, remember?"

*No. It's not.*

"It's all a show, Jackson. And maybe it's time to talk about it coming to an end."

# Chapter 34

## *Mandy*

Two weeks.

The moment I'd left that event and driven myself home, I'd decided I was done. I didn't talk to him. Blanked him entirely, missed his calls, avoided him with work. I let Harry be in charge of communication with him where it was necessary. I didn't want to talk to anyone besides my mom, Harry, and Amanda—didn't even want to go outside.

I wasn't going to let him break my heart again, even if that was already what was beginning to happen. I wasn't naive enough to let it get to the point of no return. I also wasn't about to get on my hands and knees and beg for honesty from him—I was too far above that and wouldn't dare stoop that low.

I told myself that I'd shed the last of my tears for him when he'd beaten the shit out of Harry instead of showing up for dinner, told myself I couldn't keep this thing that I so desperately had tried to hold onto when he'd only justified his actions. This had to be the end.

I wouldn't put myself through hell again for him.

Granted, I was only so strong. I'd cried a few more times since, mostly on the floor of my shower much to my own dismay, but either way, my point still stood. I was done.

I was barely getting used to the empty feeling on my left ring finger—it was still odd seeing it without the ring. I turned my clipboard over in my hand, my eyes tracing where the indent used to be, thinking about all the wrong things in my life instead of the incredible work we'd managed to achieve within the intended time frame.

The extra workers I'd asked for had been a godsend. The walls were repainted, the tile was finished. Furniture was set, art was hung, the internet was up and running, and all of the light fixtures were installed and working. The walkthrough had gone incredibly well, and now that Jackson's team had moved in and everything was up and running, today was the official grand opening. We'd opened up to the public and to the press, and as I ensured that everything was up to par and perfect throughout, Jackson cut the red ribbon out front.

Just knowing he was nearby was enough to set me on edge.

People filed in one by one, taking in the grand entryway I'd designed—the tile, the light fixtures, and the choice of textured paint. It made my heart race to see their awe, their excitement seeing this new building in the heart of Boulder that I'd designed. Well, Harry too. But in all honesty, it was mostly me.

Things turned into a blur as it ramped up. If Jackson came in, I didn't notice — too many people were talking to me, asking me questions about my designs, and offering me their cards to do work for their own businesses. Normally I'd thrive in that kind of environment, but knowing Jack was around the corner, somewhere here, was draining.

Repeating the same things over and over again to different people started to drag. I wished I could have done this with Harry, wished I didn't have to be here alone.

With all of the new potential clients, we were definitely going to need to hire more people. I made a mental note to talk to Harry about it as I left my station, and as I was weaving my way through the crowd of people, a hand roughly grabbed my arm, stopping me on my way into the grand office.

I whipped my head around, fully expecting tanned skin, dark hair, and green eyes to be staring back at me, but instead it was a face I didn't recognize. Plump jawline, short hair, stocky but small stature. "Uh, hello?"

"Congratulations on your engagement," the man said, his grin widening. "I forgot to tell you back in the foyer."

I remembered talking to him although most of the faces had become a blur at that point. "Thanks," I said, sliding my arm from his grip.

"No ring today?" He asked, his eyes grazing up and down the top half of my body. Definitely a creep, but nothing that triggered a warning.

I gave a light chuckle as I forced a smile. "No. It's uh, quite expensive and I didn't want to risk wearing it with this many people around," I lied. I'd never been good at lying, not to anyone, and it was even harder to do it on the spot with a stranger.

He nodded. "Ah, well, all the best anyway."

Too many people had congratulated me on my engagement today, and that was just the icing on the shit cake. I hated thinking about the fake engagement, thinking about the fact that I'd need to actually talk to Jack to sort out the public breakup. It was too much for my mind to deal with on top of everything else, and I could feel the stress and anxiety building in my gut as I took off toward the main office once again.

It had been converted into a ballroom of sorts, something Jackson had mentioned a while ago in his list of requirements. *Large space with intricate flooring, main offices but convertible.*

Loud music poured from the speakers as I entered the space. Lights had been set up to complement the natural light filtering in from the skylights to accentuate the hanging art we'd commissioned. Drinks were widely available, and there were a lot of people walking around with one in their hand, enjoying the free alcohol and food Jackson had arranged. He wanted to pull out all the stops, wanted to ensure good press about the grand opening.

I scanned the crowd, wishing I could will Harry to be here. I understood his hesitation at coming, even if it meant only half of the faces of L&V would be in attendance — one of those two faces was still bruised. Tensions ran high between us, too, and although I'd reassured him that we'd ended things privately, he was still uncomfortable with the public side of it. I just needed to suck it up and find the will to discuss the end with Jack even if it hurt to think about, even if I was hurting myself in the process.

*Shit.*

Green eyes clashed with mine from across the room, lit by a spare ray reflecting from the hanging fixture above. It was as if he was waiting for me to find him, to dare to look at him, for him to kick into action.

My breath caught as he crossed the space in seconds. I didn't want to speak to him, didn't want to have to deal with this today. That was wishful thinking on my part.

The crowd parted easily for him as if he was fucking Moses. Every part of my body screamed to move, to leave the room, to abandon this project and stop showing my face. *I could go home. I could run away.*

But my feet wouldn't lift. My body wouldn't turn. That small, minuscule part of me that desperately wanted to fight for whatever we still had left kicked into high gear and I wanted to snuff her out.

"Mandy," he breathed, his eyes flicking between mine wildly. They were hollow, dark circles lining the bottom edges, a hint of scruff at his cheeks. Probably working nonstop.

"Hi," I deadpanned, hoping more than anything that he just had a comment or complaint or anything else to say that wasn't related to us. The music faded, a slower song taking over from the last one. I could already tell where this was going without him even opening his mouth, but of course, he did it anyway.

"Dance with me?"

I fully intended to say no. But every part of me, every single stupid cell in my body, didn't want to say that. That small part was taking over every living, breathing cell it could manage. It wanted to say yes. Because it was *him*.

And I was shit at ignoring my body when it came to him.

"I... I guess," I sighed, taking his offered hand in mine. *One dance. That's it. Take the moment to engage for the last time, bring up ending the engagement, and then we're done.*

He breathed a sigh of relief as he pulled me toward the empty patch of the room. Only a handful of couples littered the tile floor, most people only in attendance for business, and as he wrapped his arm around my waist, I couldn't help but notice the number of eyes on us. I *hated* how easily we slotted together. I hated how easily we moved together, danced together. He kept his mouth shut, not wanting to ruin the moment, but I wasn't able to give him that kindness in return. Not after everything that had happened.

"Tell me, then," I said, locking eyes with him. "Tell me your side."

His jaw steeled. "You don't want to hear it. If you did, you'd have answered my calls the last few weeks."

"You know why I've been distant," I snapped. "I shouldn't have to explain myself. *You* should."

He sighed as he pushed me out, spinning me around as the music picked up in the chorus. "I know I should. I've wanted to. I tried to."

"I'm giving you the chance now. But this is it, Jack. Take it or leave it." I slammed back into him, my chest going flush with his own. "Tell me what happened between you and Harry. Tell me what was keeping you from me before that."

He took a deep breath, his chest shuddering against mine. "He cornered me in the garage by the old offices."

"Bullshit," I scoffed. "He said it was here. Why would he be at your old offices?"

"It's not bullshit," he hissed. "You want to see my location history? I can fucking give it to you."

I reared my head back, throwing a warning stare at him.

"Sorry, sorry." His jaw hardened again, that little tick in the muscle driving me mad. "Are you going to let me explain or are you going to pick everything apart?"

"That's not up to you."

"Fine." His tongue dragged against his teeth, his eyes getting lost somewhere behind me as we spun. "He was waiting for me in the garage. Came between me and my car, told me he wasn't letting me leave."

I narrowed my gaze at him. "Why would he do that?"

"He didn't want me to see you," he said, his jaw working. "Kept telling me how awful I am, how I'm only breaking you, how I clearly didn't think this meant anything and was just going to drop you again as if I was some spineless cunt."

He spun me out again, the movements stilted, awkward.

"He said I was chewing you up to spit you back out, and I snapped. I'm not proud of it. But *he* came to me looking for a fight."

"That's not what he said," I scoffed. "He said it was about the extra workers."

His feet came to a halt as he dragged his gaze back to me. "What extra workers?"

His words struck a chord in me, one I couldn't quite place. *Wait*. "He said you lost your mind because he took the fall for me hiring in extra hands to get this place done in time. Is that... not...?"

There wasn't a hint of deceit in his eyes as he searched mine for an explanation, flicking back and forth between them. "Why would I have a problem with that?"

"He said the budget was creeping up—"

"Mandy, I gave you a fucking unlimited budget. I told you to do whatever you needed, whatever you wanted. Did I not?"

"I—"

"He lied to you," he said, each word careful, composed, and pointed. "Fucking hell."

I didn't know what to think, didn't know how to comprehend it. Either of them could have been lying, either of them could have been keeping secrets from me. But there was the overarching issue of Jack being distant the last few weeks, of him keeping things from me, of him not fucking saying that he loved me back.

"Mandy."

"That doesn't explain why you've been distant," I

breathed, dropping his hand and taking a step back from him. This was too much to handle here, now, surrounded by people. "You're hiding things again."

The pause he gave made me question everything he'd said to me, every word he'd uttered. "Even if I am," he started, his gaze meeting mine, "you shouldn't concern yourself with it."

I could feel my heart breaking in my chest. It felt like fire, bubbling up from deep down, ten years of weight on top of it. It consumed my chest within the span of a second. "You don't love me, do you?"

His mouth formed a hard line, but he said nothing.

The fire spread, climbing up my neck, down my arms. The backs of my eyes burned, threatening to start the waterworks to cool myself down. I stepped away from him, needing the space, the distance, the *time* that he'd stolen from me. "I can't do this," I breathed.

"Mandy—"

"No," I said, my voice cracking. "I'm done."

# Chapter 35

## *Jackson*

I followed her in an instant.

I wasn't letting her walk away, not this time. Not when I had a say, not when I was present and could do something about it. I jogged toward her, catching her hand as she stepped out the doors of the grand office space. She turned, her eyes filled with flames, and before she could say a word to me, I pulled her into the private office that branched from the hallway.

Shutting the door behind me, I leaned against it, blocking her exit. "Talk to me."

Her nostrils flared, her fisted hands twitching to fight me. The knee-length emerald-green dress she had on did nothing for her if she was trying to look dangerous. "Let me out, Jack."

"I'll let you out when you actually have a conversation with me instead of running away," I hissed, taking one step toward her. "If you have something to say, say it. Don't bite your tongue."

"I have *too* much to say to you, Jack. That's the problem." She crossed her arms over her chest, a tiny, angry tear breaking free. She wiped it away with a flick of her finger. "I don't have the time to say it all."

"You do. We're alone. I have nowhere to be."

"You have interviews to do," she said, an irritated laugh escaping from her. "You have a lot of *work* to do, apparently."

"Fuck the interviews. Fuck work," I seethed. My body had a mind of its own when it came to her, gravitating toward her, taking another step closer. "If you genuinely think that's more important than this moment right here, right now, then I don't know what to tell you, Mandy."

I could see every part of her go tense at my words. "It's sure seemed more important for the last month."

"It isn't." Another step toward her and she retreated again. "It never has been. Do you think that's been an active choice I've made? Do you genuinely believe for one second, that I would rather have spent my time fucking working?"

"How else am I supposed to take that?" She snapped, her arms flying out, taking up more space. "That's all the information I've been given, Jackson. *Work. Work. Work. Beat up Harry. Don't say you love me.* That's all you've been doing."

I'd realized how she'd picked up on that back in the grand office space, but I didn't know how to explain that away. I wanted to say it to her, wanted to mumble it over and over against her fucking skin, but I couldn't. Not when everything was on the line, not when it could cost her her life, not when my affection for her that had never for a second gone away put her in harm's way. "I just... I need you to trust me. That's all I'm asking for, Mandy. Just *trust* me, please."

She cackled as she turned around, wiping her eyes with the backs of her hands. I watched as she glanced around the mostly empty office, bare except for the necessities. It hadn't been assigned to anyone yet. "I'm all out of trust for you, Jack."

I could feel the air leaving my lungs. "Don't say that."

"Do you want me to lie?"

"No, never, but *please*. There has to be some left. Just trust that I'm doing what I have to."

"Tell me what's going on and I'll consider it," she said, one shoulder lifting as she looked back at me. "Give me a good reason for snapping and breaking Harry's nose. Give me a reason that you've built me up just to tear me back down again." I winced, her words almost parroting those from Harry's mouth before I'd let my knuckles collide with his face. I wanted to tell her, desperately, but if this stupid fucking threat was real, I couldn't drag her into it. Not until we got to the bottom of it, not until we got that CCTV back from the library. It had been *hell* waiting for it, and I couldn't let this happen, not when we were so close—

"Yeah, I didn't think you would."

I didn't know how to deal with this. I never had, never grew the backbone I needed to be the bigger person. I should have. "So, what? You're going to go back to hating me and pretending there is nothing between us anymore? You're going to make me break down all of those walls again?"

She stared me down, her stare unwavering, her jaw set. "I'm going to cut myself off from you completely."

I blinked at her, rage making my muscles quake, my chest ache. "You can't do that."

"I can."

"You don't *want* that," I said.

Her lower lip quivered. "I do."

"You're lying," I said through my teeth, my feet carrying

me forward before I could tell them not to. She backed up, spine hitting the floor-to-ceiling window as my hands landed on either side of her head. Thank god I'd installed strong glass. "You're lying to me, and you're lying to *yourself*."

"I'm not," she breathed, her flared eyes searching mine as she tried to catch her breath. "I'll move away from Boulder. I'll get as far away from you as possible, stay off the internet. You won't find me."

"I will," I hissed, leaning in further, my breath fogging the window behind her. "You think I didn't track every vacation you ever took? Every quick trip to New York? I will *always* find you. Leaving Boulder is pointless."

Her breath caught before she spoke. "Then tell me what's happening."

I sucked in air as I pushed myself away. I needed to center myself, needed to gather my thoughts. I didn't want to tell her — I didn't want to *scare* her. But if that was my only option, then fuck it. "I got an email."

She huffed out a scoff, the little ringlet hanging between her eyes flying up from the puff of air. "You got an email? Wow. Revolutionary."

"Are you going to listen or make snide comments?" I snapped. I was already shaking, already reliving the fucking trauma of ten years ago. I needed her to listen.

With an exaggerated eyeroll, she went silent.

"It was a threat," I continued, flexing my hand to keep from punching the stack of filing cabinets. "A threat against *you*. They said I should have learned from ten years ago. They *knew* what happened, why I left. Why I didn't let myself go after you for years. They have to be connected. Do you understand what that's doing to me? The amount of past trauma that's brought up? I can't fucking sleep. I can barely eat. I've tried to create distance because I'm *terrified* for you."

She blinked at me, not one ounce of worry in her expression. "So someone emailed you saying that they'd... what? Kill me?"

"It was whoever broke into your house. I don't know what they want, but they spent a substantial amount of time in there before they left," I explained. Just the thought of the unknown person laying in her bed, going through her drawers, taking up space in her house made me want to scream. I'd become exceptionally good at holding that in the last few weeks until Harry had come along. "Why do you think I've had extra security outside your home? Why do you think I kept asking you to stay with me? Why do you think I lost my goddamn mind when Harry started spewing shit at me? I didn't want any of that. I didn't want to hurt him. But he wouldn't stop bringing up how I'd hurt you before, how what I'd done was horrible—and believe me, I know—but that I was doing it *again*."

"We already knew they had been in my house," she sighed, tapping the bottom of the window with one heeled foot. "It doesn't really sound like the email stated anything we didn't already know. And it definitely doesn't excuse the way you've been acting."

"No, it isn't, but if me being around you puts you in danger, then I'm willing to back off." I forced myself to look at the ceiling, keeping myself as calm as possible, fighting back the burning behind my eyes from the admission. "But I've been trying to track the email for weeks. We've traced it back to the public library, but we're still waiting on the CCTV. So, yes, I've been avoiding you because I'm fucking terrified of anything happening to you because of *me*. I punched him because I'm a coward, I punched him because

I couldn't handle the thought of all of this, everything I'm trying to figure out, breaking you *again*."

"That's..." She took a deep breath, her gaze bouncing across the room. "That's not good enough."

"Excuse me?" I breathed, my head snapping downward so I could look at her evenly. "What does that mean?"

"If that's true, and I'm not saying I believe you, but if it is — you should have told me. You shouldn't have hidden that. That's not an excuse to avoid me for almost a *month*. Do you know how I've felt? Do you even understand the amount of pain you've dished out while trying to be this white knight savior? I vomited when Harry showed me what you'd done to him. I nearly fucking drowned myself. You've caused more pain than whoever emailed you could have." She laughed again, the anger boiling over.

"Mandy..."

"No. Don't Mandy me. It's not fair, and I refuse to deal with this shit again." She stepped out from underneath my arms and took a step toward the door, her eyes daring me to move toward her. "You shattered me ten years ago, Jack. Absolutely destroyed me. I'm not letting you do that again."

"I'm trying to protect you," I insisted, taking one step as her hand met the door handle.

"I don't need your protection. What I *need* is to be free of you, once and for all. The project is done. The deal is done. It's time to do the public breakup, Jack."

"No—"

"The press is right on the other side of those double doors. Let's do it now and get it over with."

"I'm not doing that," I breathed. My hand met her arm, squeezing, *begging*.

She turned the handle. "Then I will."

## Chapter 36

## *Mandy*

I tried convincing myself that I was truly done. But nothing was ever done with Jackson.

"Please," he begged, crossing the room and caging me in again. I could have stepped out the door. I could have backed away, but my body was screaming at me to stay, to hear him out. I hated myself for it. "Please, Mandy. Give me a day. Twenty-four hours. Don't tell them yet."

"Why?"

"Because I'm not ready for it to be over," he breathed, one hand lifting to cup my cheek, his thumb swiping at the stray tear that broke free. Every part of him vibrated with worry, with fear, and although I didn't show it on the outside, it was eating me up on the inside. It was tempting me, leaving me in a paralyzing situation where I didn't know which way I wanted to go. "I waited ten years for you. Can you please at least give me one more day? One more night?"

"I can't handle one more day," I whispered, my voice breaking as I tried to turn my head away. "This hurts.

You're hurting me every second that you're making me stay in this with you."

"I know, princess," he sighed. His forehead fell to mine, his breath warming the air between us. "I'm so sorry for that. But please. At least... at least give me tonight. An hour. Anything. I'm sorry. I'm so, so sorry, for everything. I've ruined it, I know, but just... please."

He knew exactly what he was doing. He knew he was breaking me down, slithering his way inside and patching up old wounds, daring to stop the bleeding while giving me new ones. It hurt just the same. "Jack..." I breathed, barely able to justify letting him keep me in here, let alone what he was asking for.

"Let's just... pretend," he said. His lips pressed against my cheek, my jaw. One strong hand snaked around my waist, fingers digging into satin-covered skin, pulling my body toward him and away from the door. I wasn't sure I had the will to fight him anymore, but part of me felt like he'd masterminded that. "Can you do that for me, princess? Pretend, like you did before?"

"Like I did before?" I scoffed, pushing gently against his chest as he dipped lower, lips meeting my neck, my collarbone. *That wasn't pretend.* I wanted to scream it, but the words wouldn't form.

"Like you did before," he repeated, his body shuddering as his hips pressed against mine. "Let me have you."

*Shit.* Why did it feel so good to hear him say that?

His hand roamed lower, over the curve of my ass and cupped the back of my thigh as his mouth followed suit, down between my breasts where fabric met flesh. "Let me taste you."

I couldn't stop my hands from burying themselves in his hair, couldn't keep my body from reacting to his touch.

"Okay," I whispered, wishing I'd kept that one word to myself, wishing I had more control over my own heart. "Okay."

His mouth left my breasts as he cupped both of my thighs, lifting me in a heartbeat. He buried his face in the crook of my neck, teeth and tongue nipping and licking at the soft skin there as he turned us both around. Two steps and my rear hit the edge of the desk, his hips slotting so easily between them, the sensations from his mouth dragging little whimpers and moans from me.

I nearly lost my mind when he dropped to his knees.

Fingers grazed across my thighs, pushing the satin fabric up. He hooked onto the sides of my panties at the same time he planted a kiss on the inside of my leg. "Lift up, princess."

I lifted my ass, relishing in the feeling of him pulling the frilly lace down my skin. Every inch was maddening as the butterflies and warmth spread in my gut, that depraved, traitorous part of me reacting to his touch alone. His tongue dragged along my inner thigh, growing ever closer to the spot I wanted him to touch most.

"Tell me what you want," he mumbled. His teeth sunk into my flesh, hard enough to make me squeal.

"You," I said, the word feeling too much like the truth. I knew damn well there would always be a part of me that genuinely felt that in my bones, a part of me that would fold to him too easily. I'd meant it when I said I could move away. Just knowing he was in the same city as me was too tempting if I found him again. I needed to get away. "I want you."

"Where?" He chuckled, his breath tickling the little bits of peach fuzz around the apex of my thighs. "Be specific, princess."

I groaned in frustration and grabbed a handful of his

hair. "You know where." I tried to pull his mouth closer, tried to get him to go where I needed him, but he resisted.

"Say it and I'll give it to you," he purred.

I narrowed my eyes at him and shifted my ass on the desk, pushing myself into him. "Give it to me anyway."

He gave a muffled chuckle as his lips parted, his tongue reaching out and gliding across my folds almost *too* gently. His strong hands wrapped around my thighs, lifting them up onto his shoulders, and with myself laid bare from the waist down before him, he dug into his feast.

Wet warmth lapped against my most sensitive part. I leaned back on my elbows, releasing the strands of his hair, and watched as he lost himself in me. The little whimpers I made were involuntary, too easily slipping past my lips without a second thought.

Through the two undone buttons at the top of his dress shirt, I could see a hint of the panda on the left side of his chest. My breath caught in my throat, and I tucked my legs in a little tighter around his head to block the view. *It's not your fault he got that tattoo. This is for the best.*

My head began to swim as I tipped it back, the pleasure building in my gut. I'd never been eaten out like this, never had such a visceral reaction to it. I forced myself to breathe through it, to not let the way his mouth formed the words 'I love you' against me sway me any further. I could just have sex with him. Just sex, and then be done.

My body squirmed as his fingers slid inside, curling up at just the right spot. Arms shaking, I lowered myself further, laying down fully on the desk and letting him have his way. At least then I wouldn't have to look, wouldn't have to resist the temptation he embodied—

"Look at me, princess," he mumbled, the sound muffled from his mouthful. I lowered my jaw, looking down between my breasts and legs. He held eye contact as he feasted, his mouth and tongue moving against me, drawing me ever closer to that mounting precipice. "I want you to watch me while you come."

Couldn't I just pretend, for once, that this was enough?

I couldn't stop the moan that crawled from my throat. Just watching him was intoxicating enough, tossing me higher into the atmosphere, drawing out every bit of pleasure that he could. "Fuck, Jack," I whined, pushing myself up onto one elbow and grasping the strands of his hair again with my free hand.

"We'll get there," he chuckled. "Come for me first."

I tightened my grip as my orgasm met its peak, his words giving me that little bit that I needed. My legs locked around his head as he curled his fingers farther, dragging out my pleasure, forcing me to shake and buck against him as the pleasure spread through my body like wildfire.

His fingers retreated slowly, and in the haze of coming down from it, I forgot to keep myself guarded. I forgot to not care. I grabbed at the front of Jack's shirt as he stood, pulling him down toward me, my lips damp and needy as they pressed against his greedily.

He kissed me as though it were the last time, and maybe it was, but it felt like so much more.

Hands grazed up my body, pulling the straps of my dress down over my shoulders and the cowl neck down over my breasts. The fabric pooled around my waist, leaving me entirely bare above and below. He kissed down my neck, across my collarbone, my nipples.

His fingers fumbled with the buckle of his belt, loosening it as much as he could with one hand. The sound of it alone was enough to have me lifting my ass from the desk, grinding it against his waist as he refused to part from me.

Warmth pressed against the dampness growing between my thighs. My breath caught as his lips met mine again, desperate and urgent. I bucked my hips, silently telling him I was more than ready, and within seconds he'd fully seated himself inside of me, filling me entirely in more ways than one. I never wanted to be empty. *Why is it always like this with him?*

He didn't move. His hands slid beneath my back, his mouth moving against mine, and before I could process what he was doing, he picked me up. I wrapped my legs around his waist as he spun me, pressing me against the wall and making it take the majority of my weight, his cock hitting new levels of depth.

"Fuck," I grunted, the sensation making my head swim.

Arms unlatched my legs, lifting them, holding them up on either side of me. "Beg me," he whispered.

My head fell back against the wall, my eyes drifting to the door. The lock was turned, but... *which direction was locked?* "What if someone walks in?" I breathed.

"Hmm," he grunted. His hips shifted back, dragging his length almost all the way out, before slamming back in again. *Oh my God.* "I guess you better keep quiet so no one gets suspicious. Now... *beg me*, princess."

I desperately wanted to stay just like that.. "Please," I whimpered, locking my arms around his neck. "Please, Jack."

"Please *what?*"

I groaned as I tried to move my hips. I was firmly locked in place. "Please fuck me."

"There we go," he said.

He moved then, finally, and I think I might have slipped into heaven, or maybe the opposite, I wasn't sure. Strong thrusts, perfect angle, his mouth on my skin, his words in my ear. "I'm not having you end this with me without knowing exactly what you'll be missing out on."

"Jack," I groaned, my breath catching as he dropped my leg, ordering me to hold it up instead. The thoughts of it ending, the thoughts of me pushing him away, slammed back into my mind before becoming hazy again with each thrust. "Can we not talk about—"

"Yeah." His hand snuck between us, fingers grazing against my swollen and sensitive clit. It made me jump, made me buck against him as much as I could physically move. "We don't have to talk about a thing. Just let me make you feel good."

I nodded as I dropped my head against his shoulder, the sensations completely overwhelming me. It was too much, but I needed this kind of *too much*, I would always want *too much* with him. I was already building, already close.

"You're going to come again," he said matter-of-factly, his lips pressing against my temple. "I need you to, princess. I need you to come for me."

"You're an ass." The words came out in a half-moan, half-laugh.

"I know I am. But you can do it."

His fingers moved faster, swirling in little, gentle circles as he hit that perfect space inside with every thrust of his hips. I was going to lose my mind, turn into jelly, and maybe that was what he wanted. But I didn't care, not when he was touching me like that, not when he had me so close...

My release ripped through me before I'd even realized I was there, tearing apart every wall I had in place. I dug my fingers into him, cried out against his shirt, shook in his arms. It was perfect, blissful, and heaven was definitely the place. Jackson's hips stuttered as I squeezed around him, his breath faster, his moans louder. He fell over his own cliff seconds after me, shaking, whispering words I couldn't hear, one hand holding me and the other in my hair. He coaxed me through each aftershock, filling me, pushing his release deeper inside, and when we'd finally caught our breath and calmed down, he set me back on the desk to gather myself.

"The, uh," he panted, pushing the little damp strands of hair back from his face, "the door was locked. I just wanted you to know that."

I glanced at it again, taking note of the locked position. I nodded. "Thanks."

"Do you need any help?"

"No," I said. Reality was slamming in faster than I wanted, and I knew I'd fucked up. I'd bent to him again, given him myself too many times when he didn't deserve it. It hurt, and all I wanted to do was fucking cry, but I pulled my straps back up, put my underwear back on. As I stood on my heels, I gave a little shake, letting the fabric fall back down over my ass.

"Mandy."

I turned to him. Wild, tired eyes searched mine for an answer I knew he wanted, one I couldn't give.

"No. Come on. Please," he breathed, taking a step toward me, but I stopped him.

"This changed nothing."

# Chapter 37

## *Jackson*

I should've been happy. The grand opening was a success, the press was eating it up left, right, and center. Infinius was nearly finished. We were fully moved into the campus, leaving behind that shitty space I'd rented for the meantime. Morale was up. Even Angela was happy.

Yet after a week, my head was still clouded with thoughts about Mandy. How horrifically I'd fucked up, how I'd lost her *again*. Ten years later and I was still making the same mistakes by not being honest with her and letting my pride damage the people she cared about.

She'd mailed back the ring. Sent it straight to my office, wrapped in bubble wrap, and placed in a box with packing peanuts. My PR team was preparing a joint statement for us to release in the next few days. She was blanking my calls and texts.

It was enough to drive me permanently insane.

My phone rang on the table beside the treadmill. Wade's name and face popped up on the screen, and in my haste to turn off the machine and towel off the sweat, I nearly fell face-first into the mechanics.

"Hey, what's up?" I answered, doing my absolute best to hide the sheer sense of defeat in my voice.

"Hey man," Wade said. The huff and puff of his breath and the wind whipping into the speaker told me he was heading in from the slopes. "How are you? I'm sorry I didn't get a chance to text you back yesterday."

I grunted as I wiped the sweat from my face. I'd almost forgotten the string of half-asleep texts I'd sent him the day before, just one random text after another about how I should be happy but I couldn't be, how I wanted Mandy and I'd lost her. "Uh, yeah, I'm okay. Better than yesterday. Sorry about that."

"It's okay. You know you can always just call me, right? Like, whenever."

"I know."

"Are you holding up okay?"

"Yeah," I sighed. I threw my towel down on the floor, needing to let out at least a little bit of the pent-up rage that still sat heavy in my stomach after my exercise. "I just don't know where to fucking go from here. She's done. She told me that. And believe me, I get it, but at the same time, I was just trying to protect her."

"I'm not sure beating up her friend counts as protecting her, man," Wade laughed. In the background, someone called his name, the voice high and shrill. I rolled my eyes.

"I know that. I fucked up. I get it."

"Not sure how she'll forgive you for that one. But...you said something about an email?" He asked, the sound of a door clicking shut behind him.

"A threat. We traced it back to a public library, but the

gears of government grind so goddamn slowly that we *still* haven't gotten the CCTV back. It's torture."

"Was it real?"

"We think so. But considering it was from the library... I don't know." I held the phone against my ear with my shoulder as I left my home gym, navigating my way to the bathroom. I turned on the shower, letting the steam fill the room as I explained. "Whoever it was knew about my past. So that's credible enough on its own for me to take it seriously."

"Fuck," he grunted, another door shutting behind him. I could hear the creak of some kind of furniture as he sat down. "Is there anything I can do?"

"Not unless you want to use your skis to stab whoever it is to death."

Wade laughed, his deep chuckle the only thing making my lips twitch up into a smile. "You know I would. But I don't think that'll help with winning her back."

---

The hot shower was enough to make me feel slightly human again, even if I spent the majority of it thinking about ways I could try to fix things between me and Mandy. I wasn't sure if there was one, I'd come up empty every time.

The least I could do if things were truly over between us was get to the bottom of the threat and squash it. If Mandy genuinely didn't want me in her life, and it was looking more and more like that was the case, I could at least get whoever this was off of her back. That way I could scale back my security and she could really be done, even if the thought of it made my skin crawl. I could accept it. I would have to. But the idea of never seeing her again made me want to find the nearest bridge.

If I could just talk to her... I didn't expect her to forgive me, not after what I'd done. But every part of me couldn't begin to cope without knowing she'd heard me out in my entirety, heard every angle, heard how much I loved her.

My phone lit up with a text as I toweled myself off. Samantha from PR. *Meeting in ten with security.*

My muscles stiffened as my eyes scanned it over and over again. They found something. They had to. Every part of my mind was screaming at me to just call them now, but clearly, they had to pull some things together first if they needed me to wait ten minutes.

I didn't know if I was patient enough for that.

I pulled on a pair of shorts and a plain white shirt as I stumbled down my hallway, toward my home office. I sat down in my chair, eyes fixed on the computer screen, anxiously waiting for the video call.

Ten minutes felt like a lifetime, long enough for me to dive far too deep into my own thoughts. Things could have gotten worse, we could have received another threat, we still had no information and they were trying to find a gentle way to tell me. It was possible—if whoever it was knew their way around a computer like I did, they could disappear without a trace. They could have masked their IP to look like the library but could've actually been somewhere else. They could be anywhere in the world by now, but something in my gut told me they were still in Boulder, still too close to Mandy.

The video call rang out from my speakers. I answered it in less than a millisecond.

The camera was stationed at the end of a circular table, four people in suits sitting around it and two more behind them, standing up. "What's happened?" I asked, glancing between them, looking for a familiar face.

"We've received the CCTV footage," one of them said.

The breath I took was shaky. "Okay."

"We've sent it to you. We're working on facial ID, but please let us know if you recognize anyone. They've sent us the entire days' worth of video but we've timestamped the period of time the email could have been sent in."

"Okay," I repeated, my thoughts too jumbled to make a coherent sentence.

"Let us know if you need anything."

I ended the call with my trembling hand as I pulled up the video.

---

Three hours later, I'd seen absolutely nothing out of the ordinary. I'd gone to the campus, half of my shit not even moved in yet, but I needed a change of scenery. There was only an hour left of the footage, and I was rapidly approaching the end of the timestamp. My eyes were tired, but I couldn't look away. Not when we had it. Not when I could fix everything with this one video, not when I could at least protect Mandy.

I took a short break to grab myself a coffee from the cart downstairs. Gears turned as I walked, ordered, and carried two cups back toward the elevator. I had to figure this out but literally *nothing* had stood out the entirety of the three hours of video so far, and it was almost over.

Angela sat behind her brand-new, state-of-the-art circular desk. She hated it, hated that she was more available than ever now, hated that she couldn't hide behind the counter like she had at the old office.

I set down her cup in front of her.

She looked from me to the cup before her face scrunched up. "What the hell is this?"

"A drink," I deadpanned.

"It says *tea*. Is this supposed to be for me?"

"I thought maybe you were onto tea now," I shrugged, the idea suddenly striking me as absolutely ludicrous instead of another nice gesture.

"Do I look like a sad, tired, old British woman?" She hissed. She lifted the lid, recoiling when her eyes caught the bag floating at the top of it. "You didn't even put milk in it. I'm positive milk is supposed to go in tea, Jack."

"I put sugar in it," I sighed.

"Oh, I'm sorry. I must have missed the memo that milk is now sugar."

"Jesus, Angela, just say thank you," I bit out, the frustration of the lack of anything worthwhile in the video beginning to hit. "Do you want mine instead?"

"What did you get?" She asked, leaning back in her chair and crossing her arms. She spun gently back and forth.

"Black Americano."

"Absolutely fucking not." She made a fake gagging noise as she pushed the tea away from her with one finger, almost as if she was disgusted to even have to touch it. "Thanks but no thanks. What's gotten into you, anyway? This wasn't even you assuming I still liked an old order, Jack. This is, like, ten levels worse than that."

## Big & Bossy

I set my coffee down in front of her and leaned onto her circular desk. She was right. It sucked. I'd buy her a new one. "I'm sorry. I'm just... I've been pouring over this goddamn video footage from the security team for hours, and I still haven't seen anything that's piqued my interest. Nothing. It's driving me insane."

"Do you want some help? Maybe a second set of eyes?"

My brows creased as I looked down at her. "That might be the nicest thing you've ever said to me."

"Yeah, well, I'm bored. And you're not exactly solving that." She shrugged as she leaned forward, picking herself up out of her chair. "Do you want my help?"

"Yes," I sighed, standing straight and grabbing our drinks. "Please. That would be amazing."

"Sure. Just let me crawl out from under this stupid desk you insisted on."

I rolled my eyes, motioning for her to follow me. "I'll get you a new one."

---

I paused the video for a second to rub my eyes before hitting play again. Angela hummed something from beside me, her eyes trained on the screen.

"What is your coffee order nowadays?" I asked, needing a small break from the monotonous job of just staring.

"Matcha latte," she answered.

My eye twitched. "You know that's a type of tea, right?"

"Shut up." She leaned across me, hitting the play button. Seconds ticked by. Minutes. Almost at the end—

*There.*

In the far back of the screen, a man with ashy blonde hair sat behind one of the computers, the monitor obscuring half of his face. I scrubbed forward a couple of minutes, waiting for him to get up, waiting for him to move farther into view, and the second he did, I screen-grabbed it.

I zoomed in.

Closer.

Closer.

Sharpened the image.

Nearly fell off my fucking chair.

Harry Voss looked dead-eyed into the camera, the smallest smirk on his face, laptop clutched in his hand.

## Chapter 38

## *Mandy*

The clacking of my nails on the keyboard was barely enough to keep my mind occupied. L&V Interiors was supposed to have a meeting with Jack tomorrow—one final tallying up of everything we'd done and how much he owed us. Harry was on the books to go to the meeting tomorrow instead of me but considering his tardiness and the number of emails and phone calls I'd received complaining about his performance lately, I wasn't expecting him to actually follow through on it.

Which left it to me.

Harry had been off with me since the grand opening. At first I'd assumed it was just because he was still healing, but the longer it went on, the more it felt like a punishment. Like he'd somehow found out I'd had sex with Jack at the campus and hated me for it. But in fairness, I hated myself too.

But I didn't want to see Jack again. That last romp in the spare office had been the last time, and I'd promised myself that. But I also told myself I'd never see him again, never give myself the chance to act on anything stupid, and now I was stupidly going to have that chance because Harry couldn't get his act together.

I stared at my empty ring finger as I typed, that sinking feeling in my gut hitting me once again. I was having to fight myself more this time than I had ten years ago. Back then, I'd let myself fall apart because of him. I'd barely made it through my last year of college. I'd cried down the phone to anyone who would listen, distracted myself with pinball and studying but pestered Wade any chance I had. I wasn't going to do that this time, but every time I saw the lack of a ring on my finger, it made me want to. Even after what he'd done. Maybe he'd been right — maybe he was just overworked and stressed out of his skull because of the supposed threat. But I couldn't overlook what he'd done just because of that.

Surely, getting over him a second time would be easier. It had to be.

The front door of the office opened, distracting me from my task of the day. I glanced over the monitor, spotting Harry's mop of blonde hair through rows of blinds. "Hey," I called out.

He stopped in the middle of my doorway, his shoulder leaning on the frame. The hollows under his eyes were the worst I'd ever seen them, his frame thinner, his hair messy, the little cast still on his nose. Everything, for the most part, had healed — his ribs were almost normal, his bruises faded. But he still looked like a wreck. "Hey, Mands."

I stood from my desk. "Jesus, Harry," I mumbled, crossing the room in a second. I pushed his hair back, trying to make him look even slightly more presentable. "You have a meeting in an hour. I know you're not doing well, but you could've tried to make yourself a little more presentable."

His stained, oversized hoodie and joggers were enough

to make me irate, but I tried to have patience with him. He didn't want to talk about what was ailing him, and as much as I understood that, if he was going to show up to work he could at least wear a button-up shirt and slacks. "I did my best," he mumbled.

"You didn't. I think I might have something of Jack's in my car that you can wear," I sighed, giving up entirely on his hair. "And I probably have some concealer in my purse."

"I don't want anything of Jack's," he grumbled, catching my hand before I could put it back down by my side. He turned it over in his palm, taking in the empty ring finger. A smile too wide crossed his lips. "Finally took it off?"

I rolled my eyes at him as I snatched my hand back, my hand rubbing my wrist to calm me before things got heated. "I shipped it back to him last week. You'd have known that if you'd bothered to show up to work. Did you honestly think I was going to keep it on—"

"I've been busy. I told you that."

"Yeah, well, it's starting to become a problem, Harry," I said. "You've missed meetings. You've bailed on customers. Do you know how bad that looks on us? Do you know how many emails I've gotten, how many of our clients have said you've shown up late or didn't show up at all—"

"I don't really care how it looks," he scoffed, dark, tired eyes meeting mine. "We're doing fine. I just need this situation to blow over and then I'll be back up and running."

"And what exactly *is* this situation?"

"Nothing you need to concern yourself with." He crossed his arms over his chest. "So is it over, then? You and Jack?" Of course he brought it back to that. Why had he been so hung up on that lately?

"I don't want to talk about that," I mumbled as I took a step back from him.

"I'm asking as a friend, Mandy. You shipped it back, so it can't have been an easy break," he said softly, his lips pursing as I met his gaze again. "I'm sorry for the way I was reacting before, to the stuff with you two. I was just worried about you, and honestly, I think that's rightly so."

*Well, that's unexpected.* "You're right. Genuinely. But I really don't want to talk about it," I insisted, pushing down that part of me that *did* want to talk about it, the part that wanted to turn it into the big deal it genuinely felt like. But I wasn't going to let myself. "We have some stuff to go over before your meeting with Jack tomorrow if you're still going."

"Can't," he said, his word too quick, too certain. "I've got a doctor's appointment."

I sighed in frustration as I glanced at the document I'd been typing up. "You couldn't have told me that sooner?"

"I've been busy. And we didn't talk about the thing with Jack."

"Why do you keep bringing it back to that?" I whined, leaning back against my wall of filing cabinets. "I told you I didn't want to talk about it."

"Yeah, because you don't want to be proven wrong," he chuckled, a smug little smirk crossing his face. "I told you this would happen, and you chose to ignore it. He's a shitty guy, Mandy. Did you really think he'd changed?"

His mood shifts were beginning to give me whiplash. Was he sympathetic, or was he smug? "I don't need to have my stupidity shoved in my face."

"No, but I don't want you crawling back to him like some sad-eyed puppy dog desperate for attention again." He snorted at his own words, only irritating me further. I hated this side of Harry. I barely ever saw it, but it had come out in full force since the start of all of this. "Like, what kind of a man is he if some silly little email threat was all it took for his facade to crumble? A real man wouldn't just drop someone he supposedly loves. He's weak. You need someone stronger than him, someone who will take care of you."

Email threat?

*Email threat.*

"I didn't tell you about the email threat," I said, locking eyes with him from across the room.

He blinked at me as his words replayed in my mind. "I didn't say anything about an email threat."

"Yes, you did," I breathed.

"I didn't."

"Don't gaslight me." My head spun as thoughts hit me from every which way — he'd been unhappy about this from the start. He'd tried to get me to stay away from Jack. He'd been there the night that Tiana had mentioned Jackson's problem with the military project, the threats his coworker's partners were under, the kidnapping. He'd been gone so much lately, likely not sleeping, not eating. Jack had said — *Oh my god,* Jack had said he'd egged him on. Jack had said he'd baited him.

*Did he send the email?*

"You must've misheard me.."

"Harry—"

"Listen to me, Mandy," he started, taking a step toward me. "I understand your heart will always have a soft spot for him, I do. But he's not who you're supposed to be with. Not who you're fated for. I think you know that, and I think you always have."

I took a step back, my blouse catching on the drawer of one of the cabinets, the fabric tearing at my shoulder.

"I'd treat you so much better than he would," Harry

said. Bile climbed up my throat as he closed in, sunken eyes wild as they stared me down. "You know I would. I'd take you out to fancy restaurants and the press wouldn't be on our heels. I'd buy you anything you wanted. I'd fuck you the way you deserve to be fucked—raw, hard, dirty."

"I don't want that at all," I whispered, my back hitting the rear wall of my office, the photos hung there shaking from the small impact. My heart was speeding up, too much hitting me all at once. *It was him. It was Harry. It was him.*

"You do. You just don't realize it yet. And that's... that's okay, Miranda." He closed the distance, caging me in with his hands. Too easily, he slotted a knee between my thighs, locking me in place. "I always knew it would take you some time. Years, even. But I think you might just need a little push."

Cracked, dry lips met mine before I could protest, little bits of stubble scraping against my skin. His tongue darted out, swiping against my pressed-together lips, trying to part them. I could smell his morning breath. My flesh crawled at the invasion of privacy, the disgusting desperation coating him.

I placed both hands on the center of his chest and pushed hard, disconnecting us. "Get off me," I croaked. My heart hammered in my chest, my lungs hurting, my mind panicking. *It was him. It was Harry. It was him.*

"Or what?"

My palm collided with his cheek before I even knew what was happening. The slap left a stinging red mark, and as his eyes flashed with anger, I knew I'd fucked up. Royally.

His mouth slammed into mine with enough force to make me shriek, and he took advantage, forcing my lips to part further, snaking his tongue inside. One filthy hand cupped the side of my waist and dug in its fingers, coating me in the feeling of dirt and grime.

I pushed, but he didn't move. I hit, but he didn't move. His knee pressed in between my thighs, rubbing at the top of them, and I wanted to scream. I wanted to cry. He forced his tongue into my mouth again, searched out my own, and dear *God* I didn't want this.

I didn't want this.

*I didn't want this.*

His other hand fumbled with the buckle on his belt, that all-too-familiar rattling noise making the bile in my gut rise. I pushed, pushed *harder*, retreating my tongue and body as far as I could. "Stop, please, *stop*." I barely managed the words around his mouth, barely kept myself from crying—

I heard the footsteps in the main hall before I'd even noticed the door had opened. Harry took a step back, too forcefully, too quickly — and I knew he heard it too from the little smile covering his dampened lips. He turned to look, his body blocking my view, but nothing could block out *him*.

Jackson's eyes met mine over the top of Harry's head, every bit of anger and frustration hidden as he took in the sight before him. It only flooded in as he turned his sights on Harry.

# Chapter 39

## *Jackson*

I saw red.

The temptation to swing my fist directly into his face and beat him until he was black and blue and red again was overwhelming, but I'd brought the police with me, brought security. I was stronger than that. I could hold back for Mandy's sake, keep her from seeing what she'd already seen once before.

Cops filtered in on either side of me, grabbing Harry before he could protest. I watched out of the corner of my eye as they cuffed him, as he pleaded with his face smashed against the filing cabinets, but my gaze was trained on Mandy. She looked at me in horror, her fingers touching her red, puffy lips. She was shaking.

I moved toward her.

After I'd picked Harry out of the video footage, we'd gotten confirmation that he had sent not one, but hundreds of emails to me. Each one the same, each one from his own log in at the library. After comparing timestamps and videos with every bit of information we were able to obtain, we handed it over to the police. I'd had security on standby for Mandy, far enough away that she wouldn't notice, but close enough to react in case he came into the office. It had made me sick to know that he could show up at any point, but I needed to do it right. I couldn't fuck it up, not this time.

I only wish I'd gotten there sooner.

"How did you know?" She whimpered, her eyes wide as she watched them read Harry his rights.

"I've been working nonstop," I said. I used every bit of energy I had to keep my voice calm as I looked her over — every part of me wanted to kill him, leave him dead somewhere in the woods, run away, and never be caught. The temptation was nearly overwhelming considering the look of shock on her face and what I'd walked into, but I couldn't do that. I just needed to keep it together for her. A part of me knew her panicked cries of *stop* would haunt me, though. "Are you hurt?"

She shook her head at me. *Thank fuck.*

"Your shirt is torn," I said, placing my hand on her shoulder, gently turning her. She jumped at the contact, and my heart sank. She had just been assaulted, and here I was, touching her. *Idiot.*

"It caught on the cabinet. I'm fine."

"You're in shock, Miranda. You're not fine," I bit out.

"I'll *be* fine," she clarified, her eyes searching mine for something, anything. Likely reassurance. I wanted so desperately to give that to her, but I didn't know how, didn't know if I could with Harry still in the room. I could feel his presence behind me, his eyes boring into my back, his seething tongue desperate to hurtle attacks my way.

I turned to him. The officer held a knee in the small of his back, smashing Harry's face into the cold metal. "Is this what you wanted?" I snapped, my hands balling into fists.

*Calm down. You have to calm down for her.* "You wanted her, right? That's what this was about?"

He pursed his lips. An answer by omission.

"You've fucking traumatized her. You've ruined it for yourself, and it was entirely your own doing, not mine."

"Jack, stop," Mandy whispered, her hand grabbing at my suit jacket.

"Did you really think you were being thorough? Did you think you wouldn't get caught?" I continued, taking a step toward him, anger boiling up again. Mandy pulled harder, and a uniformed arm came across my chest, stopping me in my tracks. "Did you really think you could get one over on me? I own a fucking tech company, Harry!"

"It still worked," he sneered, his teeth showing as a chuckle crept up his throat. "That's enough for me."

"I'll fucking—" I started, stopping myself before I could get the words out in front of the police. Didn't need a death threat charge, not when he was going to have plenty of his own. I hoped with every ounce of my being that he at least got the shit beaten out of him while he waited on his inevitable bail, hoping he would learn some kind of lesson that wasn't at Mandy's expense.

He was lucky we weren't alone this time.

---

Mandy's body shook as she spoke to the police, my jacket slumped over her shoulders. Hopefully it would help a little with the shock, and she could have something familiar to hold on to.

With every interaction she recounted to them, every little detail of Harry's behavior lately, it made me want to vomit. The signs had been there for a while. If we'd only just communicated, elaborated with each other that something was off, not quite right, maybe we would have figured things out sooner. Maybe we'd have ended up with a better outcome.

Stories of him interrogating her about the ring I'd given her, stories of him hurling nasty comments about how she'd end up crying on the floor of her bathroom when I decided I was done with her. I knew without a shadow of a doubt the ways in which I'd gotten things wrong, but never, not in a million years, would I do *that*. And he tried to make her believe I would. He tried to make her believe that my absence from her life was me pulling back, when in reality, he'd crafted the distraction himself. He'd sought me out that night in the garage, egged me on, and laughed when I punched him. What was it he'd said? *God, she's going to love this.*

I wanted to splinter the wood beneath my feet.

The police had her sign some paperwork before they left, Harry already long gone and likely in a cell. It was an understatement to say that I hoped he never got out. I hoped he rotted in there.

I watched Mandy from the doorway. I was not about to overstep whatever boundaries she'd built up against me, but watching as the tears fall silently from the corners of her eyes as she stared blankly at her monitor was almost torture. I wanted to hold her. I wanted to make things better. I just didn't know how.

Her mouth moved, silent words falling from her lips.

"What was that?" I asked, leaning forward.

"I didn't want him to kiss me, I didn't want him to touch

me," she said quietly, only a fraction louder. I caught it, though.

"I know. I know you didn't."

"Why did he...?" Her voice caught around a sob, her shoulders hunching forward, hands twitching.

"I don't know, princess." It took every ounce of strength to not cross the room, to not hold her. I couldn't make this harder. I wouldn't.

"I just feel like—" Mandy cut herself off as she took in a trembling breath. "I feel like everything between him and me has been a lie. I turned him down years ago, Jack. Before we started our business. How much of this was planned?"

"I don't know, Princess," I repeated. My chest ached for her, ached for *myself*. I'd done the same thing as Harry. Worse, even. On a much larger scale. I'd brought myself to her uninvited, invaded her life. Was I no better than him in her eyes?

"He knew I didn't want it."

"I know."

She bit her quivering lower lip. Swollen, red eyes met mine from behind her desk, her hands grasping at the lapels of my jacket around her. "I know what you're thinking," she said. "What you did isn't comparable to him. Not at all."

I steeled my jaw. *Am I that much of an open book?* She was wrong. "You can't say that."

"So you moved to Boulder." She shrugged, wiping her eyes with the backs of her hands, streaking mascara. "And you hired me. It's not like you were trying to control the outcome of that."

"But you're wrong," I bit out. I curled my fingers into fists, needing the sting of the pain of my nails sinking into my palm. "I'm no better, Mandy. Everything, all of this," I motioned with my hands, encompassing the entirety of the situation, "was because I planned it. Do you genuinely believe I moved my business to Boulder because of the booming tech industry? If that was all I wanted, I could've gone to Silicon Valley. I could've positioned myself among the top tech companies out there, next to Apple and Microsoft and Google. But I chose Boulder. I chose Boulder because of you."

From the corner of my eye I could see her eyes blinking. "What are you saying?"

"You know what I'm saying."

She dropped her gaze to her keyboard. I could almost hear the gears turning in her head, working it out, putting me in a cage just like Harry would be in.

"I'll make you a coffee. Let you... think," I sighed, turning my sights on the break room.

---

When I came back with two mugs full of fresh coffee, Mandy had moved to the waiting area of the office. Her knee bounced incessantly, rattling the little table in front of her. The closer I got, she shifted farther over on the sofa.

"Are you asking me to sit with you? Or are you backing away from me?" I asked, the words strained as I set down our cups on the small wooden coasters.

"You can sit with me," she mumbled. Her eyes were set on the coffee in front of her, too dazed to even look in my direction.

I sucked in a breath as I sat down beside her . The shaking in her body had calmed significantly, but I could tell just by the way she looked and moved that she felt like her skin was crawling. I just wanted to hug her, comfort her, but I couldn't fucking do that after he'd forced himself on her.

I placed the coffee cup in her hands instead.

"You're not like him," she whispered. She stared straight down into the rising steam. "You're not, even if you moved here for me."

"I moved everything here for you," I clarified. "Spent millions moving my campus, seeking out your business, hiring you, and ensuring you took the job."

"You didn't send threats against my life just to get me to stop seeing someone," she said. Her thumb rubbed against the rim of the mug. "You didn't kiss me when I clearly didn't want it. I didn't have to take your contract, either. I had other options."

"But I made it so easy for you to fall into my lap." The words hurt to say. I knew it was true, but admitting it, saying the quiet part out loud — I wasn't a good person. I wasn't as bad as Harry, but I wasn't much better. "I reeled you in and left you hanging. I beat up your friend."

"He deserved it. And that was because of him."

"My actions are mine alone. I didn't have to go about it the way I did."

She turned to me, shifting on the couch. "Your actions should be taken in context," she sighed, leaning farther over and resting her forehead against my shoulder. Electricity shot through me, the need for touch just a little more filled. "I'm not upset about what you did, Jack. Any of it."

I sucked in a deep breath as I leaned back, taking her with me with a hand on the side of her head. "You should be."

"Just because I should be doesn't mean I am." She

leaned further in, snuggling down, and this was all I'd been wanting for weeks. Why did it have to come at her expense? "At least not right now. And right now, I need to calm down. Not be angry."

I nodded.

We sat in silence for a few moments, her head migrating to my chest, my hand stroking her hair. I could stay like this forever, easily. The smell of her hair, the warmth of her body... I could almost pretend this was our normal. I wanted that more than anything.

"Did you really move here just because of me?" She asked, breaking the silence with a voice so small I could barely hear it.

"I did."

"Why?"

I chuckled, squeezing her shoulders. "Because I tried to get you out of my head for ten years with no avail. I tried to move on," I said. I hooked a finger under her chin, lifting her face so I could see her. Wide gray eyes met mine. "You have been, and will always be, the only one for me, Mandy. I wanted to prove myself to you. Still do."

# Chapter 40

## *Mandy*

"You're making a mistake."

Amanda met my gaze in the mirror, her long legs propped up on the coffee table. Mom worked behind me, putting little pins in my hair to keep the top half of it up in its little bun.

"I'm telling you, Mands," she continued, looking back down at her phone. "You should have gone with the green dress. It makes your hair look unreal."

"I don't like how it hangs," I grumbled. I flinched as Mom twisted a pin into place. "Jack said it wouldn't be formal, anyway. The black one is fine."

Amanda shrugged. "I'm just saying, babes. If you don't want to get dicked-down tonight then by all means—"

"Amanda," my mom hissed, sending a glare over her shoulder.

"Sorry, Gianna. I won't talk about Mands getting dicked-down again."

I snorted. "At least not in front of my mother, okay?"

She rolled her eyes as she sunk further into the couch. "What are you guys even doing, anyway? Did he tell you?"

"No, but it's fine. I like surprises."

"Are you nervous?" Mom cooed, her hands going up in excitement after placing the final pin. "First official date. My thirty-one-year-old is finally growing up."

I glared at her reflection in the mirror. "I've been on dates with Jack before, Mom. It's not that big of a deal."

"True, but it's the first real one. Those others were just for the press."

I swallowed the lump forming in my throat. I hadn't thought of it that way, hadn't considered the fact that this time could be different. Was what he was doing before really an act? It didn't feel like one. If it had, I'm not sure I would have fallen for him again.

"Well now you're nervous," Mom chuckled. "Sorry, sweetie."

"It's fine. I just... I hadn't thought of it like that. In that context."

"I know." Mom coated her hands in hair oil, smoothing it through the ringlets of my strands that hung down around my shoulders. "To be fair, having a first date after months of pseudo-dating would feel weird for anyone. Especially after everything you've gone through."

That felt like an understatement. I still felt like we'd gone to hell and back, fighting demons as well as ourselves.

Harry was out on bail. Someone in his family had forked up enough money to get him out, and even though Jackson rushed to obtain a restraining order against him for me, he still kept trying to show up. For what felt like the hundredth day in a row, security stood guard outside my house.

"Yeah," I sighed. I stared at myself in the mirror, taking in the little curls Mom had left hanging around my cheeks, the way the gray in my eyes cut straight through the warm tones of my makeup. I was glad I wasn't alone; I'd been keeping people close after the incident with Harry, but having these two nutcases hang out and help me get ready for the first real date I was having with Jack in ten years made it feel that much more serious. "It's going to be weird."

"Oh come on," Amanda groaned, rolling onto her side to get a better look at me. "You had known him for a while before he disappeared the first time. You've been around him for several months this time. It's not like he's a stranger."

"Yeah." I said again, pursing my lips, and nodding at her. "He's not a stranger."

---

Jack's driver picked me up outside my house. Mom and Amanda waved goodbye to me from my front porch as if they were my parents sending me off to fucking prom, and I was thankful that it wasn't Jack who'd picked me up.

Steve drove in silence out into the outskirts of Boulder, up into the peaks. The city sprawled below us as we climbed higher, goosebumps prickling across my skin, my nerves building with every passing mile. As we pulled into the driveway through the automatic gates, I could see the silhouette of a man in Jackson's kitchen, dancing to music and holding a bowl against his side.

The nerves fell away.

"Thanks, Steve," I called as I pushed the car door open with my boot. Jackson had said casual.

My boots crunched in the late winter snow as I jogged up to the house, my breath fogging in front of my face. I pressed the doorbell. Chimes rang overhead and from inside the house, lights coming alive behind the glass panels above the door.

Seconds later, the door swung open. Jack stood tall in dark gray slacks and a black button-up shirt. *He said casual*, I thought, irritation beginning to slip in before I glanced down at his feet.

Slippers. Panda slippers.

*Son of a bitch.*

"Hey," he grinned, stepping to one side to let me through. "My name's Jackson. And yours?"

I rolled my eyes as I shut the door behind me, slipping my wool jacket off my shoulders in one quick swoop. He took it from me and hung it up. "Are we really going to pretend that we don't know each other?"

He chuckled as he wrapped an arm around my waist, dragging me in far enough to plant a kiss on my temple. "No, princess. We're not going to pretend with anything tonight."

———

I sat at the breakfast bar in Jack's kitchen, my legs kicking against the tiled back of the cabinets. Soft music played in the background, something instrumental, plenty of calm piano and intimate saxophone. He slid a small salad across the bar, his lips curling up into a little smirk. "Eat up."

"Don't even joke," I laughed, picking up the fork he

gave me and sinking it into the salad. "You better not hog all of the carbonara."

"I wouldn't dream of it," he crooned. He turned back to the stovetop, muscles flexing beneath his shirt as he plucked two bowls from the nearby cabinet. "You look lovely, by the way. I should have said that when you first came in."

I stuffed a bite of salad into my mouth, humming my thanks to him. "You too," I said around the mouthful. "I like the slippers."

He chuckled as he picked up a massive wad of pasta between his tongs, twisting it as he plated. "I thought you might."

"How long have you had them?" I asked as I stabbed into a cherry tomato. "Recent purchase?"

He turned, holding up the two bowls in his hand. "Ten years."

My breath caught as he set the bowl of pasta down in front of me, snatching the barely-eaten salad before I could get the tomato into my mouth. The carbonara looked incredible, like it had come straight out of a restaurant in Italy instead of an Olive Garden.

"Eat up for real this time, princess."

"Are you not going to sit?" I asked, looking up at him as he loomed next to me, his fork already stuffed into his mouth. He shook his head as he leaned forward, plopping his bowl down right next to mine, his forearms resting on the countertop. "Well, okay then."

"I considered eating at the dining table," he said, covering his mouth as he swallowed his pasta. "But as I said, casual. And I didn't want it to feel like some big thing and overwhelm you."

My cheeks warmed as he bumped his shoulder against mine. I twirled my fork, gathering as much pasta as I could fit on the end of it, and stuffed it in my mouth as I grinned at him.

It tasted like heaven.

---

"We should probably talk about the press release," Jack said as he slid me a glass of red wine. "And when you'd like to do it."

*Shit.* The press release. I hadn't even thought of that in the last few days. After our romp in the office, his team had started drafting the announcement that we were no longer engaged and would be going our separate ways. But after the thing with Harry and the mounting stress we'd both been under, it had fallen to the wayside.

His words sat heavy in my stomach as I sipped my wine. "Do we have to?"

"Have to what?"

"Talk about it," I clarified. My cheeks warmed as I caught his gaze, zeroing in on the way his lips parted, twitched at the sides.

"No, princess," he said, his fingers gently laying across mine. "We can talk about it some other time."

I nodded, squeezing his hand in return. "I just want to think about it some more. Not that it definitely isn't happening, but..."

"I understand." His lips pressed against my forehead, so light I almost didn't feel them. His breath fanned across my skin as he held himself there. "Just let me know when you are, okay?"

"Okay."

The music changed, a slower, wistful tune filtering through the surround sound in the kitchen. Jack slid his hand underneath mine, tracing the lines of my palm. "Do you want to dance with me?"

*Is he serious?*

A finger hooked under my jaw, lifting my head to him. "Please?"

My heart jumpstarted in the span of a millisecond. "Sure," I breathed. I pushed myself down from the high-top chair, booted feet hitting the hardwood floor.

He pulled me to him, half-lidded eyes meeting mine, and as our bodies came together, he started to sway. His fingers dug lightly into the fabric on my back, just a small touch that sent me reeling. "I'm half tempted to put you on my feet again like I did at Tiana's wedding," he chuckled. "I think your boots might crush the little pandas though."

I laughed as I looked down at our mismatched shoes moving in tandem. "I wouldn't want to crush the pandas."

"Take them off for me?" He pushed one of the little curls around my cheek behind my ear, his fingers dragging along my skin.

I couldn't stop the smirk from spreading across my cheeks. "Just those?"

"Just those," he confirmed, his laugh entirely infectious. "Save the rest for later."

I giggled as I leaned down, the layers of my dress lifting as I turned from him. Just a peek, just my upper thighs, but I knew it was enough to make him positively feral inside. I unzipped each boot, kicked them off to the side, and padded across the floor until I was back in his arms again.

He lifted me immediately, placing me on the soft little

heads of the pandas on each of his feet, and continued dancing.

In circles, we moved, sweeping across the floor and about the expanse of his kitchen. Song after song, he spun me, tipped me, laughed with me, and held me. It felt too natural in the best way possible — a perfect moment of this arguably perfect first date, and I couldn't not smile, couldn't be stubborn with him. I didn't want to pretend with him, not anymore. I wanted it to be real, I always had.

The song slowed, reaching its end, and he slowed us in response. His mouth met mine, tenderly, hesitantly, and I kissed him back the way I wanted to be kissed. Fully, devouring, all-encompassing. I wanted it all. I wanted him, and I couldn't lie to myself about that anymore, not after everything that had happened. Not after ten years of trying to forget the one person I needed most. The only one I ever tore my walls down for. The only one I let in, let see the real me.

"I love you," I breathed, our lips parting for just a second. "Still."

His fingers cupped my cheek, his breathing shallow. Lips brushed against lips, and when he spoke, I nearly lost it. "I love you too," he said, his voice just a little stronger than mine. "Still."

The world felt so much lighter, as if instead of holding a barrel of bricks I'd been gifted a feather hanging from a paper-thin wire. I arched up onto my tiptoes, his answering grunt telling me I was likely crunching the tops of his feet and planted my lips to his once more.

It felt right. It felt like home, like coming back after a long night lost in the frozen woods to a raging fire and a cup of hot chocolate. Like reading a book and hitting that final page, like going out in search of a Christmas tree and finding the perfect one. Like the first snowfall of winter. Like a warm bath.

"So," he said, breaking the kiss again to hold my face wonderfully close to his. "What are we going to do about L&V? You're going to have to figure that out."

I grinned up at him, his green eyes beaming. "I already know what I'm going to do."

## Chapter 41

## *Jackson*

"I swear on Tiana's life, Mandy, if you drop that box, so help me God—"

"I'm not going to drop it," she laughed, sidestepping my home office desk. The assorted non-valuables inside rustled, and within a second, her wide eyes met mine. "It's not that fragile, right?"

I wanted to laugh, but I wanted to mess with her more. "That box has the main system for Infinius in it," I deadpanned.

"Oh my God, I should put this down," she said, her voice rising in pitch as the panic set in. "Jack? Jack, take it, please, I don't want to wreck it."

I laughed as I plucked the cardboard from her hands. "So gullible."

Her wide eyes turned to slants. "Seriously? What's in there, then?"

I shrugged, popping the top open and pulling out a silver medal. "Just my participation awards from middle school." I slid the ribbon around my neck, the fake silver jingling. "This one was from... basketball maybe? I was so bad at sports."

Mandy slapped my shoulder playfully. "Why do you even want these in the new office?"

"I like having my accomplishments on display."

"Your seventh-grade basketball participation award is important enough to be on display?" She mocked, twisting the plastic medal around my neck as she inspected it.

"I don't want my employees to feel overshadowed."

"Angela's going to make fun of you," she said as if that was any point at all.

"Angela already makes fun of me. I can take it," I grinned. I popped the top of the box back on, labeled the side with a Sharpie, and set it into the To Move pile by the door. This was going to take way longer than I thought, but I was hoping I'd be in the new office by the end of the weekend.

---

The new campus was buzzing with life as I walked through the halls, Mandy padding along behind me as I pushed the crate of boxes toward the elevator.

We had a meeting in thirty minutes with security, lawyers, and Harry. Supposedly he was actually going to turn up for once, and I could tell by the way Mandy fiddled with her wrists and fingers that she was dreading it.

As much as I didn't want to put her in that position, her presence was necessary. If Harry wanted to keep this out of court, she was going to have to negotiate the terms of that agreement on her own.

"Hey," I said, dragging her attention back to me as we stepped onto the clear glass elevator. "Do you want to see something top secret?"

She cracked a grin, a little chuckle seeping out. "How secret is top secret?"

"Well, it's not technically secret. More of an off-limits thing."

"Off limits to everyone, or off limits to me?"

I pressed the B button and presented my card to the scanner. The doors closed in front of us, the elevator purring to a start and beginning to descend. "Off limits to everyone except me and a select few engineers and programmers. The list is about six people long."

Her eyes widened as she realized where we were heading, straight down to the lowest floor. "Only six people?"

"Not including myself."

The elevator slowly came to its smooth halt, the doors parting in front of us to a small room with a door. I pushed the cart forward and to the side, out of the way.

"You're not planning on, like, murdering me down here, right?"

I laughed as I stuck my key in the lock of the door, twisting three full rotations to the right and once to the left. "I guess you'll just have to trust that I'm not."

I pushed the door open, bright, faux-natural light leaking through. In an almost completed circle around the edges of the room, the supercomputer whirred, little wires embedded into the glass floor leading to the center of the circle where a pillar encased in glass sat, a locked door on the front for ease of access if we needed to do repairs.

"I was wondering what this room was," Mandy said, her

voice quiet from the shock as she took it in. "The blueprints for it looked so strange."

"Well, now you know."

"Yeah." She blinked, her eyes struggling to decide what to focus on. "So, what is it?"

I laughed and stepped across the glass, toward the second most important object in the room besides Mandy. "This, princess, is Infinius."

---

Showing Mandy the room where the most important bit of tech in the entire company sat wasn't exactly on my list of plans for the day, but I was glad I did it. If she had any lingering doubts on whether or not I trusted her completely, I hoped showing her that swayed them.

Plus, it put her in a slightly better mood for the meeting.

She breathed out a shaky breath as she adjusted the collar of her jacket, her eyes searching mine for the confidence to go in the room. "I can do it. Right?"

"Of course you can," I grinned. "And if he says a single fucking word other than 'okay', we take him to court and drain him for every penny he's worth, and then some."

"I don't want to ruin his life," she mumbled.

"You might after this."

"Why?"

"We've, uh, done some more digging," I sighed, taking her hand in mine and giving it a squeeze. "Do you want to know now or in there?"

"Now, obviously."

I bit my lip, trying to figure out the right words to say. "There's a reason your profits were down the last few months before I hired you," I began. "And I think a part of you suspected it for a while. The financial reports you gave my team…"

Her gaze went straight through me as the puzzle pieces lined up in her mind. "He was stealing money, wasn't he?"

"Technically, embezzling is the right term—"

"Shit," Mandy hissed. She pressed her palms into her eyes, her breathing spiking, her lower lip quivering. "How?"

"Overcharging clients. Pocketing the excess. Harry's work email has had quite a few complaints sent to it from your clients about how the amount they were asked to pay was significantly more than the amount given to them on their invoices."

She leaned into me, her forehead against the lapel of my suit jacket. "I'm going to kill him, Jack. I can't go in there. I'll stab a pen into his throat—"

"Shhh, my little murderer. You're not going to kill him," I chuckled, pushing her back from me and wrapping my fingers gently around her wrists. I pried her hands from her eyes, little bits of mascara stuck just below her lashes. "You're going to stand up for yourself, show him you're the better person. Lie a little and show him that this hasn't affected you in the slightest. You're strong, Mandy. You can do it."

She sniffled as I wiped away the clumps of mascara, making sure she looked pristine. If she looked it, she'd hopefully feel it, and she needed to feel it.

"You've got this, princess."

. . .

"If we take you to court, Harry Voss, you would easily get twenty years at a minimum," I drawled, leaning back in my absurdly comfortable chair. I was so happy I'd splurged on that. "We are willing to work out a deal with you, and for that, you should be grateful."

Mandy sat beside me, one hand on the arm of my chair, her knuckles white from squeezing it.

"My client would like to know the terms of the deal before he agrees to anything," Harry's lawyer said. She crossed her arms over her chest, her eyes wandering between me, Harry, Mandy, and my lawyer, Andrew, who sat on the other side of me.

Andrew clicked his pen and leaned forward. "Ms. Littleson would take over any existing clientele Mr. Voss still has. Ms. Littleson would also gain complete control of the company, and Mr. Voss would forfeit any rights he has to it, including any assets or board privileges. A payment plan would be put in place directly from Mr. Voss to L&V Interiors to cover the amount of the embezzlement, which, as it stands, looks to be just over one hundred thousand dollars. The money will then be given directly back to the clients that were overcharged during Mr. Voss's time at the company."

Harry's lawyer looked at him, leaning close to whisper in his ear.

"Oh, and one more thing," I said. My lips twitched up as I caught Harry's answering sneer that spread across his face. "You'll sign an NDA. You won't speak to anyone about my and Mandy's relationship, the situation we were put in, or even mention our names. It's outlined in the paperwork more thoroughly but do know that if you break the terms of the NDA, the entire agreement crumbles. We'll come after you for every penny you're worth, which after this, seems to be... well, not much."

"Jack," Mandy hissed.

"Her restraining order will still stand. You will keep away from her and your only contact will be in lawyer-sanctioned meetings to discuss this agreement moving forward," I added.

Harry's jaw twitched as he turned to his lawyer, whispering back to her.

"Mr. Voss would like to adjust the terms," she sighed.

"Then he can see us in the courtroom," I deadpanned.

"Just fucking sign it, Harry," Mandy said, cutting the answering silence. It was the first time she'd spoken since we'd walked in, and just hearing her voice lay into the asshole made my heart swell. "You're not going to get a better deal. It's this or prison."

Harry formed his lips into a thin line, his eyes glued on her. "Fine," he sighed, plucking the pen off the table in front of him and pulling the papers to him. "I'll sign it. You're welcome, Miranda."

"It's Mandy," she snapped.

---

The weight of the meeting was well and truly gone by the time Mandy and I made it outside. The late afternoon sun was beginning to set, and it was unseasonably slightly warm. The snow was melting, spring was beginning, and just knowing that this was another season I'd have with her was enough to set my heart alight.

Everything felt so unbelievably right. More than I could have ever imagined, even more so than ten years ago. I could die happy right now. We'd gotten our justice with Harry, we'd taken each other on for real this time, both of us all in.

I revved the engine of my Harley, warming it up as Mandy got on the back. Her arms wrapped around my waist, palms flat against my torso, her body pressed against my back. It felt like our world had come full circle.

There was one thing I still needed to do though. One thing to make it right, and I'd do it for real this time. Not for the press, not for our reputations. For us.

# Chapter 42

## *Mandy*

"Please tell me I don't look like a monster in these heels."

I turned to Amanda as she crunched in the gravel of Jackson's driveway, her ankles nearly twisting from their height. I snorted as she glared at me. "You don't look like a monster. Maybe a little overdressed, though."

"You said it was a dinner party," she hissed, grabbing her purse from the car. "He's rich as shit. Of course I'm going to assume it's black tie."

"You also know him and know that he only does that kind of stuff for the press," I laughed.

Paul and Kate, Jackson's parents, mingled at the front door. Their eyes were trained on us as Kate lit a cigarette with a match, flicking it down by her side.

"Evening, ladies," Paul called out.

"Evening, Paul. Any chance you could grab Jack? Amanda's having a little trouble walking. Might need someone to—how do I put this—pick her up," I giggled. Amanda swung her purse at me in response.

"It's fine. I'll just take them off," she said.

"And get frostbite on your toes? Absolutely not."

The front door swung open and out stumbled Jack and a ten-year-older version of Wade. I hadn't seen him since our time back at NYU, and all things considered, he looked much more attractive than he had back then. "I understand I've been summoned to carry someone?" Jack asked.

"Amanda," I clarified, pointing a finger at her.

"Oh. Wade?" Jack smirked, grabbing him by the shoulder and pushing him toward us. "Go on. I'm sure you can handle it."

"You say that like I'm heavy," Amanda grunted, wiggling her heel out from the spot it had sunk in.

"You are heavy, Amanda. Grown human beings are heavy."

I jogged across the gravel in my boots toward Jack, throwing my arms around his neck as he caught me mid-stride. "Hello, princess," he whispered, kissing my cheek, my lips. "Is your mom coming?"

I nodded. "She said she had to pick something up but she's on her way."

"Perfect. Tiana's inside, Fred couldn't make it, though," he said.

"That's okay, I'd rather hang out with Tiana anyway. She's much better company than you guys," I teased.

"So funny." Jack rolled his eyes as he released me, ushering me in from the cold, an annoyed Amanda right behind us in Wade's arms.

"You've got to come to the house sometime," Tiana said around a mouthful of bread, not a care in the world for who saw her chewed food. "We have so many photo albums. There's this one of Jack on his training bike, butt-ass naked, covered in peanut butter—"

"Hey," Jack snapped, his brows furrowed as he pointed his own piece of bread at her accusingly. "We agreed not to discuss that photo."

"Wait, that exists?" Wade chirped.

"Oh, it absolutely does," Tiana drawled, breaking off another bit of bread and dunking it in her portion of gumbo. Jack was, apparently, a ridiculously good chef. I didn't know how I managed to snag someone that could cook when I was so horrible at it, but I was more than thankful. "He's crying, too. It's hilarious."

"Tiana," Jack hissed. "Don't make me tell them about your prom photos."

Tiana's face went red instantly, the contrast so apparent against her pale skin and black hair. "Don't you fucking dare."

"Prom photos?" Mom asked, reentering the conversation as she wandered in from the kitchen, another glass of wine in her hand. "You should see Mandy's. No matter how many times I told her and Amanda that you aren't supposed to wear foundation that's two full shades lighter than your skin tone, they didn't listen. They looked like little baby clowns."

"Gianna," Amanda groaned. She leaned back in her seat beside me, her hands resting against her too-full belly. "You can't just tell people about that."

"If you didn't want people to know, honey, then you should have listened in the first place," Mom said, her giggle too much to hide.

"I would kill to see Mandy's prom photos," Jack laughed, his hand coming down gently on my thigh, squeezing just a touch. "And any other photos you have of her."

"You should come to my house for dinner sometime." Mom smirked as she met my gaze, a mirror of my own. "I've got so many childhood photos of her."

I rolled my eyes as I shoveled another spoonful of gumbo into my mouth. "I feel like we skipped over Tiana's far too quickly."

Paul and Kate looked at each other, each of them snickering. "I think I've got them on my phone, actually," Kate said. She reached behind her, fumbling for her purse, and within a second Tiana was on her feet snatching it before Kate could even make contact.

"Absolutely not," Tiana deadpanned. "I will not be having my parents show me off like that. Gross. I'm married now, Mom. I'm not some kid that you can parade on Facebook."

Jackson leaned over to me, his lips brushing against my ear. "I've got copies in my office," he whispered. "I'll show them to you later. Think Carrie, but worse."

Despite the chaos of dinner, it was genuinely a nice time. Having the people we cared most about with us was something I didn't think would happen, and yet Jackson had convinced his family and Wade to fly in. It was exactly like what I envisioned our wedding would be—intimate, cheerful, and full of mayhem.

*Big & Bossy*

Mom stood in front of the floor-to-ceiling window by the front, the vast expanse of Boulder and the surrounding woodlands glistening in the evening snowfall. She clutched a half-drank glass of wine in her hand, and gave me a little smile as I walked up to her.

"How are you feeling, sweetie?" She asked, her voice low, hushed.

I took a deep breath, considering my options. I could lie, tell her things are okay, things are slow but building. Be my usual hum-drum, dramatic self. Or I could be honest. I went with honest. "I feel... incredible," I chuckled. "I didn't think I could feel like this. Everything has fallen into place, you know?"

"Like what?"

"Well, I'm the sole owner of the company now. I'm changing the name to Littleson's Designs. And things with Jack are just so natural. So easy. I know it seems silly, but in a way it feels like when I'd look at you and Dad when I was a kid and things just felt right between all of us."

She gave me a soft little smirk as she sipped her wine. "I thought that might be the case. It's not silly at all."

"You think?"

"I know, Miranda." She was the only one I was ever happy to let call me that. She'd given me the name, and I'd own it with her. "I know exactly what that feels like."

"It's a bit overwhelming, to be honest," I chuckled. "I didn't ever see this for myself. I didn't know if I even wanted it."

"I always knew you did," she smirked.

"Yeah, yeah, moms know best, whatever." I giggled as I bumped my shoulder against hers. "I think we might actually work out this time."

"I know you will." She took another sip of her wine

before setting it on the table beside her, shoving her now-free hand into her purse instead. "I got you something."

"What? Why?"

"Because I thought it was time." Her eyes met mine, a little bit of sorrow, a little bit of happiness behind them. From her purse, she pulled the one thing I never thought I'd actually see again, the one thing she promised me when Dad died, the one thing she insisted she'd give to me when the time was right.

Dad's wedding ring.

"I..." I blinked at it as it spun around her finger loosely. She placed it into my waiting hands. "I don't understand."

"It's for Jack," she whispered, her lips spreading into a wide grin.

"For Jack?"

Footsteps sounded behind me, thick and heavy on the polished hardwood. I turned, cheeks flushed, mind racing, and found two green eyes staring back at me. The smallest smile played at his lips, his hands stuffed into his pockets.

*What is happening?*

He pressed a little kiss against my lips, shaking fingers pushing my hair back from my face, and before I could even register the kiss he had placed on my lips, he dropped down to one knee.

*Oh my God.*

"Mandy," he said, then cleared his throat. "I..."

He took a deep breath, shaking his head at whatever thoughts were racing through it.

"You know what? Fuck the speech I prepared. I'm saying what I feel," he started. "From the moment I met you, I knew you were it for me. I chased you. I spent seven months convincing you to trust me, to know me, to be with me. And when everything became screwed up, when I didn't handle things right the first time, I spent ten years trying to convince myself that I could be happy alone because I knew I couldn't win you back."

"Jack—"

"Shh," he laughed. "Let me finish. I devised a plan," he continued, "a stupid, reckless, idiotic plan to move my entire life to Colorado on the slight chance that I could fix things. And I did. But then I messed it up again."

"It's okay—"

"Mandy, please," he said, trying to control his chuckling. He pulled a little wooden box from his pocket, holding it in his hand before me. "I want to do it right this time. Right by you, right by our families, right by *us*. I only ask that you extend the gratitude you've given me that I truly did not deserve into the future in case I fuck it up again. Just know that I love you, eternally, unconditionally. Everything I've done up to this point is for you. So on that note..."

His fingers fumbled with the latch on the box, popping it open and revealing the ring. *My* ring.

I thought I was going to pass out.

"Will you do me the absolute honor of marrying me, princess?"

"For real this time?" I breathed, my body caught in a state of shock. I couldn't move, couldn't focus.

"For real this time," he nodded.

The backs of my eyes burned as I realized this was my life. This was what I knew I wanted, this was what I'd been searching for, waiting for. "Yes," I croaked, my smile coming out in full force as I finally regained control. "A million times, yes."

My mom, Tiana, Amanda, his parents, Wade, they all stood behind him on the other side of the room, their hands coming together all at once to clap as Jack rose to his full height. He slid the ring onto my finger, back into its rightful spot. I'd missed it.

Jack cupped my cheek, leaning down to kiss me and I kissed him back with everything I had, knowing I'd truly found exactly what I was hoping for, exactly what I wanted.

He was my everything. He always had been.

## THE END

BIG &
BOSSY

*Hey Fabulous Readers!*

*I hope Jackson and Mandy's sexy and heartwarming romance left with all the right feels. Read **Accidentally Engaged: A Fake Engagement with a Fertility Doctor Romance** available on Amazon. It's from my hot Single Dad Billionaires series. Check out chapter one on the next page...*

*Stay sassy and fabulous.*
*xx*
*Mia*

**A hot neighbor and a future baby daddy? Yes please!**

Hudson:
I know I shouldn't want the girl next door.
It's not fitting for a single dad or a fertility doctor of my reputation.
Plus I need a nanny... last minute.
She's the only one who can help me out.

When I finally work up the nerve to ask her, she's out on the driveway arguing with her parents. Something about her having a fiancé?
*Damn...*
But then they're all looking at me.
And I'm suddenly accidentally fake engaged!?!

So I'll play her fiancé.
Be nice to her parents.
Kiss her in all the right places.

There's one catch.
She wants a treatment for a baby.
Hell yeah!
But what happens when we also accidentally get pregnant?

Read now on Amazon.

# Sneak Peek

### Chapter One
*Hudson*

The drive home from the clinic was supposed to be cathartic. It was my alone time, my personal time, the time of the day when I wasn't Hudson, the dad, or Hudson, the doctor. No matter how much I loved my son and my job, I needed this moment of the day to decompress, to shift gears.

However, as I clutched the steering wheel with white knuckles in the thick Boston traffic, it felt anything but.

Things had been going well for too long. I knew that. I knew there'd be highs and lows, calm and unrest, but I just didn't have the energy today. Not after I'd had to sit an optimistic woman down and tell her that the treatment wasn't working, that it likely wouldn't take, and watch as she cried against her husband's soggy shirt. Not after I'd spoken to prospective parents who had lost their son—three years old, the same age as my Jamey—and wanted to try again. I didn't like having to give bad news to my patients. It hurt, especially when most of my job was giving the best news that couples wanted to hear. That was the highlight of my day, my week, my profession. I lived for it, I loved being able to tell them they were expecting. But after today, I needed the promise of a relaxing evening.

Instead, I'd gotten a cryptic text from Jamey's nanny. "I need to talk to you when you get home," she'd said.

I knew the drill already.

Driving past row after row of flashy houses and fancy cars, I pulled into my driveway, pressing the button on the sun visor that opened up my three-car garage. Beyond the house, the sky was drenched in blood-orange, little strips of fleshy pink freckled between the thin clouds. The day was winding down, soon to be over, and I'd have to start all over again tomorrow, fresh in the knowledge of whatever Jenny was going to drop on me when I walked through the door. I positioned my Porsche next to my other two vehicles—a Range Rover for towing the boat and a Mercedes AMG. I dropped my forehead against the curve of the steering wheel, measuring my breaths to keep myself calm as I savored the last few seconds I had before having to switch back to dad-mode.

*One.* Deep breath in.
*Two.* Exhale.
*Three.* Deep breath in.
*Four.* Exhale.

My fingers found the handle of the door before I'd gotten to five. Clearly, my body had decided it was go-time.

I clutched my phone and its goddamn ambiguous text message in my palm as I walked up the driveway, sidestepping an upturned bucket and a miniature, plastic excavator. The latch on the door turned as it registered my phone in its proximity.

I blew out a breath as I turned the handle, the rush of air tickling the scruff that had grown on my upper lip. *Definitely need to shave tonight.*

"Daddy!"

"Hey, hey, finish your carrots first!"

Jamey's little emerald eyes lit up in excitement as I stepped through the door. He sat at the kitchen island, his tiny feet swaying back and forth, thudding against the marble with each kick. He shifted in his seat, clearly making a move to hop down from the high-top chair, but Jenny flashed a single, pointed finger at him and he calmed.

"What did I say, Jamey? Carrots."

"Sorry, Jenny," he mumbled, picking up a baby carrot and dipping it into a tiny bowl of ranch before stuffing it in his mouth. He grinned at her with food between his teeth.

I chuckled as I dropped my keys into the basin by the door, kicking off my shoes with my toes. "Hey, bud," I called, jogging across the wooden floor toward the two of them. Jamey's carrot-ridden grin turned to me, little flecks of ranch dressing on his lips, and he giggled as I rustled his mop of dark brown hair. *Almost as dark as mine. Almost.*

I only hoped it would get darker.

"Hey, Dr. Brady," Jenny said, lifting herself from where she leaned on the counter. Her skin wrinkled as she furrowed her brows at me. "Did you get my text?"

I plucked a baby carrot from Jamey's plate and stuffed it in my mouth in an effort to seem nonchalant. Showing that I was nervous about whatever she was going to tell me wouldn't help the situation. "Yeah," I replied, speaking around the crunching between my teeth, "what's up?"

The flesh of her cheeks turned a shade darker, pinkening the skin. "Can we talk in private?"

I nodded. Shucking my jacket off my shoulders, I

threw the neckline of it over Jamey's head, and he giggled playfully as he popped himself out of the collar. "Why don't you go watch some PAW Patrol while Jenny and I chat, okay? You can finish your carrots later," I said to him, giving him a little peck on the top of his head.

"Okie dokie," he said. Before I could stop him, he scooted his butt to the edge of the chair and hopped off—something I'd told him numerous times not to do—and landed on shaky footing before taking off toward the living room.

His footsteps echoed through the quiet kitchen until they disappeared around the corner, the room instead filling with the distant sound of the PAW Patrol theme song. I sang along in my head as I looked across the counter at Jenny.

"The floor is yours, Jen."

She took a deep breath, her nervousness palpable in the air. "I need to quit."

"Well, I figured that much," I sighed, pulling the chair out from the counter and plopping myself into it. I picked up another one of Jamey's carrots but put it back down when I realized it was wet. *What had he done to it...?*

"I need to quit today."

Well, fuck. I hadn't expected that.

"Today? You can't even give two weeks' notice?" I snapped, immediately regretting the harshness of my tone when she physically recoiled. I took a deep breath to calm myself. "Sorry, it's been a long day. I didn't mean to snap at you."

She relaxed a bit as she crossed her arms over her chest. "I know it's last minute. I'm sorry. I was offered a role on Broadway for a musical I auditioned for a few weeks ago, and I just can't pass it up. They need me to relocate to New York City this weekend."

"Jesus, *they* couldn't have given you two weeks' notice?" I asked, trying to keep the conversation light.

"Apparently not. I got the call this morning after you left, otherwise I'd have told you then," she explained. She leaned one hip against the counter. "I'm really sorry, Dr. Brady. If I knew anyone else that could help you out I'd make that my number one priority, but all my other nanny friends are booked solid."

I sighed as I gave her an exasperated smile. What the fuck was I going to do? My mom lived nearby, but she had her own life, her own job, her own time. I couldn't expect her to take on Jamey full-time while I was at work, and I wasn't about to put him in daycare—not after the horror stories I'd heard. *If Becks hadn't taken off...* No. Nope, absolutely not, I was not about to go down that rabbit hole.

"Is there any chance I could get my last paycheck today?" Jenny asked, completely pulling me out of my thoughts. I was grateful for it. "It's just, I need the money for my moving fees and my flight..."

"Yeah, of course." I pulled my phone and wallet from my pocket and slapped them on the countertop. "Do you want cash or Venmo?"

---

I held Jamey in my arms, his small frame wrapped around the muscles of my hip, as Jenny's car rumbled to life. I could tell he didn't quite understand, and in his limited knowledge, he probably just thought that Jenny was going away for a little while and he'd see her again soon. Maybe at the grocery store like where we'd run into his old nanny, Caitlyn, as she worked behind the deli counter. Or maybe how we'd occasionally see Patty, our old neighbor who'd moved out last year, at the park walking her dog.

I knew he didn't get that it could be the last time he saw her because he wasn't waving goodbye like I was. He wasn't even watching as Jenny reversed down the drive. His gaze was drifting far to the right of the porch, locked on something that I couldn't see because his tiny noggin was in the way. "Wave goodbye," I whispered to him, and he snapped his head toward me instead, confusion written all over his face.

"Why?"

"Because she's moving away," I said softly.

"So?"

"So, you won't see her for a very long time. You liked her, didn't you?"

He nodded his head, his little tufts of hair flopping about his face.

"Then give her a wave. She liked you, too, munchkin," I sighed, wrapping my thumb and forefinger around his wrist and lifting his hand with it. He gave a little wave as she drove off.

Jamey wiggled his feet, his signal to me that he wanted to be put down. As his socks hit the concrete of our entranceway, he glanced one more time toward the right of the house before turning and walking back inside. I followed his gaze again, but nothing was there—just the bright blue Nissan Altima parked in the driveway of our new neighbor's house, the one that had moved in after Patty had left. I hadn't gotten the chance to meet her yet, but I'd heard good things from the neighborhood Facebook group.

I followed Jamey inside and through to the living room where PAW Patrol was still playing on the television. Immediately, he was glued even though he'd seen the episode at least twenty times. I could almost recite it by heart.

Dropping onto the couch beside him, I tucked him into my chest, letting my mind drift to the sounds of children's television. It was shocking how easy it had become to tune it out when I needed to.

I needed someone to watch Jamey. I'd already sent an email to let the others at the office know I wouldn't be coming in tomorrow and to shift my appointments to the other doctors at the practice, but that only bought me an extra day. I had tomorrow and the weekend to find someone that could look after him during the week.

If only he had a fucking mother.

My grip on the couch turned rougher, and I was careful not to let it affect the side of my body that Jamey was snuggled up to. *Don't. Don't think about her. You'll only end up more frustrated*, I thought to myself. *You can't change the past. You can't make her be a mother if she doesn't want to be.*

I'd be a liar if I tried to say it hadn't wrecked me. Becks' running away had fucked me up for far too long, and even now, I found the idea of an actual relationship daunting. I was thankful that Jamey was too young to remember his mother—she'd left just over two years ago, just after Jamey had turned two. I was also thankful that he looked absolutely nothing like her. That was a godsend, really.

I had enough money to not work if I needed to. In fact, I could never work another day in my life and be fine. I could be a stay-at-home dad if it came down to it, but I loved my job, and even on my toughest days, I didn't want to give it up. I loved being able to help women get what they craved, what they'd always known they wanted, and I was good at it. But faced with this new dilemma I had no idea what I was going to do. I was fucked. Completely, utterly fucked, and despite my doctorates, I wasn't smart enough to come up with an idea out of thin air.

"I'm gonna get some housework done, bud," I said, slowly sliding out of his embrace. I needed a distraction, and PAW Patrol wasn't going to cut it. "Shout if you need me."

Jamey nodded, his eyes never leaving the screen.

Despite how messy of a child Jamey was, Jenny always did a spectacular job of cleaning up after him and making sure he helped her with his messes, so as I found myself pacing the kitchen, there wasn't much to do. The dishes were done and put away, a final load running in the dishwasher. In the distance, I could hear the laundry tumbling in the dryer. The countertops were spotless, save for the plate with half-eaten carrots and dipping pot of ranch, so I figured I'd start there.

Wiping the soggy carrots into the hidden trash can, I noticed it was almost full to the brim. Perfect. Another job I could do.

I left the plate and the dipping pot in the sink and tugged the strings of the trash bag until it closed. "Jamey!" I shouted, lifting the bag out. "I'm just taking the trash out, I'll be back in a minute!"

"Okay!"

As I stepped out the front door, I noticed that the sky had turned mostly dark, with only a low-level blue light remaining. Soon, it'd be pitch-black and the streetlights would come on, casting the neighborhood in a warm glow that could only be described as suburban.

Lifting the lid of the trash can, I noticed something moving out of the corner of my eye. I followed it, tracking the movement as a head of brown hair bobbed behind the blue Nissan Altima, heading toward the mailbox at the end of her driveway.

She appeared behind the back of her car, keys in hand, not even giving me a passing glance. *That must be the new neighbor*, I thought to myself. Her long hair swayed behind her as she walked, moving back and forth along the small of her back. She was of average height, her slender frame covered only by a pair of lounging shorts and a tank top, definitely not the right clothes for the slight chill in the air, but my god, she looked like heaven in them.

I watched as she unlocked her mailbox and sorted through the letters, her bare feet planted on the asphalt of the road. She was almost mesmerizing to look at—stark blue eyes that I could see even from where I stood, a button nose, full lips. She didn't seem to notice me, and somehow, that made her all the more enticing. My blood pressure dipped, my mind getting the better of me and sending blood where it didn't belong. My cock twitched to life as my eyes followed her, zeroing in on that pretty mouth and the perfect body beneath it. *What I would give...*

*No. You don't want to go down that road again.*

I truly didn't. I didn't need the stress of that in my life. But from what I'd heard, she worked from home. Someone in the Facebook group had said she ran her own business and had recently started after a string of babysitting jobs as well.

No. That would be insane, right? I didn't even know her. I couldn't imagine a stranger watching after my son.

But she *was* next door, and she *was* beautiful, though that shouldn't matter. That couldn't matter. I could keep that separate if she agreed.

She looked up from her handful of mail as she came up the driveway, her bright blue eyes catching on me. She stopped dead in her tracks, as if she could sense every ounce of attraction I already felt for her.

*Salvation.*

**End of first chapter**

*Want to see how Sophia and Hudson end up fake dating? Click here to order Accidentally Engaged on Amazon now.*

"I binged the entire book in one sitting. It was just the right mix of humor, romance, and a frustration with the characters, plus a bit of sadness." - *Laci, goodreads reviewer.*

"This had a bunch of my favorite tropes, fake dating, single dad, surprise baby. And it was done great." - *Ana, goodreads reviewer.*

"This book had it all! It was funny, steamy and was heart warming. I loved Sophie, Hudson, and Jamey. I was hooked from the first page, such a great fake engagement!" - *Jackie, goodreads reviewer.*

"A great book with an intriguing storyline and captivating and awesome characters that I enjoyed reading about." - *Angelica, Booksprout reviewer.*

"Lots of twists and turns, frustrations, heartache, sadness, misunderstandings, and two MCs fighting whats growing between them until the unthinkable happens.

Loved the ending, the growth of characters. Quick and easy read, couldn't put it down." - *Nichole, Booksprout reviewer*.

"Excellent romance story, excellent couple and a HEA. So, look out because this is a HOT, SASSY and did I say it was a HOT book. :) " - *Barbara, Booksprout reviewer*.

## **GET ACCIDENTALLY ENGAGED**

Made in United States
Orlando, FL
28 June 2024

48388874R00183